BENEATH THE TRUTH

MEGHAN

NEW YORK TIMES BESTSELLING AUTHOR

MARCH

Editor: Pam Berehulke, Bulletproof Editing
Cover Designer: Murphy Rae, www.murphyrae.com

Visit my website at www.meghanmarch.com

CONTENTS

Copyright vii
About Beneath The Truth ix

Chapter 1 1
Chapter 2 7
Chapter 3 12
Chapter 4 16
Chapter 5 24
Chapter 6 30
Chapter 7 34
Chapter 8 38
Chapter 9 47
Chapter 10 55
Chapter 11 61
Chapter 12 70
Chapter 13 73
Chapter 14 82
Chapter 15 89
Chapter 16 95
Chapter 17 101
Chapter 18 108
Chapter 19 116
Chapter 20 119
Chapter 21 124
Chapter 22 129
Chapter 23 136
Chapter 24 142
Chapter 25 147
Chapter 26 150
Chapter 27 153
Chapter 28 159
Chapter 29 163

Chapter 30	170
Chapter 31	176
Chapter 32	183
Chapter 33	187
Chapter 34	190
Chapter 35	195
Chapter 36	209
Chapter 37	216
Chapter 38	223
Chapter 39	226
Chapter 40	229
Chapter 41	232
Chapter 42	238
Chapter 43	241
Chapter 44	246
Chapter 45	250
Chapter 46	252
Chapter 47	256
Chapter 48	265
Chapter 49	269
Chapter 50	272
Chapter 51	278
Chapter 52	282
Chapter 53	288
Chapter 54	290
Chapter 55	293
Chapter 56	296
Chapter 57	302
Chapter 58	307
Chapter 59	311
Chapter 60	315
Chapter 61	323
Chapter 62	325
Chapter 63	329
Chapter 64	333
Chapter 65	336
Chapter 66	339
Epilogue	344

Author's Note 365
Acknowledgments 367
Also by Meghan March 369
About the Author 373

ABOUT BENEATH THE TRUTH

I used to believe there were lines in life you don't cross.
Don't lie. Don't cheat. Don't steal.
Until I learned people don't always practice what they preach.
I turned in my badge and gun and walked away from everything.
Then I got the call no one wants, and I'm back in New Orleans.
What I don't expect is for her to be here too.
Another line you don't cross?
Don't touch your best friend's little sister.
She's always been off-limits.
Too bad I don't follow the rules anymore.
Maybe together we'll find out what's beneath the truth.

ONE
RHETT

Get home right the fuck now.

After the last year, I had become a pro at ignoring texts and calls. When you walked away from everything and everyone you knew, it was a skill you honed until it was sharp enough to slice the bullshit from your life.

Before my world fell apart, I was all about my brothers in blue. Nothing was more important to me than family, honor, and justice. And then betrayal ground those rose-colored glasses beneath its boot heel until my old way of life was nothing but dust.

My life was different now. No badge. No brotherhood. And what the hell was justice, anyway?

All I cared about was collecting fees from my PI clients. I didn't get involved, didn't let myself get invested. I turned it all off and did the job. No more. No less.

I looked at the screen of my phone again, and the gallon of coffee I'd downed to keep me awake to finish this case churned in my stomach with the burger I'd eaten.

This text was different, especially considering the sender.

My gut said so, and since that was the one thing I still trusted, I tossed my camera aside and started my Jeep. Mrs. Higgins could wait to find out if her husband was cheating on her.

For the first time in a year, I was going back to New Orleans . . . the city I'd left behind without looking back.

Just under three hours later, I slammed on the brakes, unable to get any closer to my childhood home. Blue, red, white, and orange flashing lights lit up the night sky like a jacked-up carnival. Police barricades blocked the road, and I threw my Jeep into park.

Where the fuck is the roof?

I flung open the door and charged out of the SUV, shoving my way into the crowd of gawkers.

Holy shit.

A fist gripped my heart and squeezed until I thought it might explode.

Where the hell is the house?

In place of the home I'd lived in from kindergarten to the age of eighteen was a pile of smoldering rubble.

Where the hell are my folks? A cage closed around my lungs. *Fuck. No.*

I elbowed my way through to the police barricade, gripping the top of it to vault over, but a heavy hand clamped down on my shoulder.

"Thank fuck you made it. Didn't know if you would come when you didn't answer."

I didn't tell Rix the only reason I came was because he was the one who had texted me. It didn't matter now.

"What the hell happened? Where are my folks? Jesus fucking Christ." From the complete devastation, I had to assume an explosion. Gas line? *Shit.*

"Your ma's with your aunt. She's fine."

I tore my gaze from the rubble to meet his silver one. The sympathy there had me bracing myself for the hit I sensed coming.

"Your dad . . . I'm sorry, man. So fucking sorry."

I was wrong. It wasn't just a hit, it was a wrecking ball that leveled me. My knees hit the pavement and I covered my face with my hands.

"Nooooo!" My roar sounded like a wounded animal as it echoed in the night, and everything around me ceased to exist for long, dark moments.

Pain and regret clawed at my insides. Organs shredding. Bones shearing. *Too much.* With superhuman effort, I reeled it all in and shut it down. Forced myself to go numb. Blocked out the agony.

Compartmentalization was a skill I'd learned early in my career, and right now, it was the only thing that would save me from completely breaking down in the middle of the street.

Don't think about it. It's a case. Just like any other.

I scraped my palms along the rough asphalt to steady myself before pushing up to my feet as if I hadn't just been devastated by the news.

"What happened?" I ground out the words from between clenched teeth.

"So sorry." Someone else said the words and gripped my shoulder before releasing and moving on.

I didn't bother to turn to see who it was. I didn't care. This wasn't about me. It was about the case. A year of focusing on denial in my little cottage in Gulf Shores came in handy for once.

"We don't know with one hundred percent certainty yet—"

I glared at Rix. "Spare me the bullshit. Tell me what your gut says."

Rix nodded and his expression tensed. "Warrant was finally issued for your dad's arrest. Two officers were on the way here to pick him up. Gave him a courtesy call out of respect to let him know they were coming. They might've exaggerated about how far away they were. His car was parked in the alley behind the house, and it looks like he was jamming it with important stuff. Family pictures, the cat, shit like that. They pulled up and before they could get out of the car, the ground shook and the house imploded."

Implosion? That took a whole separate set of physics than an explosion. Which meant there was no way in hell it was an accident.

My mind flipped to all the things I'd learned over the years about ordnance. "Was the house wired?"

"That's what it looks like. This was no accident."

His words echoed my thoughts. This definitely wasn't an accident. And it was no secret my dad was an explosives, demolitions, and incendiaries expert from his army days.

He wouldn't do this. Would he?

He wasn't cold-blooded enough to wire up his own house and take a chance that something could happen to Mom. Was he?

You also didn't think your dad would turn out to be a dirty cop.

The pain from earlier snaked out, a new variation this time, and I crammed it back down.

It's a case. Only a case.

"When will they know for sure?" It was a stupid question because I already knew the answer.

"This investigation won't be a short one."

"I need to see my mom. Need to know she's okay."

"I swear, she's okay. She was out for dinner with your aunt."

"Did she see this?"

Rix shook his head. "No, they didn't let her come back here. The officers told her they'd bring her when it was safe."

"My brothers?"

"I think your mom called them. I figured you still weren't answering the damned phone, so I decided to get your ass back here the only way I knew how."

No one ever knew where Rome was, somewhere down in Central or South America, but Rock was only a few hours away by plane in Vail. He'd get here quickly.

I scanned the chaos for the coroner's van, but it was nowhere in sight. "They already take . . . the body?" I forced out the words as bile rose in my throat.

The body. My father. The dirty cop who had been under investigation for the last year, and the reason I'd turned my back on my career, my family, and the only city I'd ever called home.

"Yeah. They'll be doing an autopsy."

I nodded, forcing myself to be clinical. "What's the theory?"

Another voice broke into our conversation.

"You know he can't tell you that." My old partner, Mac Fortier, held out a hand and I shook it. "So fucking sorry for your loss. We've missed you, but this sure as hell isn't the way we wanted to see you again."

Mac and Rix were probably the only people here who could say that and mean it. I'd fought to stay in the department for as long as I could after my oldest brother had been killed in the line of duty and then fingered as a dirty cop. Dad had retired almost immediately after Robin's funeral, and I didn't realize until later it was to hide his guilt.

When I released Mac's tight grip, I stared at a house that used to hold too many secrets. "You think he did it on purpose? To take out the people coming to bring him in?"

Neither replied. That was answer enough.

"You better make goddamned sure they don't screw up this investigation." My warning was for Mac. Rix wouldn't have jack shit to do with it since he was on the gang task force.

"You don't even need to say it. I won't let it go until we have answers." Mac was like a bulldog when he had a lead, so I took him at his word.

I tore my gaze away from the pile of rubble. "What a fucking disaster."

Turning back to my Jeep, I walked away. After all, that was what I was best at these days.

TWO
ARIEL

"Even though I walk through the valley of the shadow of death, I will fear no evil, for you are with me; your rod and your staff, they comfort me." The priest's voice carried through the morning air as we said good-bye to Ronan Hennessy.

I'd been to my fair share of police funerals over the years, but today's bore no resemblance to the others. No rows of uniformed officers paying their respects. No bagpipers playing a lament. No twenty-one-gun salute. Only a small crowd gathered in front of the mausoleum, fronted by three men holding up their mother with their strength.

The Hennessy family had doubled as my own for most of my childhood. Dad was on the force with Ronan, and Rebecca was the most motherly figure in my life, since I lost mine before I ever had her. Then there were the Hennessy boys . . . all of them larger than life. Dark blond hair, devastating grins, and brilliant green eyes.

My gaze zeroed in on Rhett like it always did, against my will after five years of distance. I refused to admit the slam of my heart against my chest had anything to do with the crush I used to have on him. I'd grown up, gotten over him.

I shifted on my heels and let my gaze trail across the mourners, basically focusing on anyone and anything but Rhett. Now wasn't the appropriate time.

A pall hung over this funeral that had nothing to do with the normal somberness of the occasion, and you could see it in the uncomfortable posture of the mourners. *Dirty cop* who potentially committed suicide by blowing up his own house while his former subordinates were on their way to arrest him wasn't exactly the final chapter anyone aspired to, and it broke my heart that this was how Ronan would be remembered.

I couldn't reconcile it with the man I'd known. The facts I'd pulled from the media and my own curious search of the police department computer network sounded like something out of a Hollywood blockbuster rather than reality. And no, I refused to call indulging my curiosity "hacking," because it was so basic and benign that anyone with YouTube access could have done it.

Mrs. Hennessy's head bowed, and Rock, the oldest now that Robin was gone, pressed tissues into her hand so she could dab at her tears. Rome, the youngest, who looked nothing at all like I remembered, stood at her back, and Rhett seemed to keep her upright with his grip on her other arm. Mrs. Hennessy had named her boys after classic literary heroes. Rock was short for Rochester from *Jane Eyre*, Robin for Robin of Locksley, Rome was short for Romeo, and then there was the man named after the infamous hero of *Gone with the Wind* . . .

Rhett Hennessy.

I could have kept a journal of his facial expressions in high school, because I was that girl. Okay, so I had kept a journal of them, but that was only because I had a slightly OCD list-making tendency. Like that list of his favorite things. And then the one with the reasons he would make the perfect boyfriend to my fifteen-year-old self.

I glanced around to make sure I hadn't actually said any of that out loud. Sometimes I did that too. I blamed that on living inside my own head too much. No one here needed to know how completely infatuated I had been with Rhett, bordering on creepy stalker status. It had taken me years to grow out of that crush. And yes, I did grow out of it, *thank you very much.*

The pang in my chest as I watched Rhett wrap his arm around his mother's shoulders was truly out of sympathy. It had absolutely nothing to do with the fact that the years hadn't just aged him, they'd perfected him, even with the worn-around-the-edges look he had going on today.

My mind wandered as I murmured along with the group prayer. Rhett's sharp green gaze hadn't landed on me yet, which was no surprise. He had never *seen* me; I'd always been invisible. The buzz cut he wore all through high school had grown out, and I was pretty sure its current shagginess stemmed from neglect rather than from a nod to style.

His body had changed as well. He was still about six feet tall, but his frame's former lanky youthfulness had been replaced by a solid *man.* The tightness of his suit coat looked like he'd had to force his biceps into the sleeves because they'd grown since the last time he'd worn it.

I shifted where I stood, wishing I'd never started down this familiar road of *catalog all the reasons why Rhett Hennessy is still disturbingly gorgeous and out of my league*

—like the Quiz Bowl team at a kegger. And, of course, there was the ridiculously inappropriate venue for my thoughts—a funeral. *I'm going to hell, and not just for hacking the Vatican after I read* The Da Vinci Code *the first time.*

Nothing had changed.

I was still the awkward geeky girl I'd always been. No number of patents, successful IPOs, or dollars in the bank would ever make me normal. Rhett was still the stoic one who didn't need to speak for you to know what he was thinking.

The priest made the sign of the cross, signaling the end of the service, and the Hennessy boys stepped forward one at a time to shake his hand. Rock kept hold of his mother's arm, and Rhett turned around to face my brother. He'd been best friends with Heath since they could walk, had gotten into trouble together for their first two decades, and hadn't surprised a soul when they'd both gone to the police academy to follow in their fathers' footsteps.

The younger me would have inched closer to eavesdrop on what they said, but I was older now. More sophisticated. Okay, that was a lie, but at least I'd learned the art of subtlety.

When my dad shuffled on his feet beside me, I turned to him. "You okay, Dad? Need to sit down?"

Crippling arthritis that my father had never once mentioned—not in all the phone calls we'd had, nor during his trips out to California to see me—had hit him so hard, he could no longer hide the pain or physical changes.

"I'm fine." His response was gruff, probably because he was annoyed he couldn't find his old uniform to wear to the funeral. Part of me was glad he didn't find it—there wasn't a single uniform in sight.

"We'll be going soon. We're almost done here."

He harrumphed and looked away.

Well, okay then. This day hadn't been easy for any of us.

My brother spoke to all the Hennessys, shaking their hands and kissing Rebecca's cheek before stepping aside for another group.

Rhett never once looked in my direction. Never saw me.

Because he never does.

I wanted to kick myself for that thought. We were at his father's funeral, and this wasn't about me. Nothing that had to do with Rhett Hennessy would ever be about me.

As Heath returned to offer his arm to my father, I took a deep breath and gave myself a quick pep talk.

You can do this. You will not stutter. You will not hiccup. You will be cool, collected, and the badass CEO you are.

"I'll be right back." I turned and took a single step toward the family to offer my condolences as they broke away from the crowd and moved en masse down the cracked sidewalk to a limousine waiting beyond the gates of the cemetery.

I squeezed my eyes shut and spun around again. *Great. Now I'm a crap funeral attendee too.* It was no surprise I couldn't manage to get it right. Being awkward was my jam. Designer clothes and fancy shoes would never change that.

"Let's go," my brother said, tearing my attention away from the Hennessys. "I want to drop Dad off at my place, and then I'm tracking down Rhett and getting him hammered. No one should have to face a night alone after this fucked-up day."

THREE
RHETT

"Mom, you sure you don't need anything else from Aunt Linda's before we go?" Rock asked.

Part of me wanted to protest her decision to go back to Vail with him, but it was useless. She'd made up her mind.

"No, we said our good-byes already. She's keeping everything I don't take."

Mom's suitcase was already packed and on the limo floor in front of her. She didn't have much left thanks to the explosion, so only one bag was required.

Both Rome and I had offered Rock money to cover her expenses, but he wouldn't take it. Said he could take care of her just fine. Considering I'd been sending extra funds to Mom every month since I left, I didn't argue with Rock about that either. Rome told him to shut the hell up and spend the money that would show up in his account in a few days on her. Neither Rock nor I wanted to know where the cash was coming from. Rome's mercenary lifestyle wasn't a topic of discussion for today.

"Why don't you take the limo to the airport then?" I said

to Rock. "Rome and I can jump out at the hotel." We'd all stayed at Aunt Linda's last night, on the floor in her living room like we had when we were kids sleeping over. One night was enough of that. I'd checked into a hotel before the service for a few minutes alone to pull myself together.

Rome shook his head. "I'm going to the airport too. Got a flight out in a few hours."

My attention cut to my little brother. "You're leaving already?" I didn't know why I was surprised. The fact that he'd showed up at all was a shock.

"You need me to stick around? You got plans?" Rome asked.

Mom's gaze locked on me. "He doesn't have any plans, do you, Rhett? You're going to let the police sort this out, right? It's time for you to let go and move on."

I knew what she meant. I'd been living in limbo the last year, drowning my bitterness in whiskey. I told myself that was normal after you lost everything.

"Mom—"

Her expression hardened and she considered each of us. I didn't know if it was a habit left over from childhood, but we each straightened as she did it.

"This family has been through hell. First Robin, then . . . all of this." She couldn't even bring herself to say it, and I didn't blame her. "We're Hennessys. We're strong, we're resilient, and we won't let this break us. My life is not ending with your father's. I refuse to let it."

She stared directly at me. "Rhett, you've spent a year wasting your potential. Wasting your life. Turning in that badge wasn't the end of the line. If you ask me, it was the best thing you've ever done, but instead of finding a new purpose, you're shutting everyone out. Life is passing you by while you sit on the sidelines. You're better than that. Figure out what you want and go after it. That's what I'm going to do. No more of this wallowing nonsense."

Then she moved on to each of my brothers, giving them their own tough-love speech, but instead of listening to what she thought they were doing wrong, I replayed her words to me in my head.

I was surprised she thought turning in my badge was the best thing I'd ever done. But then again, she'd buried a husband and a son because they'd been cops.

Figure out what you want and go after it. That's the part that stuck with me. But what the hell did I want?

After she finished dispensing her wisdom, Mom's eyes filled with tears as she extended both hands and we gripped them.

"I love you boys. Please be safe. This family has borne too much loss. It's time for happiness." Her lips formed into a trembling smile despite her tears. "And maybe some grandbabies to spoil."

When she released our hands, Rock offered her another tissue to dab at the tears clinging to her lashes.

None of us volunteered to go out and impregnate someone, but if I had to guess what Rock was thinking, I'd say he was running through a list of women in his head to decide if there was anyone suitable.

An image of one woman flashed through my mind, and it wasn't the dark-haired beauty I'd lost to Rix last year. I had already moved on from my hang-up with Valentina before my life went to shit. No, the woman who came to mind was a redhead with a quick smile and an even quicker brain.

Ariel Sampson. The girl next door. My best friend's little sister. A woman off-limits to me who I'd worked hard to forget since the last time she blew in from the West Coast and then left just as quickly.

That red hair of hers had stood out like a flame against the slim-fitting black dress she'd worn to the funeral, bright enough to penetrate even the haze of my grief.

She hadn't approached me. Hadn't approached any of us.

And I probably wouldn't see her again for another five years, if ever.

"You getting out?"

Rock's question shook me from my thoughts, making me realize we were parked in front of my hotel.

"Yeah. Sorry." I shook each of my brothers' hands before hugging my mom tight. "Take care, Mom. I love you."

She squeezed me in return, and I climbed out of the limo to watch them turn the corner and disappear. My family would never be the same again.

The missed calls still registered in my phone's memory would haunt me for the rest of my life. What was Dad going to tell me? Why the fuck didn't I answer? Regret and shame consumed me in equal measure.

I stood before the tall building, dreading the idea of going up to my room and staring at the TV for hours, hoping it would drown out my grief. No. Not tonight. Tonight, I was getting drunk.

I headed inside, ready to get the hell out of my suit and into jeans so I could make my way to my old haunt where people would leave me to drink my whiskey in peace.

FOUR
ARIEL

Heath took Dad back to his place since the windows were blown out of our childhood home from the force of the blast that destroyed the Hennessys' house next door. The city had announced that all affected dwellings must be inspected and cleared before people could return, so it was going to be at least a week before Dad would be allowed to move back in.

I would have offered a bedroom, but I wasn't sure how long I was staying in town. After I saw how bad Dad's arthritis had gotten, I decided a few days would be a good idea. It didn't seem like he was taking care of himself the way he should, and his repeated questions about his uniform seemed like more than normal forgetfulness.

Carver, my driver for the time I was in New Orleans, navigated the streets toward the house I'd rented on Lake Pontchartrain. My last-minute travel plans didn't leave me with many options, but this place worked out well. Tonight, I planned to indulge in a glass or two of bourbon, a bubble bath, and sleep. What I wasn't looking forward to was the call that was supposed to be coming from my on-again/off-again boyfriend, Carlos. We were overdue to be *off* again.

My phone chimed in my purse and I pulled it out. *Heath.*

"Everything okay?" I asked.

"I tracked down Rhett and I'm heading to the bar. You should come. I know you missed him at the funeral."

My brother knew about my crush. In fact, he'd gone out of his way to make sure *everyone* knew about my crush. Even now, I wasn't above putting him on the no-fly list out of spite for the angst he'd caused me as a self-conscious teenager.

I opened my mouth to decline because saying "no" to social activities that required leaving my house was normally one of my favorite things, but something stopped me. One of my other special skills was avoiding reality when I didn't want to deal with it, and finding the right words to tell Carlos that we were done fell firmly into that category.

"Where are you going?"

"Molly's on Toulouse. You know the place, right? I know you've barely been home in the last decade, but you should remember a few things." Bitterness crept into Heath's tone.

"Twice. I've been home twice in the last decade, and yes, I remember where Molly's is." Did I sound defensive? Maybe.

"Good. Meet us there." He ended the call without waiting for a response.

Ugh. I hesitated for a full sixty seconds before asking Carver to change direction.

The last time I went to Molly's was when I was twenty-one and finally feeling like I'd come into my own. Four years in California not giving a shit about what anyone thought, along with developing and selling a few apps while

I was in college, had improved my confidence measurably, not to mention my finances.

It had only taken one night at Molly's to grind all that newfound cool-kid attitude into dust, though, and of course it was all because of one guy. Rhett Hennessy. I swear, he could be linked to every good and bad memory I had in this town, which probably had something to do with why I only came back when it was absolutely necessary.

To this day, I hadn't forgotten what it felt like to walk into that bar with my newly legal ID and see my brother and Rhett in the middle of a group of girls vying for their attention, each one taller, skinnier, and prettier than me. I was going through my Cali no-fucks-given phase, so I was wearing ripped boyfriend jeans and a worn white T-shirt shredded on the sides with a black bra under it. For me, it was the height of daring, especially knowing who I would be seeing.

Except Rhett hadn't teased me like usual. Hadn't asked me why I'd stolen his T-shirt (except I hadn't . . . not this time). No, he'd ignored me. Pretended I didn't exist.

The only saving grace was that he'd been blind to the pack of girls too, or so I'd thought. When he left an hour after I arrived, and I might have kept track down to that last minute, one particularly gorgeous stacked blonde exited the bar through the same door two minutes later.

The next morning at breakfast with my dad, I caught a glimpse of Heath's texts with Rhett giving him shit about going home with someone.

I still couldn't help but wonder if the escape happened because he was taking pity on me, not wanting me to see him leave with someone else because he knew about my ridiculous crush. *How pathetic, right?*

But tonight, I wasn't worried about any of that. Not my crush, not the past. Tonight was about helping an old friend, even if I used the term loosely, escape from some heavy stuff. My heart clenched when I thought of how Rhett must be feeling. His father, the man he'd looked up to his whole life, had been accused of terrible things. And then to know his dad had been blown up? Possibly by his own hand?

I cringed at the horrific reality.

Honor was a cornerstone of Rhett's character, and to think that his father had betrayed what he held most dear . . . how devastating.

Carver navigated his way through traffic and pedestrians to get as close to the bar as possible. "Would you like me to park and find a discreet place to wait inside?"

What he really meant was *will extra security be necessary?* But with Heath and Rhett both there, I wasn't worried about my safety.

"You don't need to stay. Go find a place to grab dinner, and I'll text when I'm ready. I'll be a few hours." *Long enough to miss any potential call with Carlos.*

"Yes, ma'am. Enjoy your evening."

"Thank you, Carver." I hopped out of the car and headed for the door to the bar.

Molly's was a bit of a dive. Even with its proximity to Bourbon Street, it had a distinctly different crowd from the tourist-jammed bars a hundred yards away. Locals filled the stools here.

"Flounder! You made it!"

The yell came from beyond the pool table, where my brother and Rhett had taken up position at a high-top with a bottle of whiskey between them.

That mental groan? It was for my childhood nickname being shouted across the bar.

Cue the question I'd gotten all too often during my life: are you named after the little mermaid? *Why, yes. Yes, I was.*

My mother was diagnosed with cancer while she was pregnant with me, and lack of medical technology at the time meant she couldn't be treated until after I was born. I lived, and she didn't. I steeled myself for the full-body wave of emptiness that came every time I thought about the woman who gave up her life so I could have one. My eyes burned with familiar tears.

How can I miss someone so badly when I never knew her? My logical mind railed at me every time, but there was no reasoning away the pain. My brother didn't realize that every time he used that nickname, it reminded me of the story my dad had told me about my mom spending her whole pregnancy watching Disney movies and telling me all the things she wouldn't be able to share with me as I grew up.

How different would my life have been if I'd had a mom? Rhett might have just lost his dad today, but despite everything that happened, he had over thirty years of good memories he could recall, regardless of whether the last one was shit. I didn't even have that. I had nothing. The sense of loss dogged my every step as I blinked back tears and crossed the floor, avoiding meeting anyone's eyes.

"Shut up, Scuttle." My brother laughed as I reached the table, the scent of whiskey wafting off him.

Another couple of blinks and I finally looked up. *Bam.* Rhett's brilliant green gaze slammed into mine.

"And miss my chance to tease my little sister in person

for a night? Not likely. You don't give me enough opportunity, so I gotta get it in while I can."

It was another jab at how rarely I came home, but I ignored it.

"How's it going, Ari?" Rhett asked, his voice rumbled as deeply as I remembered.

"I'm so sorry for your loss. I didn't get to tell you that earlier. I meant to. Just missed you at the service," I blurted, finally getting my chance to pay my respects.

Rhett's gaze dipped to his whiskey glass. "Not talking 'bout that tonight." He tossed back all three fingers in a single gulp.

I didn't watch the movement of his Adam's apple as he swallowed. *Okay, that's a lie.*

"Duly noted." My words came out bright and chirpy, at least until I choked on the saliva in my mouth and coughed twice. *I'm such a hot mess.*

Heath raised a hand to signal the waitress. "We need another glass over here."

"I'm more of a bourbon fan than whiskey these days," I mumbled as I pretended to study the drawings carved into the table. *Wait, is that an abnormally large penis and hairy ball sac*? No longer pretending, I tilted my head to fully appreciate the detailed carving. *Impressive.*

"Guess you're gonna have to slum it with us anyway," Rhett replied.

My attention snapped to him as his gaze traveled up from my hips to my face.

Is Rhett Hennessy checking me out? Surely not. I had to be wrong. Heat started in my belly and licked up my chest and face.

"Balls," I blurted. *Oh no. I did not.*

Both my brother and Rhett stared at me.

"What?" Rhett asked, probably thinking he heard me wrong.

I pointed to the table. "Dick and balls. Good work. Nice shape. Could use a few more veins." *Oh sweet Jesus, someone shut me up before the verbal mudslide starts.*

Heath's laugh boomed through the bar.

Why am I talking about penises? My gaze darted to Rhett's lap, and my cheeks burned as I looked away.

Great, now I'm going to be as red as my hair. I had to distract myself from the disaster. I snatched Heath's glass and tossed back the liquor.

Oh shit, that burns too. I coughed as soon as I swallowed, trying to mask it by clearing my throat. *At least now I have an excuse for the tears in my eyes.*

"Good stuff," I said, attempting nonchalance as I set the glass back down on top of the bar version of a dick pic.

The corner of Rhett's mouth tugged upward in a semblance of a smile.

Heath choked, sounding like he was hacking up a lung as he tried to stop laughing, slapping the table and nearly toppling the bottle of whiskey. "Damn, my little sister is all grown up, and I missed most of it." He grabbed the glass and sloshed another measure of booze in it.

Rhett's partial smile disappeared.

"I swear," Heath said to me, "I spend more time talking to your assistants than I do with you. I'm tight with Erik and Esme."

Deep slashes appeared between Rhett's brows. "You have two assistants?"

Before I could reply, Heath jumped in. "Yeah. In case you didn't know, my little sister is kind of a badass these days." He gave Rhett a quick rundown of my accomplishments over the last few years, stunning me by how much he knew about my adult life, considering he hadn't played much of a role in it.

Rhett's expression was unreadable.

Oh, great. Now I was the geeky girl who also happened to be a workaholic.

At that moment, I would have given anything, even my prized Funko Pop! collection, to know what was going through Rhett's head.

FIVE
RHETT

Little Ariel grew up, not that I needed a news flash to tell me that. I saw it with my own two eyes just fine. Who the hell was I kidding? I'd seen it the last time she'd come home and knocked me on my ass just by stepping out of a car in her dad's driveway.

Everyone knew about her crush in high school, including me. Then and now, there wasn't jack shit I could do about it. There were lines you didn't cross in life, and your best friend's little sister was one of them. Those lines put her completely off-limits.

Back then she was a brainiac with a case of social anxiety who carried a stack of books that probably weighed more than she did, but not anymore. Now she was a frigging CEO who could no doubt buy and sell me. That made her just as untouchable, in my book. If I'd been out of her league as a popular high school jock, she was out of mine as a loaded businesswoman. Apparently, that was my type lately. Valentina Noble had been one too. Learned my lesson there, and was happy as hell she and Rix had made it work.

There was no question now, though—high-class women like that weren't for me.

But watching Ari toss back two fingers of whiskey like she was an old hand and blurt out something about a dick and balls somehow made her seem more attainable. Or maybe it was knowing that she'd carried a torch for me for years. By the way she rolled her eyes at her brother when he referred to anything from the past, I had to assume she'd gotten over all of it, including me. She'd moved on.

Probably for the best. I'd honed plenty of *pretending Ariel doesn't exist* skills over the years. An eighteen-year-old had no business thinking about his buddy's fifteen-year-old sister the way I had. So I'd cut it off. Put on blinders where she was concerned. Heath would have ended me with his dad's service pistol, and I would have handed him the bullets to do the job.

Tonight, those blinders slipped. I couldn't stop noticing just how sexy she was. The dress she'd worn to the funeral still hugged her curves, but that wasn't the sexiest thing about her. No, it was how *real* she was.

She didn't put on a show. Didn't preen. And surely didn't have a clue how gorgeous she was.

Ari had wandered into the bar ignoring the attention that followed her every step, including mine. That was a refreshing change for me, and damn if it wasn't sexier than everything else combined. Well . . . maybe not. There was that wild mane of red hair that she tamed into loose waves, the legs that I didn't remember being quite so long, and that big brain of hers I'd always found fascinating.

A quick glance around the bar told me that the eyes that had followed her hadn't looked away yet. Plenty of them watched as she accepted a glass from the waitress and poured herself another two fingers from the bottle. She held it by the neck and read the back of the label while she lifted the tumbler to her lips. As long as I'd known her, the girl read everything she could get her hands on. Some things never changed.

Apparently satisfied with her study of the label, she returned the bottle to the table and scanned the room before looking from me to her brother. "Who wants to play pool first? Table's free."

I groaned inwardly. I wasn't sure I could keep my eyes to myself if I had to watch her stretch and position herself with a pool cue.

"Rhett'll take you on. I'll play the winner." Heath's words were proof that my best friend had some of the worst ideas.

Didn't he know I was doing my best to keep my hands *off* his sister?

"Nah, you go on—"

Ari stiffened. "Fine. If you don't want to play me, I'm sure there's someone in this bar who will."

She rose from the bar stool and smoothed her dress down her thighs. I swore it looked longer at the cemetery than it did right now, inching up her toned legs. The shoulders and chest were sheer black lace, as sophisticated as could be, but the lace took on a sexier edge in the dim light of the bar. I'd lay money on her being the classiest thing this place had ever seen. And damn, what those heels did for her . . .

I ripped my gaze away from her ass to focus on her face.

Her lips flattened in obstinate challenge before she strutted toward the pool table. And yeah, I used the word strutted because there was no other way to describe how she walked in those stilettos now that her attitude was flaring.

Heads turned to follow her progress, and two guys jumped off their stools to follow her.

Oh, hell no. *Not a chance, assholes.*

I pushed off my seat and stalked toward her. Ari's back was to me when I stopped behind her at the cue rack. She spun around, unaware of my presence, and smacked into my chest, a pool stick trapped between us. She sucked in a breath, jerking her head up.

"Sorry. Didn't realize you were so close."

Years ago, she never would have lost track of where I was if we were in the same room. The realization was a blow to my ego, although not unexpected. I no longer made the cut on her priority list, and that stung.

Rather than move and give her space, I reached around her to snag a cue off the rack, letting my arm brush her shoulder.

Ah . . . there it is. Her facial expression remained static, but her involuntary shiver gave her away. *Maybe I'm not off the list completely.*

I didn't know why it mattered, but after the last few brutal days, I needed something good to distract me from the shit show that was my life. And there was no doubt in my mind that Ariel Sampson was everything good.

Her spine straightened and she bobbed around me, avoiding contact in favor of racking the balls and lining them up.

"Do you want to break?" she asked.

"Ladies first."

Ari rolled her eyes and reached for the chalk. With her stick prepped, she leaned over the edge of the table, her ass jutting out and the hem of her dress riding up her thigh.

Lord . . . I groaned silently. This was torture.

Haven't I been through enough? I tossed the question skyward and received no sign the big man had heard me.

I tore my gaze off her ass and scanned the bar. *Mistake.* My fist tightened around the pool cue as a reflex, but that didn't mean I wouldn't use it to smack every jerk in this bar back into line if they didn't quit staring. Double standard? Sure. But I didn't care.

With a step behind her, I blocked the most direct view and turned to glare at all of them. Thankfully, Heath's interest was hooked on the waitress working our table. One by one, the gazes dropped away, and I turned back to Ari, marginally satisfied that they picked up what I was throwing down. *Off-limits, assholes.*

Ari cursed and stood up straight, leaning lightly on her pool cue. "Dammit. I had that shot."

I scanned the green felt and found half her balls were missing. "Jesus, what were you doing? Trying to clear the table?"

Her nose went up in the air. "Trying? If I wanted to clear the table, it would be clear. It's just angles."

"Brainiac as always."

Ari shrugged, but I caught a hint of a smile. "Didn't you hear? It's cool to be a geek now."

I had no doubt that wherever she lived in California, she was exactly what was cool. Shit, she had every man's attention in this bar.

"You were always cool in my book, Red. My turn." Even though I wanted to wait for her smile, I chalked my cue and sank two shots before missing the third.

"Not bad." Her nonchalant tone made me grin.

"I try."

Her eyes finally locked on mine. "I succeed."

Hell. Why was that statement so damned sexy coming from her lips?

She pushed off her pool cue and spun around to face the table again, her dress sliding up another inch as she bent over the table.

My dick pulsed against my jeans.

Heath is going to kill me.

SIX
ARIEL

I could feel his eyes on my ass. I knew it was impossible to truly feel someone's stare, but I didn't care because I knew it was there, just like I knew for the first time in my entire life, Rhett Hennessy was *seeing* me. I made one shot and deliberately missed the next because I didn't want to end the game too quickly.

Spinning on my heel with something snarky on my tongue, I slammed into Rhett's solid chest again, just like I had when I'd grabbed my cue. I wasn't saying I didn't do it on purpose.

Wham. My heart slammed against my ribs as it sped up about twenty beats per minute.

The heat and delicious woodsy citrus scent radiating from his body did good things to me. Things that made me want to do very bad things to him. I wasn't a seventeen-year-old virgin anymore. I knew my way around a man, but I had to admit, the hipsters in Cali had nothing on a homegrown Louisiana man like Rhett.

When he spoke, he leaned in so close that I could feel his breath on my ear. "You missed that shot on purpose."

My gaze jumped from the sexy five o'clock shadow shading his jaw to his piercing green eyes.

"Wha-what are you talking about?" I smacked myself mentally when my old stammer kicked in. *Of course he would cause it.*

"That shot. You missed on purpose. I saw you adjust at the last minute. Why?"

I swallowed the saliva pooling in my mouth and decided to take the safest exit from this situation. *Lying.*

"Cue slipped."

His eyes narrowed on me. "You're lying and you're terrible at it, just like you've always been." He reached up and pressed his thumb to my left eyebrow. "You get a twitch right here."

Oh my God. Rhett Hennessy is touching me. And what's more . . . he knows my tell. He noticed me!

The fifteen-year-old inside me did a terrible cartwheel at the realization. Okay, more of a round-off. With a tumble in the grass to finish. Whatever.

But outwardly, I was trapped in that green gaze until he decided to let me go—or until I came to my senses.

I cleared my throat and sidestepped him. "Whatever you say, hotshot. I need another drink."

Focusing on putting one four-inch heel in front of the other without biting it, I escaped to the table and reached for the whiskey glass I'd left behind, interrupting my brother and the waitress. They both stared at me as I chugged the contents.

I'd always wondered what it would feel like to have

Rhett's attention, and now I knew. In a word, it was . . . unnerving.

"How's the game going?" my brother asked.

"Fine." Keeping my answer short meant he couldn't tell that I was lying. Heath wasn't nearly as observant as Rhett.

"You winning?"

Thanking the Lord that Heath obviously hadn't been watching, I shrugged. "I guess."

He glanced toward Rhett and then back to me. "The sister I know and love doesn't lose at pool. Ever. Even to Rhett Hennessy."

I lowered the glass to the table and straightened my shoulders. "Like they say, things change."

He nodded slowly. "That may be true about most things, Flounder. But you're a pool shark and we both know it."

Before I could respond, Heath's attention jumped back to the waitress. I took another ten seconds to gather myself, also known as *drinking offensively* in my mind, before I crossed the floor to face off against my former obsession.

"You all right, Red?" Rhett asked.

"Don't call me that. And I've never been better."

His gaze dipped to my feet and dragged up my body. "I can agree with that statement."

Whoa. Who is this guy with the innuendo? A glance at his empty whiskey glass told me he was drinking heavily as well. Was this the booze talking? Or was Rhett Hennessy not just noticing me, but *noticing* me?

Either way, I had to play it cool. Or at least pretend to play it cool, since it seemed I might fall short.

"Your turn, hotshot. Better not miss, because I'll clear the table next time," I said, but my cocky attitude backfired.

Rhett didn't miss. He sank his balls and then the eight,

ending the game almost as quickly as it started. He returned his cue to the rack and turned to face me, all traces of the earlier heat banked, his expression shuttered.

"Game over."

What the hell just happened?

SEVEN
RHETT

When you play with fire, you get burned.

I knew the rules, and I saw the line. I wasn't breaking them, and I wasn't crossing it.

But damn if flirting with Ari hadn't made me say things I shouldn't even have been thinking. How many times did I have to tell myself she was off-limits before I got it through both my heads?

Standing next to the pool table with a hard-on, watching her walk across the floor to talk to her brother, *my best friend*, did the trick faster than you could say *bad plan.*

I knew what I had to do—end the game and get the hell out of this bar before I did something stupid, like get close to her again and catch a hint of the coconut scent coming from her hair. Or maybe it was her skin. I didn't know, but the fact that I *wanted* to know firsthand was bad enough.

Shutting it down was my only option. A shaft of regret stabbed into me when I sank the eight ball and Ari's expression deflated. It reminded me of how she'd looked when a kid in her class picked on her, and I had to go make threats to ensure it never happened again. Except this time, I was the one who caused it.

It made me an asshole. Not surprising, since that's what I was good at being now.

"Here, I'll put your cue up." I took it out of her fingers, careful not to breathe again until I stepped away.

Heath held out Ari's phone to her as I returned. "Your boyfriend texted. Might want to tell that douchebag to fuck off once and for all."

Wait. A. Goddamned. Second. Ari has a boyfriend?

Her gaze slammed into mine, a thin veil of guilt slipping over her features. That answered that.

If my hard-on hadn't already been gone, it would have died right then. Never again would I make the mistake of turning my attention on a woman who was involved with someone else.

Ari strode to Heath, yanked the phone from his grip, and unlocked the screen to read the text.

Even though I wanted to walk out the door, I followed them back to the table, and Heath took that as his sign to fill me in on the situation.

"You'll never believe this jackass. He's not nearly good enough for her. I don't get why she doesn't cut ties for good."

Ari stiffened at his words. "You know I can hear you, right? I'm standing right freaking here."

"Good. Then hear this—Carlos is bad news. You need to drop him." Heath was acting like the protective older brother he'd been on occasion, but there was one difference now. His little sister wasn't all that little anymore.

Ari turned her icy gray eyes on him. "When I want your opinion on my love life, I'll ask you for it."

"But—"

"But nothing. Besides, I was going to tell him we were over the next time I talked to him anyway. I was going to do it before, but I—"

"Didn't have the nerve to break it off?" Heath asked.

"Look, I was busy, okay? This isn't exactly something I can delegate to Esme or Erik and have them deal with it."

"No, but that doesn't mean you shouldn't suck it up and get him out of your life. For good."

Heath's adamant tone surprised me. This Carlos guy had to be an asshole for Heath to hate him this much. I would have said it was a case of no one being good enough for his little sister, but this felt different.

"Is he abusive?" I didn't intend to ask the question, but it came out anyway.

Ari's gaze cut to me. "No. Of course not." Her eyebrow didn't twitch, so I knew she wasn't lying.

"Then what the hell is wrong with him?" There had to be something, otherwise Heath wouldn't be talking about him like he needed killing. Even without having met the guy, I didn't like him. No one was good enough for her. Especially not me.

"Look, I'll deal with him when I feel like it."

It was obvious from the finality underlying Ari's words that the subject was closed. Heath didn't look like he agreed, but he kept his mouth shut and didn't say anything else.

Ari's fingers flew across the screen as she tapped out a text in response before shoving her phone in the side pocket of her purse, where Heath must have snatched it when the text chime came through.

"I think I need another drink. What about you two?" Ari grabbed the bottle and sloshed a measure of whiskey into all three of our glasses, but didn't wait for me or Heath before tossing hers back.

If a text from this jerk-off had her swigging whiskey like that, the first chance I got, I planned to ask Heath for his full name so I could run him through all my databases.

Heath's a cop. He would have already done that, I reminded myself. Except his detective skills had never been quite as good as mine. We were talking about Ari here, which meant a second look wasn't going to hurt.

Besides, even though Heath wasn't a top-grade detective, which was why he worked in internal affairs, his gut was solid and that was all I needed to know. Open season on Carlos was coming up.

EIGHT
ARIEL

Three sheets to the wind wasn't my normal state when leaving a bar, but when Heath laid off the Carlos issue, he launched into a trip down memory lane. It might have only been a year since he'd seen Rhett, but apparently that was sufficient time to require a rehashing of their High School Greatest Hits, or so I liked to refer to all their legendary exploits that got more impressive every time Heath told the stories.

After a second bottle of whiskey, I fumbled for my phone and dialed Carver.

"Yes, Ms. Sampson?"

"I think I need a ride soon. Probably a good idea."

"Yes, ma'am. Of course. I'll be there in under five minutes."

"Thank you, Carver." Both men were looking at me when I hung up. "What?"

"Who's Carver?" Rhett asked with heat in his green eyes that I would have loved to attribute to jealousy, but even I wasn't that intoxicated.

"My driver while I'm in town. He came highly recommended."

Rhett let out a whistle. "Fancy. Someone's come a long way from selling computer advice to the neighbors."

It was the truth, but not something I focused on. My bank balance didn't have anything to do with what kind of person I was, just how good I was at making money.

"Whatever." I surveyed them both. "You both want a ride?"

Rhett stood, gripping the table to keep himself from wobbling. "I'm not driving." He jerked his head at Heath. "Him either."

"No shit," my brother shot back.

I hooked my purse over my shoulder and the three of us made our way toward the door. One of the guys at the bar mumbled something under his breath as we passed, and Heath stopped in midstride.

"What did you say?"

The guy's expression hardened. "Didn't say shit."

"Thought I heard you say something rude about my little sister here."

The barfly's eyes widened. "Didn't mean anything by it. My mistake."

Heath yanked his badge from his pocket and held it in front of the man's face. "Damn right, that's your mistake. Watch how the fuck you talk about women next time."

I pushed open the door to see headlight beams cut through the darkness outside as Carver pulled up. "Oh-kay. Time to go now. Our ride's here."

I linked my arms through Heath's and Rhett's and dragged them both toward the door, using my heels as leverage.

Both men followed me, one spouting off another threat to the random guy at the bar, and the other silent, his bicep flexing beneath my hand.

Good Lord, I was right. Rhett did have to stuff his arms into that suit.

Carver had already opened the back door of the car, and his eyes widened when he saw me dragging two grown men out of Molly's. He released the handle and stepped toward me, his hand going to his shoulder holster.

"Ms. Sampson, can I be of assistance?"

His tone carried an air of lethal calmness that I recognized. I had a specific phrase I could speak to let him know I was in danger.

"No danger, Carver. Just my idiot brother picking a fight over nothing, and I've never been quite sure what this one's problem is." I jerked my head toward Rhett. "That'd require a lot more thought."

Rhett tugged out of my hold at my sarcastic comment, and I wobbled on my heels. Carver took a step toward me, probably intending to keep me from falling on my face or ass in the muck coating the streets of the French Quarter, but Rhett beat him to it, catching me around the waist with both big hands.

"Careful, Red. I don't think you want to swim in this sludge."

Rather than focus on the fact that Rhett was touching me, I lifted my gaze over his head. A wave of nostalgia washed over me as I took in the brick buildings with rusty wrought-iron balconies, the thick white molding with peeling paint, and the neon lights coming from Bourbon Street that never went dark.

"Ma'am, are you sure you're okay?"

My gaze cut back to Carver. “I’m fine. We’re getting in. I swear. There might have been a little more whiskey involved tonight than was advisable.”

“Yes, ma’am. As long as you’re safe.”

I pulled away from Rhett’s grip, telling myself I couldn’t feel the outline of his hand burning through the sheer sleeve of my dress.

Once we were in the back of the car, with me sandwiched between Rhett and Heath, Carver maneuvered us away from the bar.

“Were you going for a gun?” Rhett asked Carver. “Because I’ve seen that move before. And if I’d been carrying . . .”

Carver’s gaze lifted from the street to the rearview mirror to meet Rhett’s and mine in the backseat. “Ma’am . . .”

That was my cue to explain the situation or end the conversation so Carver didn’t have to violate the confidentiality agreement that came with providing services to someone like me.

I shrugged. “Cab drivers carry guns. Why shouldn’t he?”

Carver’s attention went back to the road, but Rhett leaned closer, pressing our bodies together from shoulder to knee.

Why is he so damned hot? Is he running a fever? There’s no way his body temperature is 98.6.

And, of course, thinking of ninety-eight degrees reminded me of the band by the same name and their cheesy love songs I used to listen to while I signed my name *Ariel Hennessy.*

Let’s hope Dad burned those journals I left behind.

An elbow bumped into my ribs from Rhett’s direction.

When I didn't look at him, he reached out and gripped my chin, forcing my attention to him.

"Was that necessary?" I asked, my jaw working against the calluses on his fingertips.

"Your eyebrow twitched. I don't believe you."

I rolled my eyes.

"Still waiting for those to fall out of your head from rolling them so damn hard."

"Hasn't happened yet, and I've perfected my eye-rolling technique since you last saw me."

"It was perfect then. Just like the rest of you."

I stiffened, and his hand dropped immediately. *Did he really just say that?* Rhett looked just as surprised by the comment as I felt. His gaze shot over my shoulder, but a soft snore came from Heath's direction.

Rhett cleared his throat. "Tell me about the security guy. Why do you need one?"

"I'm pretty sure that's none of your business."

"You've always been my business."

I snorted out a laugh. It wasn't very attractive, and all I could hope was I didn't accidentally land a stray booger on Rhett's hand.

He frowned. "What's so funny? I stood up for you all the time when we were in school. I think our history entitles me to a little leeway here."

When I was fifteen and a boy from my class broke into my locker and jammed it full of Nerds, rumor had it that Rhett clotheslined him during football practice and almost broke his collarbone. So he wasn't wrong.

I didn't want to tell him the truth, but since Rhett was a human lie detector where I was concerned, it was the least complicated solution. "Let's just say that once upon a time, someone I fired thought it would be fun to pose as a cab driver and kidnap me when I got in the car."

Heat flared in Rhett's eyes, flame-hot and furious. "Are you fucking kidding me?"

I shook my head.

"Why didn't I hear about this?"

"Because I didn't tell anyone."

His nostrils flared. "What did you say?"

"I. Didn't. Tell. Anyone."

"Are you insane?"

I shook my head, starting to get pissed. "No. I made a calculated decision that the drama it would evoke wouldn't be worth the hassle, so I told Heath I was hiring security out of a generalized concern, and he bought it. No one gives me the third degree about my decisions anymore, and no one else can tell when I'm lying."

"You need to be more careful."

My gaze darted to the mirror to find Carver splitting his attention between us and the road.

I jerked my head in his direction. "I'm being careful, hence the driver with a gun and hand-to-hand combat skills."

"Who the hell are you, and what happened to Ariel?"

I laughed in disbelief. "She grew up and made a boatload of money when no one was paying attention."

Apparently, I didn't regulate my tone appropriately because Heath jerked against my side.

"What? What's going on? What'd I miss?"

"Nothing. We're taking you home."

I rattled off his address to Carver, who had cleared the traffic in the Quarter. Gentilly wasn't all that far geographically from the estate I was renting on Lake Pontchartrain, but it was light years away in economic terms. The middle-class families in the neighborhood where I grew up would go for a Sunday drive by posh weekend places like mine and wonder what it was like to live that life.

But I didn't have to wonder anymore. It was my life.

As we closed in on Heath's house, only a half mile or so away from where Rhett's parents' home exploded days before, Heath shook off some of his drunken stupor and spoke to Rhett.

"Dude, I'm sorry. My dad took the pullout in the den. I don't have a spare bed for you."

Rhett cursed under his breath. "My shit's at my hotel anyway. I can grab a cab over there."

Heath leaned on me, shoving me tighter against Rhett's side. "Nah, dude. That's too big of a pain. Go stay with Flounder. She's probably got like seventeen bedrooms in that mansion she's staying in. If Dad wasn't so against change, I would've insisted he stay with her."

Rhett stiffened. "It's fine. I'll take a cab back downtown to the hotel."

"Ari, tell him you don't mind, or this stubborn asshole is going to be standing in front of my house waiting for a cab for a half hour."

What could I say except, "You can stay at my place. I have plenty of extra room."

I took Rhett's grunt for an affirmative answer, but he remained stiff for the rest of the ride, even after we dropped Heath off at his place and I slid over to the spot he'd vacated.

Carver checked the backseat, and for the first time, I wondered why I didn't insist on sitting in the front instead of being squashed between Rhett and Heath.

Oh, wait, that's right. I was close to my former crush who smells like fantasies and dreams, and my brain stopped functioning normally. Silly me.

When Carver pulled up to my house's fenced entrance moments later, he punched in the code. Rhett watched with interest as the gate slid open to reveal the well-lit colossus of a house.

Carver parked in the garage and opened the door for me to step out. Rhett opened his own door and followed us silently into the house.

"Do you require anything else this evening, Ms. Sampson?"

I shook my head. "No, thank you. Have a good night."

Carver retreated to the garage where he stayed in one of the two apartments above the eight-stalled monstrosity. Heath exaggerated when he said this place had seventeen bedrooms. There were only twelve, including the two garage apartments.

"You have changed. A lot."

Rhett's voice came from behind me as I walked into the kitchen and dropped my purse on the counter.

I wrestled with that comment. It was true to a certain extent, but I wasn't about to get into a drunken introspective discussion.

"Maybe. Maybe not," I answered simply.

"Ms. Sampson, is there anything else you require this evening?" Rhett's attempt at mimicking Carver's tone came off sounding hollow.

I spun on my heel. "At least I'm taking precautions and not being stupid. Because if I weren't, I'm sure you'd be lecturing me about my personal safety right now instead."

Surprisingly, a deep chuckle filled the room as Rhett's whole body shook with laughter. "Fuck, you're probably right. I'm sorry, Red. It's been a shit day, topping off a shit week, a shit month, and a shit year. It's not personal. I'm just being a dick."

At the word *dick*, it took everything I had to keep my eyes from dropping to his crotch. Again.

Instead, I plastered a sincere smile on my face. "You get a pass, hotshot. *I'm* sorry. I wish . . . I wish none of it had ever happened. I wish I could turn back time and fix it all for you before it went wrong."

His chin dropped to his chest, hiding his eyes. He lifted it after a few beats. "I believe you. Out of every person I know, you're one of the few who would move heaven and earth to save me from that."

For long moments, we both stood frozen in my kitchen, staring at each other. I didn't know how to respond, but Rhett saved me by turning to survey the house.

"So, which of the seventeen bedrooms do I get?"

I knew what I wanted to say.

Mine.

But we both knew that would never happen.

NINE
RHETT

You'd think I would have learned my lesson by now when it came to drinking, but last night it was either tip too many back with my friends, or drown myself alone in shame, regret, and whiskey. There was plenty of time for that, though. I'd be carrying this with me for years to come.

I rolled over on crisp white sheets I didn't recognize, my head pounding and my mouth dry. *Where the hell am I?*

I cracked open my eyes, hoping like hell there was no stranger beside me, but it was empty. Not even a wild red mane of hair on the pillow.

Where the hell did that thought come from?

I knew better than to let myself think about things that would never happen. Ari was so high above me, she might as well be in a different stratosphere now.

Wait a minute. For as long as I could remember, I'd told myself Ari was off-limits because she was my best friend's little sister. When had my thinking changed?

Last night. When I finally saw her as more than Heath's sister.

My mother's voice echoed in my head. *"Life is passing you by while you sit on the sidelines. You're better than that. Figure out what you want and go after it."*

It didn't take a genius to figure out I wanted Ariel Sampson. But what the hell was I going to do about it?

I rolled out of bed slowly, stretching as I went. It felt like a group of street kids had used my head for a drum on a street corner in the Quarter instead of a five-gallon bucket.

Going out last night had been a mistake, not because of the hangover, but because of everything else it shifted.

I should have stayed at my hotel. But I hadn't. And now I couldn't get the picture of Ari's hair spread across my pillow out of my head.

Turning away from the bed, I walked into the massive attached bathroom. Probably nicer than any I'd ever seen, but all I cared about was the new toothbrush on a tray between the double sinks.

After ridding myself of the gutter-sludge taste in my mouth, I used one of the glasses to drink a half gallon of water before opting for a shower. The steam killed the headache, and I finally felt like a functioning human again.

I pulled on my jeans, wishing they were sweats instead, and walked out in the hallway. I was hoping my nose would lead me toward the scent of coffee or breakfast, but no such luck. Instead of finding the kitchen like I intended, I got lost in the maze of hallways and heard a thump coming from one of the rooms on the back side of the house. I approached the door and heard a grunt and a groan followed by a moan.

I froze two feet away.

What the fuck?

Another thump and a groan.

No way. Ari was not having sex in there. Not in this house while I was here.

Because if anyone was having sex with her in this house, then goddammit, it was going to be me.

I froze, realizing I'd made a decision this morning that changed a hell of a lot. Now that I knew what I wanted and was going after it, no one was going to get in my way.

Especially not . . . who the hell was in there with her? If Ari's boyfriend showed up last night . . . No. Not after the way she acted when Heath talked about him. She said she was done.

Then I heard her grunt again, and with my ear practically pressed to the door, it sounded more like a noise caused by frustration rather than pleasure.

I shoved open the thick wooden door and burst inside—to find a full gym and Ari on her back, struggling against a much larger man, her face twisted.

Oh, hell no. No one puts their hands on her. He was going to die.

Rushing forward, I didn't think. I reached for the first weapon I could find, a dumbbell. I poised to strike.

Ari flipped the much larger man onto his back, keeping hold of his arm in a classic arm-bar submission move. "Tap, dammit!"

Her face red from exertion, Ari widened her eyes when they locked on me. Through labored breaths, she said, "What the hell are you going to do with that?"

She released her grip on the man and he jumped to his feet, his expression wary.

I lowered the dumbbell and Carver surveyed me carefully, something like respect settling onto his features.

"I heard you. Thought you were in trouble."

"And your plan was to bludgeon someone with a thirty-pound dumbbell?"

I glanced at the weight in my hand before looking back at her. "If necessary."

"Brutal," she said as she held out a hand, and I used my free one to pull her to her feet. "But thank you."

Carver retreated to a small fridge, retrieved two water bottles, and walked toward us, tossing one to Ari. He didn't look all too interested in getting close to either of us, probably because he almost died of blunt-force trauma to the head.

Instead of catching the water bottle with a feat of coordination like one would have expected given the level of skill she just demonstrated, Ari batted it away with both hands, hopping backward. "Whoa. Just because I can submit you with an arm bar doesn't mean I can catch things."

For some reason, it was comforting to know that certain things never changed.

Carver clearly didn't know her that well after all based on the look of surprise on his face. "But you just—"

"Planned out a series of movements to gain a submission and followed through with them while making adjustments in form to compensate for your changes? That's strategy, practice, and execution. Impromptu is not my forte."

I wanted to laugh, but my mind was already skipping ahead. Why the hell was she grappling and submitting a guy? Was there more of a security threat than she'd let on?

"You studying self-defense for fun or out of necessity?" I asked.

"Does it matter?" Her question to answer a question didn't satisfy me.

I dropped the dumbbell and lunged toward Ari, catching

her off guard by locking one arm around her stomach and the other around her neck. Then I hauled her back against me like an attacker might.

For a moment, she didn't move, frozen in shock. Probably like she would if someone actually attacked her in real life.

"Fight me," I growled into her ear. "If I can get you out of this room, I can get you in a car and no one ever sees you again."

Still she didn't move, but Carver looked like he wanted to pull a gun and go for a head shot. *Fuck him.* I was more invested in her personal safety than he'd ever be. This wasn't a paycheck to me, this was personal. Vital.

"Fight me, goddammit. Show me what you've got. What you'd do if your life depended on it."

I dragged her toward the door, and six feet from it, Ari finally snapped into action. Elbow to the gut. *Good.* Stomp to the top of my foot. *Damn, that hurt.*

Adjusting my grip, I moved my hand up from her neck to cover her mouth as she started to swear. Partially cutting off her ability to breathe would scare the shit out of her, but hopefully force her to fight harder.

We were three feet from the door when she bit my hand, and I jerked it away. Exactly the move she was waiting for. The next thing I knew, I was lying flat on my back on the mat with Ari standing above me, her chest heaving and a troubled expression on her face.

Carver stepped beside her, holding out her bottle of water. "You need to work on your reaction time." As soon as he delivered his advice, he strode out of the room, shutting the door behind him.

"You bit me," I said, acutely aware we were now alone and I was already flat on my back.

"You manhandled me," she snapped out, outrage coloring her tone.

"I think you liked it. That's why you didn't fight me off at first."

Her indrawn breath was indignant. "I did not!"

"Your eyebrow just twitched, Red." With a grin, I spun on my back and swept her leg so she tumbled to the floor, landing on top of me.

"What are you—"

"Going after what I want." Her gray eyes widened as I gripped the back of her head and pulled her down until her lips almost touched mine. "Kiss me. You know you want to."

She opened her mouth to protest, just like I knew she would, and I seized the advantage, crushing my lips to hers and sweeping my tongue inside.

One thing was for sure, her reaction time for kissing me was a hell of a lot better than it was for fighting me off. Sweet, sweet heaven.

And when she moaned into my mouth, my instincts shot into overdrive. I palmed her ass and squeezed, pressing her into my throbbing dick. With only a couple of layers of fabric between us, there was no question of her knowing exactly how I felt about her right at that moment. Another shaky inhale, and her hips bucked against me.

Fuck.

Without thinking, I released her ass and rolled her under me, and she spread her legs so I could settle my hips between her thighs. Her full tits, which I already knew would be spectacular, pressed against my chest, the nipples hard through her sports bra.

Her hands speared into my hair and she tugged at my lip with her teeth, urging me on, thrusting up against me.

I'd never allowed myself to think about what it would be like to have Ari under me, and it was a damn good thing. I wouldn't have been able to stop myself. Without thinking, I gripped the hem of her tank top, ready to yank it up and over her head, and I stilled.

Not like this. Not yet.

Ari noticed my hesitation when I released her shirt and scooted out from under me so fast, I was surprised she didn't knee me in the junk.

"I don't know what just happened, but I—" She turned away. "Oh my God. What did I do?"

I pushed off the floor with one hand, a hand that minutes ago had been wrapped around the curve of her ass. "I think it's safe to say not all of your reaction time needs work."

Ari's face flamed. She opened her mouth but nothing came out.

I would have given everything I owned to be able to see inside her head at that moment. Her gaze flicked from point to point on my face and then around the room, never making eye contact.

No, Ari hadn't completely gotten over whatever she'd felt for me once upon a time, and the bastard that I was wasn't above taking advantage of it so I could taste heaven again.

If I didn't try, I'd be adding *missing out on this* to my list of regrets.

Not happening.

Ari spun toward the door, grabbing a rolled towel off a stack on the table next to the mini-fridge. "I need a protein shake. My muscles . . . they're clearly tired after my workout, which came after last night's drinking but before the grappling and jujitsu. If I'd been properly rested and not dehydrated, I would've been quicker to react the first time."

I could almost hear her brain clicking into analytical mode as she tried to process what had just happened. I'd thrown my little genius for a loop, and she escaped from the room without ever making eye contact, so I couldn't even tell if her eyebrow twitched.

Alone in the empty gym, I walked toward the wall of windows, hoping the view of Lake Pontchartrain would make my dick stand down. My stomach rumbled a few minutes later, but I was hungry for more than just breakfast.

TEN
ARIEL

I *may never shower again.*

That's what the sixteen-year-old me would have said if she'd experienced the feel of Rhett Hennessy's naked chest against her skin. Spontaneous human combustion was real, and I was pretty sure I just came close to experiencing it.

Good. Lord.

I didn't know what just happened in that gym, but it wasn't something I could have ever predicted. In fact, I would have estimated the probability at less than one percent.

I touched my mouth, amazed at how my lips still tingled from where his teeth had scraped along them. Did I leave a mark when I nipped him? Part of me hoped so, and the other part was so embarrassed, I wasn't sure I could handle it. My ass burned where his hand had kneaded it, and let's not even talk about the state of my panties or the rest of me.

With a calming breath, I made my way into the kitchen, hoping just a little that Rhett got lost trying to find it. I needed about a hundred yards of space between us right now if I were going to get my head straight again.

Do I really want to get my head on straight?

Yes. Yes, I did. This was counterproductive. I'd spent years getting over him, and while that had obviously only been semi-successful, I refused to spend any more time thinking about getting *under* him.

Sweet Lord, it had been better than I could have imagined. I'd wondered whether my mind had inflated the size of that bulge in his pants. Probably more than I should ever admit. The conclusion? My estimates had been *way* off. Because now that I'd had the real deal pressed against me, I knew certain things were bigger than they appeared.

Good thing I didn't grind myself against him like a cat in heat, and maintained some of the dignity I've developed over the years. Even I could feel my eyebrow twitching at that lie.

Not thinking about this anymore. Also a lie.

I made it to the kitchen intending to make a protein shake, but one was already waiting on the counter and Carver was nowhere in sight. *He's efficient.* I wondered what I was paying for his services, and decided a hefty tip was in order.

Turning toward the wall of windows that looked out over the pool, grotto, and lake, I chugged my shake and waited to hear footsteps signaling Rhett's entrance to the kitchen. He would follow me, right?

Maybe not. Maybe his reaction to rubbing up against a sweaty woman's body would be to go shower like a normal human being. Where maybe he'd jack off.

Oh my God, I am not picturing him stroking that big, hard, probably veiny and perfect penis in the shower until he comes all over the travertine wall and the spray washes it down.

My pulse skipped up about twenty beats per minute at the visual, and my nipples peaked against my top.

Then I heard footsteps. I gulped down a huge mouthful of shake and tried to pretend I wasn't just thinking about Rhett naked in the shower. I spun around in mid-swallow and almost choked.

A shudder worked through my entire body. In the gym, I hadn't been able to fully appreciate the fact that he was shirtless and his body looked nothing like the lanky youth who'd washed his car in his parents' driveway while I perved from my bedroom window.

His thickly muscled and well-defined chest was sprinkled with a light smattering of hair that did nothing but accentuate how freaking manly he was. His abs had enough ridges to scrub laundry. And then those arms. Sweet Lord, they were my biggest weakness. Thick and strong, they looked capable of lifting the weight of the world from my shoulders and handling anything I threw at him.

From Rhett's hooded expression, he looked like he was having impure thoughts of his own. *Oh hell. Is he looking at me thinking things like I am while looking at him?* I couldn't process the idea, so I did what I was best at—rambled awkwardly.

"You want breakfast? I'm going to make eggs. Well, eggs and egg whites. Because it's healthier to get your extra protein from the whites and not have the yolks. But don't worry about shells. I don't crack and separate my own because I'm usually in a hurry, so I get them in handy cartons."

Stop, Ari. For the love of God, stop.

"But then again you probably know all about that because you look like you probably drink a carton for breakfast. Maybe lunch. Brunch? Or do you just eat meat?" I held out my cup. "Protein shake?"

Rhett looked around the kitchen. The corners of his mouth twitched like he was fighting a smile, and his chest shook like his laughter was internal. "You don't have to cook for me, Red. I'm capable," he said as he peered around me.

"What are you looking for?"

"No personal chef?"

I appreciated his change of subject more than he'd ever know. I smiled like a fully functioning, non-rambling human being. "I don't travel with one. It seems pretentious."

Apparently, that was the right answer. Rhett threw back his head and laughed. "Have you seen your digs? I think you're a little beyond worrying about what's pretentious."

I took a deep breath, feeling like we were back on level ground. I took a drink of my shake with another well-practiced eye roll before turning to the fridge. "It's not like my assistants consult me with details when they lease places for me. My requirements are outlined in the file, and they find something appropriate within those parameters."

"Exactly what are those requirements and parameters? A mansion big enough to fit an entire neighborhood, a pool bigger than at a resort, a view to die for, and enough bedrooms to host an NBA team?" His joking tone kept the question light.

I gave him my back as I opened the fridge. "At least twenty minutes from downtown, preferably thirty. Walled and gated. Fully monitored security system. There are a few other key requirements, but those are the basics. I set the budget, and Erik and Esme get creative trying to outdo each other on how ridiculous a place they can find."

I managed not to blush as I reached inside to grab the egg whites and a carton of eggs. Once the ingredients were laid out on the counter, I ducked down to reach for a bowl. "You should've seen this pink palace they leased for me in Dubai. It was absolute insanity. Some sheik's party pad. I stayed two nights, then got the heck out of there to go home."

When I set the bowl on the counter, I'd finally calmed down enough to make eye contact. Rhett stared at me like a complete stranger had stolen into the kitchen to replace the girl he'd known his whole life. I wasn't sure how I felt about that, but I wasn't going to dissect it right now.

"So," I said as I glanced down at the bowl. "You good with eggs, heavy on the whites?"

"You really don't have to cook for me. I've been doing it myself for a long time."

I shrugged. "Then it'll be a nice change for you." With a jerk of my chin toward the bar stools surrounding the massive kitchen island, I told him, "Sit. I'll make sure you get fed."

I kept up the chatter as I cooked, but it was mostly one-sided. Rhett answered when required but for the most part, he just watched me. I gave myself permission to ramble at will because it was the only way I could handle his stare.

You technically have a boyfriend, the voice in my head reminded me. *So you should take care of that situation before you roll around on the floor with another guy again.*

Wait, was I planning to roll around on the floor with Rhett again? Dumb question. *Obviously.*

Also, Carlos wasn't really my "boyfriend" in the traditional sense. He was a guy I dated on occasion, so it wasn't like he was a true barrier. One phone call and he would be gone. But . . . did I need a barrier? Every time I let myself get my hopes up about Rhett, it ended the same way—me leaving New Orleans with my head held high, telling myself I didn't care that he'd never want me. I'd go back to being Heath's little sister and totally invisible.

From the feel of Rhett's stare on me as I cooked, I most definitely wasn't invisible right now. *What is happening here? Has the universe gone crazy?*

By the time I plated the eggs, his gaze had switched from my every move to the wall of glass facing the lake.

Had he blocked out what had happened between us this morning? Maybe he was telling himself it was never to be repeated.

I snipped off a couple of sprigs of fresh dill from the artistic vertical herb garden at the end of the kitchen counter, then dropped them on the eggs before sliding the plates across the island.

Rhett finally turned around at the sound of a fork dropping next to the plate. Instead of commenting on the breakfast I'd prepared, his question threw me completely off-balance again.

"How long are you staying?"

ELEVEN
RHETT

I had to get out of here before I forgot why I'd forced myself to let go of her in the gym. I shoveled the eggs into my mouth, which were delicious, chugged a half gallon of coffee, and rose from the kitchen island, all while trying to forget Ari's response to my question.

"I haven't decided yet. Longer than I originally planned."

"Thanks for breakfast, Red. I appreciate it. You're a good cook."

"Glad you enjoyed it. If you need a ride back to your hotel, Carver can give you one."

That's one guy whose hand I should probably shake before I left. It was only his presence that had kept me from fucking her on the floor of the gym. If Ari and I had been alone this morning, that's exactly what would have happened, and that couldn't happen yet. I needed to make this right with her brother before I took things any further.

"I'll get a ride. It's no big deal. Thanks for letting me crash. I'll get out of your way."

As I said the words, I dragged my gaze up her body, knowing it was a lie. I didn't want to get out of her way. I wanted to be in her way so she'd remember everything she'd ever felt for me. I didn't want to give her a chance to forget.

"I do have work I need to do."

I'd spend all day working on her.

Her cheeks flushed like she could read my mind. *Good.* I wanted her thinking about it too.

"Then I'll see you around, Red. Soon."

She bit her lip as if she was stopping herself from saying something else. Like *stay*, maybe?

Even if I wanted to, I couldn't. Not until I talked to Heath. I might be an asshole, but I wasn't going to be the asshole who screwed around with his best friend's sister behind his back.

As I edged toward the door, she finally found her tongue.

"Have a good one, Rhett. If there's anything I can do to help with your mom, let me know."

Her offer reminded me of the Ari I'd known before. Always going out of her way to give. For the last year, I'd been the douchebag who took without giving anything in return. That was going to change.

I left the house and walked down the long driveway to the gate, pressing an inside button that sent it sliding to the side. Once it closed behind me, I knew it was the right choice.

I couldn't have her today, but that was going to change too. I knew what I wanted, who I wanted. But first, I had to get answers and sort out this disaster I called a life.

So I pulled out my phone to call for a ride.

Four hours later. I walked into a place I hadn't been to in over a year. The fact that the inside of Voodoo Ink hadn't changed a bit gave me some comfort, but the massive guy with the man bun and covered with tats sure as hell wasn't Con Leahy. I knew they'd hired someone else, but I didn't remember the guy's name.

Either way, it didn't matter because the man I was here to see was in the other chair, not moving a single facial muscle as the tattoo machine permanently marked him. Like always, stepping into this shop made me itch for something new, but that wasn't my purpose today.

Rix's silver eyes landed on me as I stopped outside the room he occupied. "Figured you'd be tracking me down sooner or later."

"What else have they figured out?" I didn't bother with an intro. Rix wasn't stupid. He knew exactly why I was here.

"Can't talk about an ongoing investigation."

"That's bullshit and you know it. If you were in my shoes, you'd be demanding answers."

Rix looked at the artist. "We clear here, Bish?"

He nodded. "We sweep regularly. With Eden's dad being nosy and shit, we don't much have a choice."

I blinked and stared at the man. I couldn't name another tattoo shop on the planet that regularly swept for bugs . . . at least, I assumed that's what he was talking about.

Rix's silver eyes locked on me. "You're lucky Bishop's girl is a mob boss's daughter, and he's up on security protocols and shit."

I wasn't sure why I was surprised. Voodoo Ink had never been your average tattoo shop. Why start now?

"What can you tell me?"

Bishop lifted the tattoo machine and wiped away the

excess ink with a paper towel, and Rix stretched before settling back into place.

"Not much. There's a rumor going around in the department that there's still a dirty cop among us. I'm starting to wonder if shit'll ever be right even after . . ." He trailed off, but I knew what he wasn't saying.

Even after the department was clear of Hennessys.

"Who?" The question came out with more force than I intended. If there was still a dirty cop on the city's payroll, that meant there was a chance my dad could have been set up. Slim chance, but a chance.

"Hell, Hennessy, if I knew that, I would've already arrested his ass so we could finish cleaning house. Everyone's on edge, looking at each other like their partner could be the one."

No police department should be running that way. I knew what it was like to have people constantly look sideways at me when I had a badge. Before my dad's role had been uncovered, my brother had been killed in the line of duty and fingered as a dirty cop working for the cartel. If I'd let that lie—let my brother forever be known as dirty—I never would have found out that it was my dad who was on the take, and that his fuckup had gotten his own son killed.

For the first time since I'd pulled up at the scene at my folks' house, I wondered if my father could have wired the house and pressed the button to blow it all to hell. Maybe he couldn't live with the guilt of knowing he'd killed his son any longer.

I didn't want to believe any of it.

"What do you think, Rix? You think my dad did it?"

"Wired his own house and planned to blow it up?"

The part about taking out the guys coming to bring him

in made my gut twist, but I gave Rix a curt nod anyway, even though I wanted to rage that there was no way in hell my dad could have done it. What stopped me? I remembered the mother of a serial killer screaming that her baby boy could never hurt anyone, despite the fact that he'd been caught with seven bodies in his deep freezer.

No one ever wanted to believe that someone they loved could do awful things, but the sad reality was that they were wrong. And if my dad did this, what did that say about me? What was I capable of?

"I don't know. I didn't get to see the file, and without that, I'm not gonna speculate." Rix shifted in the chair as Bishop moved on to another part of his arm, and met my gaze with a serious glint in his. "But knowing how bad the captain needed to close that case, it wouldn't surprise me if they took shortcuts and found a convenient scapegoat."

"Wouldn't be the first time politics outweighed justice," Bishop added.

"But then again, your pop wouldn't have been the first cop wanting to avoid prison bad enough to do something stupid and crazy."

I wanted to put my fist through Rix's face for suggesting it, but I knew he had a point. "Either way, I'm not letting this go."

"Didn't figure you were, but you might not like what you find."

I crossed my arms over my chest, knowing that he was right. "I owe it to my family to find the truth."

The creak of a door opening shut me up, but when Con strolled up the back hallway and around the corner, the stiffness in my spine faded.

"Never thought I'd say this to a cop, but I missed seeing

your face around here, Hennessy. Really sorry about your loss." The sympathy on his face was genuine.

I didn't have to point out that I wasn't a cop any longer. Everyone here knew.

"Thanks. Appreciate it."

"If you need a throwaway to take care of business, I have a guy that could hook you up," Con said.

Life without a badge never ceased to amaze me. What had always seemed so black and white before was all sorts of gray now. And how did I know this? Because I already had an unregistered pistol I could toss if I needed to.

Rix scowled at him. "Why would you say that shit in front of me? I know I was deep cover for a long fucking time, but I'm still a cop. You keep that shit to yourself until I get out of here."

Con looked sideways at Rix. "You want that tat finished? Then you'll shut the hell up and not comment on what I say in my own damn shop."

The two men eyed each other, the mutual respect obvious.

"Where's Delilah when we need her to tell you to just get your dicks out and compare?" Bishop said with a laugh.

Con looked around. "Where the hell is Delilah?"

"No clue. Probably getting her cards read. She doesn't have an appointment until three."

"Maybe her reading will tell her to get her ass back to work," Con said. "I'm grabbing last night's deposit and I'm out of here. Got kids to prep for at the gym."

It still amazed me that Con, the guy who didn't used to care about anything but avenging his parents' murder, had stuck with his pet project and made it into something that impacted hundreds of kids' lives. It probably helped that his woman was at his side every step of the way.

"Good seeing you, Con."

He clapped me on the shoulder. "You too. If you need anything, we're here for you. You've done me more than one solid, and I owe you. Just say the word."

I tucked that offer away, not about to turn it down. "Thanks."

"Don't be a stranger. If you decide to bail on NOLA again, at least let us know so we can throw you a going-away party. The girls love that shit. Any reason for a party, right?" Then he disappeared down the back hallway.

After a few more minutes of me asking Rix questions that he couldn't or wouldn't answer about my dad's case, I headed for the front door. Before I could reach it, a woman entered with a familiar cloud of black hair swirled around her shoulders.

Valentina Noble.

Wait, scratch that. Valentina Hendrix.

"I thought you were working this afternoon, not getting a tattoo?" she said as soon as she walked in the door, completely blind to anyone but Rix.

One more reason I knew she picked the right guy—he was all she saw. It hadn't taken me long to realize things had worked out the way they were meant to. I was glad my feelings for her didn't go any further. Seeing her so happy, it was one thing I could be proud of—that I hadn't tried to come between her and Rix when it was clear that they were strangely right for each other.

"Who told you?" Rix asked.

"Who do you think?"

"Eden," both Rix and Bishop said at the same time.

Rix shot Bishop a look. "You told your girl I was coming?"

The bearded guy shrugged. "Might've mentioned it."

"Duchess, you're gonna turn around and walk your ass back to your gallery and pretend you never saw me here."

Valentina crossed her arms over her chest. "Oh, really? Because that's not at all what I'm planning."

Bishop lifted the tattoo machine away from Rix's skin and slid his stool back so the man could lever out of his chair and stalk toward his wife.

"Yeah, really. Because you don't want to ruin my surprise."

Valentina's eyes went soft as she looked at him, and there wasn't a hint of envy running through my veins. No, there was something else entirely, and it didn't have anything to do with her. It was all wrapped up in wanting a certain redhead to look at me the way she used to.

It wasn't until Rix stopped two feet away from me that Valentina noticed me standing there.

"Oh my God, Rhett. I'm so sorry. I didn't see—"

Rix wrapped his other arm around her shoulders. "Don't bust the man's ego, duchess. He already lost the most incredible woman to walk the earth."

Her eyebrows shot up. "Stop it. That's not very nice."

"Never said I was nice. You knew that."

Valentina rolled her eyes. "Sorry, Rhett. I wish I could've been at the funeral, but—"

"It's fine." I stopped her before she could say any more.

She reached out a hand and laid it on mine, squeezing it tight. "Know that we've all been thinking about you. If there's anything we can do at all . . ."

"Appreciate it. I better get going."

When Valentina released her grip on my hand, Rix shook it next. "Take it easy. I'll let you know if I hear anything I can pass along. Don't do anything stupid in the meantime."

"I'm not making any promises."

My day looked like it was heading straight for the crap hole, but on my way to the car, I caught sight of Heath holding the door of one of my favorite oyster restaurants open for his dad. He must have seen me before I saw him, because he was already waving me down.

"Hey! You eat?"

I shook my head.

"Then come on. I'm buying."

Maybe today was looking up. I could tell him that I wanted to see where things could go between Ari and me, and the last roadblock stopping me from making a real move would be gone.

I followed him into the restaurant, working out what I should say, but as soon as I saw a flash of red hair, I knew that wasn't in the cards. But it could wait, because Ari's whole face lit up with a smile when she saw me before she could school her expression.

Yeah, this is happening.

TWELVE
ARIEL

I didn't expect to see Rhett again so soon. Even more than that, I didn't anticipate that his eyes would soften when he saw me like I was a welcome sight. This morning, part of me wondered if he was trying to get away from me as quickly as possible after our . . . um . . . *run-in.* Yet only hours later, his expression said he wouldn't mind if I were on the menu.

To every guy who has cursed women for giving off mixed signals, screw you. Guys are worse than women on every level. Just when I decided I was well and truly over Rhett Hennessy, he sucked me back in with a single look. And some groping. And rolling around on the floor of the gym. But how was I supposed to act now?

Too bad there wasn't facial-recognition software out there to interpret mixed signals. I pulled out my phone to make a quick note to check into the concept and brainstorm commercial applications.

All through lunch, I forced myself to keep up with the flow of conversation instead of disappearing into my own head like I would have done under other circumstances. Being fully engaged instead of distracted, I noticed two things. First, my dad's forgetfulness was worse than I'd realized. I'd flown him out to California to see me three times in the last year, and it had never been as apparent as it was now.

He'd asked the waitress twice where his order was, and that was after he'd devoured a plate of fried oysters. I was glad he was staying with Heath, because I was concerned about his ability to function by himself. I added another note to my list to research doctors for blood work and cognitive testing as soon as possible. Dad would bitch, but we needed to know if this was the gateway to dementia. I wasn't leaving Louisiana until we had answers, which meant I needed to get Esme and Erik on the phone to sort things out for an extended absence.

The second thing I noticed was that my brother had taken a turn for Crazyville. He asked Rhett about his plans for staying in town, and when Rhett said he didn't know yet, Heath shocked the crap out of us both.

"Flounder has that rental place for at least a week. You should just crash with her. I'm sure she wouldn't care."

I choked on a sip of water, and all the noise in the restaurant seemed to go silent as my heart pounded while I waited for Rhett's response. Using only my peripheral vision, I studied him as subtly as possible. He seemed as stunned by the suggestion as I was.

"Where's my dinner? I ordered an hour ago," my dad said.

This time, I didn't try to explain, but continued holding my breath, waiting for Rhett to speak. I counted the seconds as they passed, all twenty-seven of them.

"I've got a hotel."

"But she's got tons of room, and you could hit that kick-ass pool. Might as well make your trip back a little better by enjoying it."

Rhett didn't have a chance to give a definitive answer because my father stood up and yelled across the restaurant.

"Where's my damned dinner?"

Heath and I shot to our feet to calm Dad down, and the conversation was over.

THIRTEEN
RHETT

Stay with Ari? What was Heath thinking?

I still had no answer when I left the restaurant and headed out to deal with the less pleasant part of my day.

The image of Ari's wide gray eyes and sleek curtain of red hair stayed firmly fixed in my mind as I pointed my Jeep in the direction of my parents' house, hoping I could get a better look at the scene in the daylight.

When I arrived, I found the street had been cleared of debris, but crime scene tape still wrapped around the lot that used to hold my childhood home. Three black-and-whites were parked along the curb, and members of the crime-scene unit were crawling all over the rubble. I ducked under the tape, but a uniformed officer I didn't recognize stopped me before I made it six feet.

"Sorry, sir. You can't be here."

"This is my parents' house. I'm not going anywhere."

Knowledge flashed across his face. I might not have known who he was, but he sure as hell knew me.

"Mr. Hennessy, you need to step back."

Mr. Hennessy. It sounded so foreign even now. I'd been Detective Hennessy for enough years that it was strange to be addressed as anything else.

Arguing with him wouldn't gain me any ground. I didn't have a badge, and the law wasn't on my side, so I tried a different tack.

"How long before you clear the scene? I need to start figuring out cleanup and disposal." I had no idea if my parents' insurance would cover it or if I'd be looking at massive debts to split with my brothers, but it needed to be done.

"I couldn't say, sir. The department will let you know as soon as you're able to have access. In the meantime, I would suggest that you leave this to the professionals."

The last part was a dig, and it burned just the way he'd intended.

"Thanks for nothing." I turned away from the uniformed punk, wondering if I'd ever been that big of a prick. Probably.

Instead of giving him the satisfaction of watching me get in my car and drive away, I headed to the house across the street. I might not have a badge anymore, but that didn't mean I couldn't canvass the neighborhood for information. Eyewitness statements might be notoriously unreliable, but skipping out on taking them wasn't an option. Occasionally there was a single nugget of information that could change the trajectory of an entire investigation.

"Oh my goodness, Rhett Hennessy, is that really you?" Mrs. Thurman greeted me at the door with a warm smile. "It's been an age since I've seen you around. Do you have any idea when all those police officers are going to let Minnie back into her house?"

Minnie Myers had lived on the other side of my folks for as long as I could remember.

"I'm not sure, Mrs. Thurman. They wouldn't give me any information either."

"I swear, there aren't any good cops left anymore . . ." She trailed off, probably because she assumed it was a sore subject with me. She was right.

I also noticed she didn't ask about the Sampsons, and I knew why. About ten years ago, Mr. Sampson decided to have a neighborhood party and didn't invite Mrs. Thurman. The grudge had lasted an entire decade with no signs of fading. Her dedication to it made me smile to myself. It was good to know some things in the old neighborhood hadn't changed.

"They've been going through that pile of brick piece by piece. I've been watching them for days, and I can't see that they've found a single useful thing. Sure, they've put stuff in baggies like it meant something, but it looks like a whole lot of nothing. No one lit up and jumped around like they'd found the answer they're looking for."

And that was why I started with Mrs. Thurman. She was the stereotypical nosy neighbor with nothing but time on her hands to people-watch from her window. It drove my mom nuts, but I hoped it would turn out to be my saving grace.

"Have the police been by to talk to you?"

She harrumphed. "They sent a wet-behind-the-ears kid in a uniform who wasn't even old enough to be my grandson. He didn't even ask me about my day before he started in on the questions. Beyond rude."

"So you didn't have anything to tell him?"

She smiled, looking awfully proud of herself. "I had

plenty I could've told him, but I decided I'd wait until they sent someone who would treat me with a little respect."

And that's when things got interesting.

Apparently, for months now my dad had been heading out within minutes of my mom leaving the house every day. Mrs. Thurman didn't want to speculate on what he was doing, but she said he was constantly looking around like he suspected he was being watched. When she'd tried to confront him about it, he'd blown her off, so she'd decided to keep it to herself but hadn't stopped watching. My folks had also had several unusual repair people, or so she assumed, because an unmarked white van had been parked on the street in front of the house a few times over the last couple of weeks.

I took down notes in my phone, wishing I could ask my dad what the hell had been going on. If I knew my father, which I'd been questioning for a while, he wouldn't have involved my mother in anything, so asking her would be a dead end.

After I ate the stale cookies Mrs. Thurman offered and drank her lukewarm coffee, I left with more questions than answers.

What the hell were you doing, Dad?

I spent the rest of the afternoon interviewing other neighbors, none of whom were as helpful or as observant as Mrs. Thurman. However, all of them were nosy and not afraid to pry into my life. I finally left the neighborhood that held all my childhood memories around six o'clock and returned to my hotel to order a crappy room-service dinner.

If I'd jumped on that offer Heath had made, I could be at Ari's right now. Why the hell hadn't I?

After an hour of staring at the blank notepad that was

supposed to contain all my brilliant theories about what had happened with my dad, I'd had enough. I needed to get out of this room before I lost my damned mind.

Heath must have had a sixth sense, because my phone lit up with his name on the screen. After a year of not answering calls, it was strange not to ignore them.

"What's going on, Heath?"

"Can you do me a favor?"

"Sure. What's up?"

"I got into it with Ari tonight. She stormed out of here pissed off, and if I go track her down, she's going to be even more pissed."

As soon as he said her name, all my senses kicked into overdrive. "What happened?"

"I had a cop buddy of mine out in Cali keeping an eye on her boyfriend, and, well . . . he sent me pictures this morning that were damning. I showed her today after we got Dad home from lunch, and I'm a little worried that she's gonna do something stupid."

The fucking boyfriend. He had to go. Now more than ever, because Ari wasn't his anymore. Not if I had a damned thing to say about it.

But Heath didn't know I'd staked a claim on his sister, and that discussion wasn't happening over the phone. That would make me a spineless dick.

"What kind of pictures?" It was more of a demand than a question.

"The kind where he's wrapped around another woman, buck-ass naked."

Dammit . . . the kind of pictures I'd delivered to more than one spouse after catching someone cheating. The aftermath was never pretty. I'd seen it all—people flying into a rage, curling up into a ball and crying, or staring out the window like their soul had been sucked out of them. I never left them alone without asking them if there was someone I could call.

"And you just let her go?"

"It's not like I had a choice. She doesn't listen to me. Not sure she ever did before. I would go track her down, but Dad's riled up and I can't leave him here alone. I need you, man."

Did Heath know something had happened between us? What was his angle here? Either way, there was no question about whether I'd go after her.

"Where'd she go?"

"I don't know. She won't answer my calls, and I don't like the idea of her out hitting some bar by herself."

"You really think she'd go out?" The Ari I knew wasn't a barfly, although she'd held her own last night.

"I know so. I got in touch with her driver, and he told me he dropped her at Molly's an hour ago and she sent him away. He didn't feel comfortable leaving, so he's parked as close as he can get. But unless she asks for him to come inside and babysit her, his hands are tied. He can't go against her orders unless there's an immediate threat."

Shit. Molly's? I'd seen the way those guys had stared at her last night, and on a Friday, it had to be even more packed.

"I'll be there in fifteen. I'll make sure nothing happens to her."

"I know you will. There's no one else I'd trust with my baby sister. Thanks."

When Heath hung up, his words echoed in my head.

"There's no one else I'd trust with my baby sister."

Tomorrow, I'd find out if he really meant that, because our come-to-Jesus talk was due.

I didn't waste any time before heading out to jump in my Jeep and point it in the direction of Molly's.

The French Quarter was so packed with cars and people that traffic moved only inches at a time. I cut down a dark street that I knew would be mostly overlooked and found a parking spot I'd used many times before. Even after being gone a year, this city was still my home, and I knew the tricks.

When I climbed out of the car, a couple of homeless punks paused in trying to jimmy a gate open and ran in the other direction. Before, I would have chased them down, and it was hard to suppress the urge. It wasn't my job anymore, and I had more pressing business tonight.

I strode down the uneven concrete sidewalk and swung into the open doorway of Molly's. My first thought when I walked inside was pure instinct. *I'm going to paddle her ass when I get her out of here*. I couldn't miss Ari, and neither could anyone else in the bar.

A black sweater hung at her elbows, revealing a tiny white tank top that barely covered her bra or the tits pushing up over the top of its cups. With the sweater on, she might have looked like a sexy librarian waiting to be unwrapped, and with it off, she could stop traffic. The red-and-white plaid skirt that completed her outfit was no doubt giving every man in the bar schoolgirl fantasies.

What the hell was she thinking? Her red hair spilled

down her shoulders, and every eye in the bar followed as she bent over the pool table to take a shot.

Was that . . . Oh, hell no. Please tell me I *could not* see the bottom curve of her ass when she leaned too far forward.

Three other men had their heads tilted to the side in a way that would have been comical if she weren't my woman. Whether she knew she was mine wasn't the important point in my mind. It was inevitable.

I stalked across the room and slipped the pool cue from her hand before she could twitch her ass again or take the shot.

"What the hell—" Ari straightened and spun at the same time.

"What do you think you're doing?"

Her eyes, already bright from liquor, narrowed on me. "Not that it's any of your business, but *whatever the hell I want because I'm a single woman.*"

When she flipped her hair over her shoulder for an extra punch of attitude, my dick stood up and took notice. *So she's officially single now.* Good to know.

"We already covered this. You're my business. Always have been."

"Hey, the lady and I are playing a game here."

I twisted my head toward the guy leaning on a pool cue at the other side of the table. He looked pissed at the interruption. Too damn bad.

"Game's over."

"Says who?" Ari narrowed her eyes on me. "Me and Jack were just getting to know each other."

"It's John—"

"Thanks, John. I got this." I swung my gaze from her

pissed-off pool partner to her and said, "We're going home," loud enough so everyone in the bar heard me.

"No, we are *not*," Ari snapped back, and my gaze stuck on the bright red slicking her lips.

Jesus, that would look amazing around my cock. As soon as the thought entered my head, I shut it down. That wasn't why I was here.

"Look, Heath told me about the boyfriend shit. Glad you're done with him, but trust me, this isn't the way to handle it."

She dropped a hand to her hip. "Don't tell me what to do. You're not my father and you're not my brother. You've only kissed me once, so that means you can go ahead and keep your opinion to yourself."

I laid the pool cue on the table and grabbed her hand. "Let's go, Red."

She tugged out of my grip and spun around to face John, who'd come around the table. "I'm not leaving without finishing my game."

I wrapped an arm around her waist and yanked her back against me. "You want a game, Ari? Then you'll be playing with me. Not some damned stranger."

She let out a grunt of anger and struggled against my hold.

"Hey—" John interrupted, but my fierce glare shut him up.

Ari whipped back around, no doubt to rip me a new one, and I silenced her the best way I knew how.

I kissed her.

FOURTEEN
ARIEL

I had no idea how it happened, but Rhett Hennessy was kissing me. *Again*.

The heat from the alcohol buzzing through my veins blended with the adrenaline dumping into my system from sparring with him. The result? Enough combustion to create an inferno.

I moaned against his lips as he buried his hand in my hair and tugged my head to the side for better access. The kiss morphed from a maneuver to an obsession in a flash. All day, I'd told myself it wasn't as good as I remembered. I'd built it up in my head. I might be suffering from some exotic disease.

But no. I was wrong. *It was better*.

Without thinking, I lifted my leg and wrapped it around his hip, wanting to get closer, to feel more, as his tongue dived inside.

Oh sweet Jesus, he tastes even better too. Spearmint and spice this time, mixed with the bourbon I'd been drinking.

Rhett reached down and cupped my ass—under my skirt—and I melted, drenching my panties.

Even on my boldest day, I wasn't an exhibitionist, but in that moment, I wouldn't have cared if he'd boosted me up onto the pool table and taken me in front of the whole bar. Actually, it didn't sound like the worst idea I'd ever had.

But Rhett came to his senses and tore his mouth away. His hand squeezed reflexively, and my hips bucked against him again.

"We're leaving." He growled the words, and I hoped the promise they carried was really there and not a figment of my drunken imagination.

"You should probably kiss me again first." I leaned up on my tiptoes and pressed my lips to his, and his growl vibrated through my body.

Within seconds, I found myself flying through the air and upside down, landing over his shoulder.

"Hey—" My surprised screech filled the air, and everyone in the bar started shouting.

"That's the way to handle her!"

"Nice move!"

Men. Screw them all.

When I struggled against Rhett's hold, a heavy palm landed on my ass to hold me in place. My cheek stung where it landed.

Oh my God. Did he just spank me? As quickly as that question flew through my head, it was immediately followed by another. *And why do I like that idea so much?*

While I was trying to come up with answers to both those questions, Rhett carried me out of Molly's to the sound of the patrons cheering him on.

I was too stunned by what had happened to protest—or to flip them off.

Rhett set me on the sidewalk on my heels, grasping my shoulders to steady me. "You ready?"

I crossed my arms, trying to block out the fact that my panties were soaked, and summoned up the proper level of indignation. "Are you seriously asking me that question right now? Shouldn't that have been the question you asked before you threw me over your shoulder like a caveman and decided to carry me out of the bar?"

One corner of his mouth quirked upward, and there was zero remorse in his expression. "I think you liked it."

"I most certainly did not!" The denial was instant, and the other corner of Rhett's mouth lifted as he grinned.

"Eyebrow's twitching." He grabbed me by the hand and hauled me against him.

I opened my mouth to sputter something. *Anything*. But Rhett was quicker.

"Good thing, because I sure did."

He covered my lips with his, tasting me like a starving man, his hands roaming over every inch of my curves.

"Ms. Sampson, are you okay?" Carver's voice came out of the darkness in an unwelcome interruption.

I tore away from Rhett and twisted around to face him. "Uh—"

"She's fine," Rhett answered for me.

Gathering my wits, I spun back to glare at him. "I'm perfectly capable of speaking for myself."

I turned toward Carver one more time, straightening my

hair as if that would somehow make me not look like I'd been two steps from begging Rhett to take me up against a wall in some dark corner.

"I'm fine, Carver. No need to be alarmed."

He nodded, his expression giving nothing away. "The car is this way, if you'd like to follow me." He held out an arm to direct me.

"I'm taking her back to her place," Rhett replied.

His answer surprised me, and Carver's attention jumped between us, finally landing on me.

"Ma'am?"

"You can meet us at the house. Thank you."

With a deferential nod, he stepped back. "Yes, ma'am."

I twisted back to Rhett, but before I could open my mouth, he pinned me with his green stare.

"You and I are going to have a talk. Let's go."

"I get to have a say. I'm a freaking CEO. No one makes decisions for me, but me."

Rhett's eyes narrowed. "Not when your decisions put you in the middle of a meat market like you're out trolling for a random rebound hookup."

"So what if I had been? I'd be well within my rights!"

"Because I had you under me this morning, and I'll be goddamned if you're going to let someone else put his hands on you before we figure this out."

He guided me down the sidewalk, and I let him, because I was too busy processing his words.

"Figure what out?" I asked a few steps later.

Rhett paused beside the Jeep. "You and me."

My mouth dropped open as he unlocked the door and lifted me to deposit me on the seat.

You and me.

Holy. Crap.

Rhett shut the door and rounded the hood to hop inside. I was struggling to catch up with the point where *you and me* had become a thing when he pulled out of the spot and the Jeep rolled forward.

As Carver pulled out behind us, I mumbled, "I feel like I need a flowchart to keep up with what's happening here."

Rhett shot me a pointed look. "What's happening here is I'm taking you home. You're not going to Molly's again without me. You want to rub up against a guy in a bar? It's gonna be me."

"Did I miss something?"

"What?" he asked, maneuvering the Jeep through traffic.

"This massive shift? You've gone from never noticing my existence to all of a sudden hauling me out of bars and kissing me. Yeah, a flowchart would be helpful."

Rhett said nothing at that point, leaving an awkward silence that hung in the car until we hit the causeway over Lake Pontchartrain and toward my place.

"Last time you were home," he finally said, "your hair was about four inches shorter. You had blond highlights that looked more like the sun had turned your red into gold. You had on a green dress I wanted to peel off you. Your heels were tall and black, and I spent the entire night trying not to look at you because I kept imagining what they'd feel like digging into my back. I went home and jacked off thinking about how good it would feel to come inside you."

Oh. My. God.

I didn't realize I'd whispered the words aloud until Rhett glanced over at me, the heat in his gaze even stronger.

"Don't tell me I didn't notice you. I noticed every goddamned thing about you. But because of your brother and the respect I have for him, I wasn't about to let you know that I've been noticing you for longer than I want to admit. You think I don't see you? I have to pretend I don't, or I'd end up with my head mounted on Heath's wall. He's my best friend, closer than my own brothers, and I wouldn't have disrespected him like that."

Okay then. Wow.

Rhett was attracted to me. For real. And I'd be damned if my brother's existence was going to be a Rhett-proof chastity belt.

"My brother doesn't get to have a say in that part of my life. I'm an adult."

"I know. He might not get a say, but he does deserve my respect. I'm going to tell him."

My entire world shifted on its axis tonight. Rhett wanted me. And he had for years. It pissed me off that he'd held back because of Heath, but it also made sense.

Loyalty. Respect. Honor. Those were qualities Rhett had in spades, and without those, he wouldn't have been the man I'd been wanting in my life for so long.

And now when I was faced with photographic evidence of Carlos's cheating, those things meant more than ever.

What would it be like to be with a man who prized his principles as highly as he prized his woman?

I had no idea. I'd told myself I was over Rhett, but I'd been making decisions with incomplete information, which basically meant I was making a different decision. I needed to analyze all these new facts.

But the biggest question was—*what am I going to do about it tonight?*

My time for evaluating anything was gone because we'd

reached the gate and Rhett had stopped next to the keypad mounted outside.

"Code?"

Oh, good grief. I changed the code to every place as soon as I got there . . . and this one was embarrassing.

I rattled off "111723" and Rhett punched it in. It wasn't until the gate closed behind us that he spoke.

"My birthday and football number."

Everything inside me cringed. Dammit, sometimes I forgot he was a good detective.

"Coincidence, Ari?"

I looked over at him and focused on my words. "Complete coincidence."

"Your eyebrow just twitched."

FIFTEEN
RHETT

Get her inside. Do not fuck her. And for the love of God, don't blow your load in your pants like a kid on his first date.

Before I could let this go any further, I had to clear it with Heath. Otherwise, I'd feel like shit.

Although I had my self-imposed marching orders, I doubted my confidence to stick to them as I parked under the porte cochere and hopped out of the Jeep. Ari had her door open by the time I got there, her legs stretching for the ground and looking longer than ever in that short skirt. It wasn't the first time I was glad my Jeep had those six extra inches of height on it.

I reached out to grab her but she jumped at the same time, stumbling forward when her feet connected with the ground. My outstretched hands connected with her perfect tits.

Christ. I had no doubt they were one hundred percent perfect based on how damn good they felt in my hands.

Instinctively, my fingers closed around them, and the nipples hardened against my palms.

My dick flexed against the zipper of my jeans like it was testing just how tricky it would be to find its way out and into the woman I'd never been able to admit I wanted.

Until now.

The expression on Ari's face was priceless when she realized I was holding her up by her tits.

"Steady there." I slowly positioned her upright and released my grip, even though I didn't want to.

When she wobbled on her heels, I grasped her around the waist this time, not able to talk myself into breaking contact completely.

"You're bossy all of a sudden."

A smile slid over my lips, tugging one corner up. "I've always been bossy. You just never realized it."

Her eyes widened, telling me she put it together in the context I meant. Heat crept up Ari's cheeks, and there was nothing I wanted to do more than bury my hands in her hair and kiss her again. But that would be dangerous, considering we were within sprinting distance of her bed.

And I meant what I'd said—I wouldn't go down this road without clearing it with Heath first. Sure, Ari was a grown woman and made her own decisions, but loyalty and friendship were concepts I valued.

Apparently, Ari wasn't willing to be patient. Her hands moved from my shoulders to my neck, pulling my mouth down to hers.

Wait, did it count if I wasn't kissing her, but she kissed me?

Loophole. This is what those fucking lawyers would call a loophole.

As soon as her lips pressed against mine and she took the lead, all thought left my head except how damn good she felt.

Ari moaned against my mouth, rocking her hips against my erection.

I was going to hell. My hands dropped from her waist to grip her hips, and when her tongue stole inside my mouth, I pushed her skirt up to her waist and squeezed my next favorite spot—her ass.

She bucked into me, tugging hard on my hair as she lifted a leg and wrapped it around my hip for more contact just like she had at the bar. I'd been two seconds from laying her out on the pool table and fucking her in front of an audience then, and now that there wasn't one . . .

My fingers slid when she moved, and before I could draw them back, they swept across the wet panties covering her pussy.

Fuck. Me.

Ari was drenched, just like she was always meant to be for me.

One move, that's all it would take to bury a finger inside her. I rubbed along the soaked lace as Ari moaned into my mouth, urging me on.

One finger slipped under the fabric—seconds away from finding heaven—when the front gate opened and headlights cut through the darkness before they came down the driveway.

Ari either didn't notice or didn't care, because she was still writhing against me. There was no way in hell I was going to let Carver see her like this, though, and I was pretty sure she'd agree.

I pulled my mouth away from hers. "We gotta stop."

"But—"

"Company."

As soon as the word was out, Ari jerked back, dropping her leg and shoving down her skirt. "Shit. Carver. I forgot."

One of the garage doors opened, and as the car turned, the beams cut across us.

There was no way Carver could miss Ari's wild hair or flushed face, so I took charge. "I gotta get the hell out of here before we do something we might both regret in the morning."

Ari shrank back from me, but I was too preoccupied with getting her inside to notice. As soon as we stepped into the gargantuan house, she crossed her arms over her chest again, but this time, there was nothing seductive about it. All that delicious heat and intensity was missing.

"You can go. I'm fine."

"Ari—"

"I would hate for you to make a mistake you'd regret in the morning."

Fuck. "That wasn't what I—"

"Just so you know, I don't require my brother's permission to do anything."

"And what happened with the boyfriend? Is it really over this time?"

My question came out of nowhere, and Ari sucked in a breath before narrowing her gaze.

"Not that it's any of your damn business—"

"My hands all over that sweet body of yours says it is my business."

She bristled. "He cheated on me. I saw the pictures. Heath had them. *Of course* it's over for good this time. I do have some self-respect, you know." As the anger faded, her vulnerability broke through.

"I'm sorry you had to go through that." I pulled her into my arms, and she didn't resist. "So damn sorry."

She sniffled, and I wanted to wipe that dick off the planet for causing her a single moment of pain. "I should've done it a long time ago, then I wouldn't have had to go through that awesomely humiliating experience with my brother. I called him after I left Heath's and confronted him about the pictures."

"What'd he say?"

She stiffened in my arms, and I loosened my grip so I could see her face. The expression on it gutted me, but morphed into rage before I could say anything else.

"He told me that they were none of my concern."

What a fucking asshole. I kept the comment to myself.

"So I very politely explained that he was right, it wasn't any of my concern because I was done with him, and I would appreciate it if he never contacted me again."

A wave of approval surged through me, and I swiped a thumb along her cheek to catch the couple of tears she'd let fall. "Way to stand up for yourself."

Ari lifted her chin, and I could practically see her armor closing over her emotions. "Thank you. Now I hope you'll understand why I'm asking you to go before I say something I won't be able to take back because I'm frustrated. I refuse to be anyone's mistake. If anything, I'm a goddamned privilege."

Only Ari could make me smile while throwing me out of her house.

She's always been special, and this is more proof.

"I'll go, but I'll be seeing you tomorrow. And just so we're all clear, I'm going to see your brother first."

The promise in my words made her eyebrow shoot upward. "Is that so?"

"Damn right." I turned for the door.

"Good night, Rhett."

I paused with my hand on the knob. "Tomorrow, Red."

SIXTEEN
ARIEL

It took me hours to fall asleep with Rhett's words ringing in my head, so when my phone went off at three o'clock in the morning, I wanted to crush the SIM card and go back to bed. But instinct, and a healthy dose of fear, had me grabbing it.

"Hello?"

"We just had an attempted hacking incident." The voice on the other end was one of my assistants, Erik.

I shot up in bed, fumbling for the light switch to turn on the nightstand lamp. "What? Did they breach? Wait, you said attempted."

Esme's voice joined the call. "They made it past the second firewall before the threat was contained and our adaptive security measures crushed them like the little roaches they are." She had always been more bloodthirsty than Erik, so her comment didn't surprise me.

"They got through the second?" I sounded like a demented parrot with my repetition, but shock had me fumbling for coherent thoughts.

"Yes, through the second," Erik confirmed.

"What the hell?"

"That's what I said. No one has been able to get that far since you designed this system." This came from Esme.

"Who was it?"

I didn't bother to ask if they were able to trace it because it would be an insult. My team was good. I wouldn't have hired them if they hadn't been kicked out of Stanford for some creative grade switching, also known as hacking into student files and failing three guys on the swim team who wouldn't stop harassing a friend of theirs. They were expelled, black marks solidly placed on their record, with no chance of getting a decent job with most companies.

Except mine. I appreciated their sense of justice and creativity.

"Some idiot savant in Miami who didn't know how to cover his tracks well enough to hide from me."

"Get a name, get the information. Find out everything you can to determine why we were targeted."

"It might be another punk just trying to prove himself, you know? We've got a reputation as being impenetrable because of your genius brain, which makes us a big, beautiful target."

Esme had a point. By being virtually hack-proof, there was always an idiot out to test his skills against my security. So far, we'd napalmed anyone who had gotten past the first barriers, and this jerk-face would be no different. But it did worry me that he'd gotten further than most.

I took a deep, calming breath, inhaling the lavender diffusing at my bedside. *Look for the opportunity when presented with a problem.* That was how I'd built an incredibly successful business, and I wouldn't let emotion get in the way here.

"This just means I need to get more creative and do some tweaking. It's time to adapt and change, something I've clearly been neglecting this week."

Normally, I updated my security protocols at least twice a week, but since being back in New Orleans, my schedule was off. It proved, once again, that complacency represented weakness.

While I had one big glaring weakness in my personal life who'd left me needing to take care of business myself tonight, I didn't have them in my professional life.

Immediately, my mind went to Carlos. Had he hired the hacker out of spite? Just to prove to me I wasn't as good as I thought I was?

Even though the possibility burned, I voiced it. "Check for any connection between the idiot savant and Carlos."

"Really? Why would he want to . . ." Erik's question trailed off.

"I dumped his cheating ass today. Cut all ties. Maybe this is his way of telling me that he didn't like my methods."

"You go, girl! I never liked that douchebag." Esme's response was quick and to the point.

"And you never mentioned this because?" It came as a little bit of a surprise that she hadn't shared her opinion sooner. Esme was nothing if not assertive.

"Didn't you notice that I brought you celebratory sushi every time you flipped the switch to off-again mode? And I'm pretty sure I made enough snide comments about that ridiculous Lamborghini he drove to compensate for something he's obviously lacking."

Thinking back, I remembered both, but I hadn't made the

connection. "Why didn't you just come out and say it? You know I don't pick up on hints. I would've listened."

Erik choked out a laugh. "Ari, no offense, but you're about as good at taking suggestions on your personal life as you are at tennis."

Oh, he did not just mention "the incident."

"That's not fair."

The phone went completely silent, telling me they hit MUTE so I couldn't hear them laughing. Assholes.

Nine months ago, the CEO of a very prominent Silicon Valley tech company invited me to play tennis with him as we discussed a potential project we could pursue together. My tennis lessons had stopped when they started costing money the summer after fourth grade, so my skills as an adult were basically shit.

After two days of intense private lessons, I'd convinced myself I was good enough to play a casual match.

I was wrong.

My first serve landed right in his ball sac, and the match was over before it could even start. In a high-pitched voice, the other CEO had said maybe we should have our project managers get together to discuss it instead.

I swore up and down that my serve was no indication of my interest in partnering on the project, but he was too busy icing his balls to listen.

I'd sent a bottle of Macallan and a slow-thawing ice pack I'd invented years ago after a bike accident as an apology, and I hadn't heard anything from him since.

"You can take the phone off MUTE now if you've gotten your laughs in . . ." My tone was devoid of humor.

Esme and Erik's chuckles immediately became audible.

"I'm not sure I'll ever be able to think about that without

laughing, Ari," Esme said. "I'm just putting that out there in case you need to fire me now."

"I have a buddy who works there who said he still shields his balls whenever someone makes a sudden move in his direction." Erik's words were barely understandable through the giggles.

"Are you *cry-laughing*? I swear to God, Erik."

"I'll stop. I promise."

"Moving on. I'll dig into the security issue as soon as we're off the phone. It's not like I was getting much sleep tonight anyway."

"Oh, really? Why is that?" Esme didn't bother to hide the interest in her tone.

"I'll give you one guess."

My assistants were no strangers to the history surrounding my ridiculous crush on Rhett. Heath had taken care of that a few visits ago when we went out for dinner and drinks, and all the stories came out.

"No way!" Esme yelled. I could picture her doing a fist pump.

"What happened?" Erik asked.

"He kissed me. Or maybe I kissed him. I don't know. There was kissing."

"Eeep!"

I swore I heard them trade a high-five.

"This is huge," Esme said.

"I want to know what else is huge," Erik added. "Wait, I take that back. I don't want to know. Forget I said anything."

Rather than reprimand him as would probably be more appropriate in this situation, I let it slide. I didn't have a normal employee-employer relationship with these two, and that was the way we worked best.

"He won't make a real move without my brother's approval, though."

"Really? I'm not sure how I feel about that. You're a grown-ass woman who doesn't need anyone to give her permission to do anything."

"Exactly!" I yelled. Esme obviously understood where I was coming from.

"Cut the guy some slack." Erik took the devil's advocate position, as always. "He was a cop and all about honor and serving others. Why would he want to do something that he sees as a betrayal of his friend? He probably shouldn't have kissed you to begin with, and I bet he's wrestling with that hard now." A slap of skin on skin came through the line. "Dammit, Esme, don't hit me."

"Then don't say stupid things."

"Stop. It's fine." I'd played peacemaker between these two often enough to start feeling like their big sister, which was a signal it was time to wrap up this conversation. "I'm jumping off here, and I'm going to spend some quality time with our defenses. Have alpha team attempt entry in the morning. You two can call it a night."

"You swear you'll keep us up-to-date on the hot-detective saga?" This came from Erik.

"He's not a detective anymore, but yes."

"Stand your ground, Ari. Don't settle for scraps from this guy just because he's been your holy grail for fifteen years."

"Thank you for the reminder. Now, go to bed."

I hung up before they could give me any more advice, but as soon as the room went silent, I missed their presence. Now I was alone in a big empty house with nothing but work to keep me company.

Story of my life.

SEVENTEEN
RHETT

As soon as I left Ari's, I texted Heath saying I'd dropped her off. His response was a suggestion to meet at our regular place at ten o'clock tomorrow.

Looked like I wouldn't have to track him down.

How was I going to tell my best friend that I'd manhandled his sister, kissed her, and planned to do a hell of a lot more? I climbed into bed at my hotel a little while later, still without an answer to that question.

When I woke up at seven the next morning and jogged to the gym, I was still coming up empty. Even a punishing workout didn't knock any ideas loose.

Didn't matter. I was going after what I wanted. No more sitting on the sidelines. No more allowing life to pass me by.

I rolled up to our regular breakfast spot just beyond the boundaries of the Quarter and decided to wing it. Heath was already inside, a mug of coffee in front of him. Black with two sugars. That was how well I knew the man.

As I sat across from him, the waitress swooped in and

poured me a cup as well. When she disappeared, Heath slid his phone across the table toward me.

"We got a problem."

I expected to be staring down at information relating to my dad's case, but instead I saw a picture of Ari on the screen, walking out of a restaurant with another guy's arm around her shoulders. I'd put money on that asshole being her ex. The gossip rag that had posted the pic had captioned it RECLUSIVE TECH CEOS VACATION IN NEW ORLEANS.

What the hell?

"He's here?"

Heath shook his head. "No. Old picture. She definitely never brought him home. I'm guessing this is Carlos's last attempt to keep her by forcing the issue in the press."

My hands clenched into fists. "They're done. Ari was clear about that. Obviously, someone needs to make it even clearer to this asshole."

I looked up at Heath in time to catch the satisfaction flashing across his features.

"If he comes here, there's no way I'll let him get close to her." He leaned back in his chair and held my gaze. "If she wasn't living in Cali, I would've told her she'd be better off dating you."

If I had a mirror, I was sure my face would be the picture of dumbstruck. "What did you say?"

"When we were in school, I knew she was crazy about you. We all did. You never let on that you knew, which made me respect you even more. Some guys would've taken advantage and tried to hook up with her because they knew she'd be an easy lay."

"I never would've—"

Heath held up a hand. "I know. But we're not in high

school anymore. She's not my virgin little sister. We both know I have no say in what she does with her life. But I'm just throwing it out there because I know she's never totally gotten over that crush, and I know you're too good of a guy to make a move behind my back."

Guilt formed a fist in my chest, wrapping around my lungs, and I had to come clean.

"I kissed her last night." I left out the rest for obvious reasons.

Instead of his features twisting with anger or betrayal, Heath smiled. "Fucking finally. All I'm going to say is this, and then we're never going to talk about what happens between you and my sister ever again. You're the best friend I've ever had, the best man I know. You fuck her over like that asshole did, and I'll deal with you shotgun-and-shovel style. You guys try it out and it doesn't work for whatever reason, I'm not gonna hold it against you. If it does work out, I'll welcome you as a brother with open arms, because you've already been one my whole life. That's my way of saying you've got my blessing for whatever you decide."

With each word Heath spoke, the fist loosened its hold a little more. When he finished, all I could do was shake my head in amazement.

"It would be the understatement of the year to say this went how I was planning."

Heath chuckled as he shrugged. "I know I was an asshole in high school about anyone who looked twice at her. I'd like to think I've grown up a little since then. Besides, if I could pick a guy for her then or now, it would be you."

I appreciated his vote of confidence. "I don't know what's going to happen—"

He held up both hands in a gesture of surrender. "I know,

and that's why I'm backing away and not worrying about either of you when it comes to that. But," he pointed down at the picture on his phone screen, "I am worrying about this. Now people know she's in town, and although she's not a celebrity, I don't like the level of visibility it gives her. Ari keeps a low profile for lots of reasons, but most of all because of the incident she doesn't think I know about."

It was clear Heath kept closer tabs on his sister than she knew, based on his comment and the pictures he'd produced. If I were in his shoes, I would too.

"What can I do?"

"I was hoping you were going to ask that." Heath's smile widened. "I was thinking you should pull your head out of your ass and stay at her place instead of at whatever cheap hotel you probably picked."

He knew me well. When I didn't shoot down the idea, he continued.

"She could use an extra set of eyes, and this wouldn't feel like she was crushed by security. Just the fact that she made her guy leave her alone last night scared the shit out of me."

His words made me wonder if there was another threat Ari hadn't told me about, but he didn't elaborate.

"What aren't you telling me?" I asked.

He reached for his coffee. "She's my little sister. I might be cool with the thought of you dating, but I still get to worry about her. I'd move Dad into the mansion, but he won't even leave my den after the scene at the restaurant yesterday. I got my hands full. Do me a solid."

I thought of how Ari and I had left things last night. "I can't just show up with a bag and move in."

"Don't see why not. I'm sure you'll figure out something that works. You're smart."

The waitress returned to take our orders, and we both ordered the same thing we had every time we sat in this very same booth.

"Some things don't change," Heath said as she walked away with our orders. Omelet for me, and eggs Benedict for him.

"Yeah, except you're the one sitting there with a badge and I'm not." The hint of bitterness that crept into my tone was unavoidable.

Heath's easy smile faded. "I know. And that's straight fucked up."

"You hear any more on the investigation?"

Lines bracketed the corners of my friend's mouth. "You know I could lose my badge for saying anything to you."

"So all those years of friendship you talked about meant nothing?"

Was it fair for me to play on his loyalties? Maybe not, but I'd do whatever it took to get to the bottom of what happened with my dad. It didn't feel right. Something was off in a big way.

"I don't know much except what's going on in IA, but the whole department has been talking about the case and no one knows what the fuck happened. The wiring and triggering device weren't what they would've expected your dad to use."

"What do you mean?"

"He knew military demolition but old-school style. This was new school. Sophisticated shit. Unless your dad kept up with technology as it advanced, it looks like someone else might have wired it. If they did, it was like they went out of their way to make it clear he didn't do it."

A shaft of hope jabbed into my chest. "So you're saying he's going to be cleared? And if he didn't do it, who did? What was the motive?"

Heath held up a hand. "Slow down a second. The only thing they're saying is that he might not have done the wiring. Forensic accountants are going through all your parents' finances to see if your dad might have paid someone else to wire it. The timing of everything seems way too convenient."

Typical of the department not to look at every possibility. They weren't searching for a reason to clear him; they were digging for a reason to pin this all on him so they could close the case as fast as possible.

I knew exactly what I'd have to do in order to clear my dad—figure out what actually happened and bring in irrefutable evidence to support it.

"Think about it. Why would he pay someone to wire the house when he could've done it himself? And let's get real, there's no way in hell he would've done it himself either with my mom coming and going. He never would've put her at risk like that. You can't tell me you believe it."

Heath jammed a hand into his hair. "You know I don't want to believe any of it, but we gotta look at all the angles. He was a lifelong cop looking at sitting in a cell for a long damn time after they arrested him. None of us would want to go through that. He wouldn't have been the first cop to . . . take another way out."

My jaw clenched at the suggestion. "I don't believe it. Leave my mom homeless so he could avoid being arrested? It doesn't make sense. If he wanted to end it all, he could've walked out of the house with a gun in hand and gone out old-fashioned suicide by cop." It turned my gut to say it, but it was the truth.

"Your old man was stubborn, there's no doubt about that. Look, let us do our job. If there's any evidence to the contrary, it'll come to light."

"Yeah, because you can tell me with a straight face that's really what the department wants."

Heath's expression darkened. "We're not all dirty cops. Some are still in this to protect and serve. You know that."

"I know."

"Did you know Ari might be sticking around longer than she'd planned?"

The trajectory of my thoughts did a one-eighty. "Really?"

"She said she's not going anywhere until we sort out all this stuff going on with Dad, no matter how long it takes."

"Shit, I'm sorry. As much as I'm glad she'll be around longer, the reason sucks for you both."

"Getting old's a bitch, that's for sure. I'm hoping for the best, but from what I've been seeing the last week, he's going downhill fast."

"If there's anything I can do, let me know."

"Appreciate it. Best thing you can do is keep an eye on Ari."

The waitress delivered our orders, and the rest of breakfast passed with the same easy camaraderie Heath and I had always had. But as we ate, my mind kept bouncing between two different thoughts.

What the hell actually happened with my dad, and how long would I have with Ari?

EIGHTEEN
ARIEL

"Ha! I still got it!" I jumped up from the chair and did a little dance around the office where I'd set up shop in the house. I didn't care that Erik and Esme could see me shaking my groove thang through the live video stream.

"You've definitely got something . . ."

My tweaks to the security system had rendered it impenetrable once again, and my top team of internal hackers, along with Esme and Erik, had failed miserably.

"What I don't understand is why you won't take one of the hundreds of offers we get for you to do this for other companies? Do you have any idea how much money you could make?"

"She's already got plenty of money. Why would she want to go work for someone else and follow their rules, even if it were on a contract basis?" Esme pointed out.

"This is something I do for my personal satisfaction, not for money."

"But . . ."

"No buts. On to the next subject."

"Speaking of butts . . . did Mr. Hot Former Cop grow a pair and talk to your brother today to get permission to bang you?"

Esme's question sent a wave of heat up my cheeks. "We're not talking about that either."

Heath texted me this morning to tell me that he and Rhett were having breakfast at ten. A glance at the clock showed that it was now noon and I'd received no updates. Not that I was expecting one, or, you know, Rhett to show up with a giant bouquet of flowers and toss rose petals all over my floor as he led me to bed.

Actually, that would be creepy, despite what I thought when I was eighteen. Officially scratching that one off the fantasy list.

But what if we took that next step and it didn't come anywhere close to living up to what I'd imagined? I'd expended an undisclosed amount of brain power on how it could be between Rhett and me, and the more I thought about it, the more I was terrified of the possibility of disappointment.

"Uh-oh. I recognize that face. I don't see it often, but that's the face of hesitation. Maybe even second thoughts," Esme whispered.

It took all the adult willpower in my body not to flip off the screen. Both Erik and Esme read me too easily.

"What if . . . what if something happens and . . ." I pressed my lips together, not even wanting to put my fears out in the universe.

"What if it's not as good as you've always hoped it would be?" Esme suggested.

"You think you've built this guy up to have a Jack-in-the-beanstalk-level magic cock, and he might just have regular beans?" Erik asked.

Neither waited for me to respond, opting instead to discuss it amongst themselves.

"He can't suck," Esme said. "I've seen pictures of that guy, and he looks like the real deal."

Erik speared her with a skeptical look. "Oh, and your track record with identifying winners is so good?"

"Shut up. That was one internet dating experience gone bad. It's not like—"

I hit the END button on the screen and wondered how long it would take them to realize I'd hung up on them.

I gave it *three, two, one . . .*

They popped up onscreen again.

"Hey, not fair."

"Moving on now."

After knocking out a long list of items I needed to discuss with Erik and Esme, I clicked out of the video conference and looked at the time. Two more hours had passed, and still no word from Rhett or Heath.

Okay, I'm just pathetic. I've got plenty of things to do to keep me busy, and none of them involve mooning over Rhett Hennessy.

Years ago, I'd spent way too much time up in my tiny room, staring out the window at the Hennessys' driveway and front yard, hoping for a glimpse of Rhett coming or going from school or practice or . . . ugh, on dates. Instead of studying and preparing to rock my future life, I'd make up stories about how Rhett would scale the chimney and sneak in through my window and tell me he couldn't live without me. Followed by him carrying me out of my childhood bedroom and down the stairs without getting shot by my dad.

Needless to say, that had never happened. What did happen was watching Rhett bring his senior prom date, Valerie Hebert, to his parents' house after picking her up so his mom could take pictures of them in front of the blooming magnolia tree out front. The day before, Valerie had spent a good twenty minutes preening in the girls' locker room after PE, smiling smugly about how Rhett Hennessy was going to try to hit a home run after prom, and she was thinking about letting him.

She still had that smug look on her face before he led her to the passenger side door of his dad's classic Corvette and helped her inside.

I'd been near tears and ready to give up my hopes and dreams about all things Rhett Hennessy at the thought of them together in some hotel room, when the long skirt of her pink princess dress had touched the exhaust pipe running under the door. It melted instantly, ruining her perfect look and causing a bloodcurdling scream to echo through the neighborhood.

Now, I hadn't been rejoicing at any girl's dream prom getting ruined, but from the way she'd lit into Rhett in front of his entire family, and the way he'd looked skyward as if searching for patience and had accidentally met my gaze through the panes of my bedroom window . . . I knew that he wasn't going to be scoring any runs that night, and I'd felt marginally better.

Then I'd let myself daydream about what it would be like for Rhett to show up and take me to my senior prom.

Spoiler alert—he hadn't.

I'd gone with Donny Jenkins, who'd tried to shove his hand up my dress as I walked out to his car. I had to tell him my brother was the top shooter from his academy class and would happily put holes in him if he tried it again. Donny had left me in the parking lot, and I'd had to get a ride home with all the girls who'd gone stag. I'd never heard from him again.

Maybe I should have said something similar to Carlos . . .

To this day, I wondered if Donny had crapped his pants as he'd run to his mom's Suburban and torn out of the parking lot. I'd never thought about him since.

Ah . . . trips down memory lane. So not useful.

I stood up, stretched my arms behind my back, and shook out my wrists to prevent carpal tunnel. Then I walked into the kitchen to dig up some food before I got back to work.

Waiting on Rhett Hennessy was like hoping your hair wouldn't frizz up in the Louisiana humidity—pointless and frustrating.

With a bowl of stir fry in front of me, I went back to work, determined to knock out everything on my to-do list before I let my mind wander in the direction of Rhett Hennessy again. Since my track record of being able to stop thinking about him was *so* great.

Resolute, I shoved in my earbuds and crunched into a piece of broccoli as I opened the document I needed to review to decide whether to invest in a new start-up. They had an app that they claimed would become as addictive as Facebook and Instagram.

I've got an empire to build. Watch out, world.

I'D LOST TRACK OF TIME WHILE BEING WILDLY PRODUCTIVE, electing to invest a couple hundred thousand dollars in the first start-up and another half million in another company. Reviewing other people's business plans and proposals always made me proud of what I'd accomplished. Had I taken a different path, I would have been applying to people for angel financing, giving up over half of my equity stake just for a shot at making it.

Instead, I'd taken a big risk that could have blown up in my face. I cashed out my college tuition account and used that instead of fake money during the day-trading portion of my finance class. I was either going to be a dropout or a success, and luckily, I'd learned I had a solid gut instinct and could recognize patterns. I'd tripled my money, paid my next semester's tuition, and used the profit to hire a couple of friends to help develop my first successful apps.

My phone lit up, its vibrations carrying through the table to get my attention.

Unknown Number: Your plane ticket home is in your email. We'll be discussing the situation you raised last night in person.

I'd blocked Carlos's number on my phone, so while it didn't surprise me he was texting me from another number, it pissed me off.

Oh. Hell. No.

As I picked up my phone to reply something along the lines of *No way in hell am I coming home* and *We have nothing to discuss because there is no us*, Carver came into the room.

"Ms. Sampson? You have a visitor at the gate. Shall I let Mr. Hennessy in?"

I sat my phone on the table and stood. "Rhett Hennessy?" Yeah, as if some other Hennessy was going to show up at my door.

"Yes, ma'am."

Mentally, I tugged up my big-girl thong and straightened my shoulders. "Sure. Let him in. Feel free to give us some privacy, Carver." My gaze landed on him long enough to ensure he got the message loud and clear. "When Mr. Hennessy is around, I'm not under any security threat, so consider yourself off duty."

No matter what else ever happened with Rhett, I knew those words were unfailingly true. He would protect me with his life.

"Understood, ma'am. I'll let him in, and will be in my apartment if you need anything at all."

"Thank you, Carver."

"Of course, Ms. Sampson."

He strode away, and I looked down at what I was wearing. A *Namaste in Bed* T-shirt that had caught a splash of soy sauce during lunch, and sweats I'd turned into cutoffs with a dull pair of scissors.

Looking hot, Ari.

But I'd been working all day, and part of being the boss meant I got to wear whatever I wanted when I was in beast mode. Which was all the time. *I might be a geek, but I'm* always *a beast-geek.*

Rhett was going to get the real me. No makeup, my hair a little wild from putting it up and taking it down as I mulled over decisions, and a hot mess of an outfit. I was too old and too awesome to worry about being someone else.

With that positive thought firmly fixed in my mind, I tried to calm down the flock of seagulls that took up residence in my belly as the doorbell rang. Rhett Hennessy was on my doorstep.

Be cool, Ari. Be cool.

Okay, scratch that.

Pretend.

NINETEEN
RHETT

After we left breakfast, Heath shot me a text saying the cops were getting ready to release the crime scene that was my parents' house, so I'd hauled ass over there to start my own investigation before it was corrupted. I put in a call to an old friend who owned a barricade company, and he agreed to bring over enough metal construction fencing to surround the entire property and lock it up. Any assholes who thought they'd go searching for scrap metal or anything else of value would be blocked.

That began my day of digging through rubble and looking for evidence that the crime scene unit might have missed. I couldn't decide if it was working in my favor that they'd missed a few pieces of the wiring and device, or whether they were screwing my family by not being better at their jobs. When it came down to it, I didn't trust anyone to solve this case except for me, so I was going to take it as a positive.

Evidence collected in my own baggies and the fence in place around the yard, locked up, and security lights armed, I babysat the glass installers at the Sampsons' house next door to make sure Mr. Sampson would be able to move back into his house sooner rather than later. That was, if Heath and Ari decided he could live on his own.

Either way, I was doing my part to hopefully make their lives easier.

Once that was finished, I shot Heath a text to let him know it was done. He didn't reply.

As I looked up at the two windows I knew belonged to Ari's childhood bedroom, I remembered seeing her face in them more than once over the years, watching me, even though she didn't know I saw her.

She'd thought she was invisible to me, but she'd been dead wrong. It was always the opposite. I'd been as hyper-aware of her as you tended to be of something you couldn't have.

Breakfast with Heath had changed that.

Now, how am I going to make her mine?

More than ever before, I understood completely that life was short. You got one ride, and you didn't know when your number was going to be up.

If this was my only shot with Ari, I wasn't going to screw it up.

I cursed when I realized it was already four o'clock by the time I pulled away from my parents' street. I thought about calling her, but what I needed to tell her had to be said in person.

Turning my Jeep in the direction of my hotel, I worked out a game plan.

All right, Red. I hope you're ready for this, because I sure as hell am.

Fifty-five minutes later, wearing a white dress shirt I'd pressed with my crappy hotel-provided iron and black dress pants, I stood on the front steps of Ariel Sampson's massive digs. It wasn't like I needed a reminder about just how different our situations were in life right now, but I got it anyway.

Still, we had something that spanned the differences—history, and years of it.

I waited after I rang the bell, finally hearing footsteps padding toward the front door. I wasn't sure what I expected to see when Ari opened it, but the smile that stretched across her face when she saw me told me everything I needed to know.

I'll take her any way I can get her.

Her chin lifted as she took me in. "I was wondering if I'd ever hear from you again."

I stepped forward and pulled her against me, one hand wrapped around her hip and the other speared into her hair. I closed my lips over hers and kissed her the way I'd always wanted to—with nothing hanging over us. No guilt, no barriers, no hesitation.

Just me and Ari.

Exactly the way I wanted it.

TWENTY
ARIEL

I didn't know how Rhett's conversation with my brother went, but from the way he was kissing the hell out of me, it must have gone well.

Good Lord, Rhett Hennessy could kiss. I wondered how long it would take me to stop thinking that every time his lips touched mine. I was willing to make an experiment out of it.

My fingers found their way into the long ends of his shaggy blond hair, my nails raking his neck as he groaned and pulled me tighter against him until I could feel his hard-on pressing into my belly. Bursts of heat shot through me.

I was about to climb him when Rhett jerked away from me.

"Wha—" The partial word, not even a fully formed question, fell from my lips before Rhett interrupted.

"Go put on a dress, Red, because I'm taking you on a date. A real date." He took another step back and tucked his hands in his pockets. "God knows I could turn this kiss into something that'll last all night, but you deserve better than that and I'm going to give it to you."

So this is what it feels like when your insides are melting into a giant puddle of oh-my-God-is-this-really-happening goo.

"A date?"

He nodded. "Yeah, and I'd be honored if you'd put on a dress, unless you'd prefer I take you out like this. I don't care either way, but I figured you might . . ."

Go out on my first date with Rhett like this? Oh. Hell. No.

"I'll be right back." I spun around and shut the door. Two steps later, I realized I'd closed it with Rhett *outside*.

"Shit!"

I yanked the door open and took him in, standing on my front stoop with a smile on his face. I didn't even attempt to lie. "I'm flustered. This is all because of you. Would you like to wait inside?"

Rhett stepped in the house, leaving barely an inch between us, and closed the door behind himself. "Take your time. I've been waiting what seems like my whole life for this. I can wait a little longer."

Oh. My. God.

His hooded green eyes told me he spoke the truth, and it took everything I had to turn away and put one foot in front of the other until I reached my bedroom.

As soon as I eased the door closed behind me, I broke into a dance that was way more enthusiastic than the one Esme and Erik had witnessed earlier. With both fists in the air, I spun into my closet.

You can get what you want. Sometimes it just takes half your life.

With a deep breath, I surveyed my clothes. *Now, what in the world am I going to wear?*

The need to balance not wasting too much precious time on getting ready warred with the need to look hot as hell. After an objective scan of my closet, I opted for a little black dress that went everywhere with me because it was so versatile. The draping V-neck was low enough that it was sexy, but the extra swath of fabric teased more than it revealed, keeping it classy.

Once I'd selected a pair of simple black stilettos and jewelry, I rushed to the bathroom with my armful and stared into the mirror.

My hair was every bit as much of a disaster as I'd thought it might be. It had reached bird's-nest-level proportions, and it was painfully obvious I wasn't wearing a bra under my T-shirt.

And still Rhett had kissed me like he was a man coming back from war.

That was a *very* good sign, in my opinion.

I stripped in minutes and kept my hair in a knot on my head before I hopped in the shower and did the fastest shaving job of my life. I was taking no chances that things might end up in a bed later—or up against a wall, in a car, or on a table, because my imagination was very well-versed in creativity when it came to Rhett.

Luckily, no blood was spilled in the shower and I was dressed, made up, and my hair had been tamed into a sophisticated twist with tendrils falling around my face in under twenty-five minutes. I considered it a minor miracle, although not the type that would reasonably put me in contention for canonization.

Slipping my right foot into my second stiletto, I adjusted the strap and buckled it before straightening and preparing myself to walk back into the living room.

I'm going on a date with Rhett Hennessy.

I will not worry about being cool.

I will not worry about being awesome.

I will be my own damn self, and if that's not good enough for him, it's not meant to be.

With that pep talk bringing me solidly back to earth, I strode in his direction. He rose from his seat on the sofa, his face unreadable.

He kissed me when I was looking like a hot mess, so he has to appreciate this effort, right?

Rhett stepped forward, meeting me in the middle. "You're beautiful, Ari. Whether you're wearing a T-shirt with a pencil jammed in your hair or a ball gown, you're the most beautiful woman I've ever seen. Thank you for not telling me I missed my shot."

His words, ones I didn't realize I needed to hear, echoed with sincerity.

"I wondered if you were ever going to let me know what happened with my brother. I kept myself busy all day trying not to think about it."

Rhett reached for my hand and gripped it. "Turns out he's a hell of a lot more levelheaded about the situation than I would be if I had a sister. But I don't, and he's not standing in our way. So let's go see what we think about this."

As I let Rhett lead me to my front door, I appreciated his no-nonsense approach. With all the waiting, longing, hoping, praying—on my side of the fence, obviously—it was hard not to wonder if reality would be anything near what I'd dreamed of as a teenager.

Neither of us were in high school anymore, and those old feelings might not have faded, but they weren't relevant here. This was new ground for us to cover, and I was going to put everything else behind me.

Except . . . I did have one tiny confession to make. As Rhett led me around to the passenger side of his Jeep, I had to tell him.

"Remember that hit-and-run, the one that smashed the taillight of your Jeep when you were a senior?"

He paused, his fingers gripping the door handle. "Yeah?"

"It wasn't exactly a hit-and-run. It was more of a hit-and-walk."

"You and a Louisville Slugger the day that the rumor went around at school that I knocked up Kim Leander."

My mouth dropped open. "You knew?"

"That you were pissed I could throw away my life like that? Yeah, I knew. I watched you do it. It put a hell of a lot of things in perspective for me."

I jerked my head back. "Like what?"

"Like that I wasn't going to back myself into a corner by making stupid mistakes when I was eighteen."

"Well, I guess that's a good thing."

He met my eyes, and his green gaze shone. "I never touched Kim Leander, Red."

"You didn't?"

"No."

"Oops."

He smiled. "I'll let you make that taillight up to me sometime. Don't worry."

And so started my first real date with Rhett Hennessy.

TWENTY-ONE
ARIEL

I couldn't help but keep trying to guess where Rhett was taking me. Maybe a regular place he took his dates? A New Orleans classic? I flipped through the possibilities but came up empty.

"Where *are* we going?"

He glanced over at me with a smile. "Sometimes I forget you've been gone a long time."

That didn't answer my question. "And?"

He raised an eyebrow at me. "Patience, Red. Patience."

I folded my hands together in my lap, resisting the urge to tug my dress down when it rode up my thighs further as I fidgeted in my seat. When we pulled up to a stoplight in an area of old warehouses, I was officially lost.

"Where are we?"

The car in front of us laid on the horn because the truck first in line at the light wasn't moving.

Rhett twisted to look at me. "You don't know New Orleans that well at all anymore, do you?"

I glanced out the window, trying to place the street. I had

nothing. "If you recall, I left when I was seventeen, and before that, I never had my own car. I went from home to school and church and not really anywhere else."

Rhett drove through the green light and took one more turn before pulling into a parking lot across from a warehouse that looked like it had been rehabbed and then upper stories added with new, modern construction. The red brick that colored the surrounding buildings was missing on this one, as it was black with a giant gold logo painted between the old storeroom-type windows. The newer-looking upper stories had solid glass walls supported by thick wooden timbers.

The building was breathtaking. I'd never seen anything like it in New Orleans.

"What is this?"

"The Seven Sinners Distillery. It's been around longer than I've been alive, but the family gave it a facelift and opened it to the public with a restaurant just before . . . well, just before I left town."

My gaze traveled over the exterior, marveling at the gorgeous design of the building, marrying the old and new, and the bold logo. "It's amazing."

Rhett opened his door and climbed out of the Jeep. "I'm glad you like the looks of it. The food and drinks are supposed to be just as good, if not better."

I latched my purse, which had somehow become unlatched in all my fidgeting, and reached for the door handle. Before I could grasp it, Rhett was there swinging it open.

"Wow. Full gentleman treatment."

His smile turned wolfish and his eyes flashed. "I wouldn't say I'm fully a gentleman."

My mind went to all the places it probably shouldn't, and Rhett's had obviously gone there too. What would it be like if he carried through on all the thoughts I could see blazing in his gaze? That thought made me wish I'd tossed a second pair of panties into my purse. The ones I was wearing were a lost cause, which seemed to be a theme around him. *Maybe I could just take them off . . .*

"What could possibly be going through that head of yours right now?" Rhett asked as he helped me out of the car, his rough palm clasping mine with a possessive grip.

"I have no idea what you mean," I replied, keeping my tone light and joking.

Rhett closed the door of the Jeep, but instead of leading me forward like I expected, he backed me up against it. His chin dropped so it was only an inch from my ear.

"You know exactly what I mean, Ari. I see that look on your face, and I know that incredible mind of yours is thinking something naughty enough to turn your cheeks pink. You watched me, but I watched you too. Even when I should've been blind, deaf, and dumb where you were concerned, I couldn't help but look."

"How's that look-but-don't-touch angle going for you?"

His palms glided down my sides before stopping and gripping my hips. "I plan on doing a whole lot of touching."

My body was so acutely aware of Rhett that shivers started at the indent of each of his fingertips into my skin. I wanted him to squeeze harder or maybe shove my skirt up and . . .

"That. That right there. I wish I could look inside your head and see exactly what made your breath catch. I'm making it my mission to figure out every single thing that puts that look on your face."

An involuntary shudder started at the base of my spine and shook my upper body. “Is that right?”

“You better believe it.” Rhett’s breath ghosted over my skin before his lips feathered across the same path along the edge of my jaw. “Now we’d better get inside to claim our table before I pin you against the car for a whole different reason.”

“Oh dear Lord.” I didn’t mean to say it out loud but the words escaped my lips, and Rhett’s lips curled into a satisfied smirk.

“Come on, Red, before I lose my willpower.”

At that moment, I would have been totally and completely fine with skipping whatever was waiting for us inside the building across the street in favor of whatever Rhett had on *his* mind, but when he stepped away and threaded his fingers through mine, I followed behind him. And not mostly because of the view it gave me of his ass in those dress pants of his. Sweet Lord, I didn’t know what that man did in the gym, but I hoped he kept doing it.

We waited for a few cars to drive by before Rhett led us across the road. I glanced back at the parking lot, which was partially full. But for such an amazing-looking place, I would have expected more patrons.

I guessed our experience would be the determining factor of that.

When Rhett pulled the door open wide for me, my heart melted. He was a gentleman, despite his claim to the contrary.

A large reception desk, whiskey barrels with a live-edge wooden slab on top, was manned by a petite dark-haired woman.

"Welcome to Seven Sinners Distillery and Restaurant. Do you have a reservation?"

"Yes, Hennessy for two."

I couldn't believe I was on a date with Rhett Hennessy, and he had made a freaking reservation. I wasn't sure why that struck me as even more surreal, but it did.

"Of course, Mr. Hennessy. If you would follow me upstairs, I'll show you and your guest to your table."

The woman led us toward a shiny silver elevator that carried us to the top floor of the building. When the door opened, she held out an arm. "Right this way, please."

I stepped out of the elevator to be amazed by an incredible view through the walls of glass of downtown New Orleans and the Mississippi River beyond. "Wow."

The woman turned toward me. "Wait until the sun sets. It's magnificent. With our solid glass walls and height, you get a three-hundred-sixty-degree view. We're very proud of our renovated space."

"I can see why. It's phenomenal."

Rhett squeezed my hand, and I knew this place would always be special to me. No matter what happened for the rest of the evening, I would remember it forever.

TWENTY-TWO
RHETT

Ari's wide gray eyes scanned every detail, taking them all in. Despite the sweet building and killer view, I was way more interested in studying *her*. This building would stand for a century or more, but I had no idea how long I'd get with Ari. I'd already wasted years, so I wasn't about to waste another minute.

"As you requested, Mr. Hennessy, we have a table for you in the corner." The hostess led us toward a table that had a decent amount of privacy, for which I was grateful. "Is this acceptable, sir?"

Ari's surprised gaze was already on me, as though she was shocked that I'd request something private. We might have known each other for years, but we still had a lot to learn about each other. One thing she'd quickly figure out was that I planned to take every advantage of our limited time together and make the most of it.

"It's great. Thank you."

The hostess motioned to a piece of wood on the table between us, which looked like a section of a stave from a whiskey barrel. Burned into it was the whiskey tasting list. "I'll leave you with this for now. Your server will bring you the cocktail menu and a list of tonight's specials." She left us with a smile as Ari and I slid onto the high stools of the tall table.

"This place is really nice and so unique. Thank you for bringing me here."

"I figured I'd have to get creative to impress the girl who has hundreds of fancy California restaurants to choose from on any given day."

Ari laughed. "And I rarely see the inside of those restaurants because I'm too busy working. I can usually identify their take-out containers, though. I see those too often."

My little workaholic. "What do you do besides work? I know you've got some self-defense skills that you practice regularly, but tell me about your other hobbies."

"Hobbies? Like things I do in my free time?" She sounded completely confused by the concept.

"Pretty sure that's the definition."

This time she threw back her head and laughed. The deep throaty chuckle hit me right in the chest . . . and elsewhere. I shifted on my seat to make sure my thin dress pants didn't strangle my dick.

"Free time isn't exactly something I have. If I could create a thirty-hour day, I might have time for both sleep and fun."

The thought of Ari never taking time to enjoy life bothered me, which was ironic since I didn't do it often either.

"You have to do something to blow off steam or keep you entertained when you take a break from work."

A guilty look flashed over her face, and an image of her masturbating behind a big desk slammed into my mind. In my fantasy, her head was thrown back as she came, and my name was on her lips. Fuck, now my dick was rock hard. Thankful for the table blocking her view, I pushed the image out of my head. Or at least I tried.

"What was that thought?" I asked, my voice coming out with a husky edge I couldn't control.

"Nothing."

Ari snatched up the whiskey menu and scanned it. I tugged it out of her grip, taking possession of her hand and squeezing until her gaze locked with mine.

"Tell me."

She attempted an innocent, confused expression, but she wasn't good enough at it. She swallowed, but didn't break our stare. "Sometimes I play around on the computer."

It made sense because she was the ultimate computer nerd, but why would that send guilty signals?

"Wait, you watch porn?"

Her mouth dropped open. "No! I mean, yes, but I was talking about hacking."

Hacking? "What the hell?"

Her gaze darted from side to side and she leaned closer to me. "You can't tell anyone if you don't want me to go to jail. Or you know, federal prison. It's not like I do anything bad. It's more to make sure my skills stay up to par. It's like a foreign language—if you don't use it, you lose it. And, obviously, I like to make sure my conspiracy theories aren't crazy, but in fact are reality. If people only knew . . ."

"You've gotta be joking."

Her brow furrowed. "No joke. I've been doing it for years. Just ask Kim Leander. She's been on the enhanced screening list since I learned to get into the TSA."

"Are you frigging serious?"

"That Kim Leander gets a more-than-friendly pat-down and bag search every month when she travels for work? Yes. Yes, I am."

A mental picture of what Ari described filtered into my mind and I couldn't help but laugh. "You're ruthless."

She shrugged. "Long memory. No one screws with the people I care about and gets away with it. I can make someone's life a nightmare. She shouldn't have lied."

"I'm not sure whether to be scared or impressed."

Another shrug from Ari. "It's not like it's hard. Any amateur could do it."

I was sure that wasn't really the case, but before I could respond, our server arrived at the table.

"Welcome to Seven Sinners, we're so happy to have you join us. Can I get you a complimentary taste of any of our whiskeys this evening? We have some fabulous ones available for you."

Clearly wanting to change the subject after her confession, Ari asked, "What would you recommend?"

"Are you a whiskey drinker, ma'am?" When Ari shook her head, our server smiled. "Then I'd recommend a glass of the Spirit of New Orleans. It's smooth and warm with a nice kick, but not too hot. You'll enjoy it, even if you're not normally a fan of whiskey. It's my favorite of everything we offer."

"I'll try that."

"Excellent." The server looked to me. "And for you, sir?"

"I'll try the single malt."

"Perfect. I'll bring those to you along with today's menu and water."

When our server disappeared again, my attention was

one hundred percent focused on Ari. "Tell me more about the hacking."

She shook her head. "I'd rather not. It's not a big deal. Just something I do when I feel like entertaining myself. The only useful aspect is when I find ways to keep other people out because I'm better than they are."

One thing Ari was never shy about was how smart she was. "Like the hackers the Feds arrest and then later hire to make their systems impenetrable?"

"In theory. But nothing is truly hack-proof. There's always someone out there who can beat it, at least so far."

It was as good a moment as any to find out exactly how much time I had with her. "When are you going back to the land of sun and surf and hacking?"

My question must have surprised her. She didn't answer right away; instead, her expression fell and she looked out the window.

"What's wrong?"

"Dad. I don't know what to do to get him to agree to go in for testing so we can figure out the next steps."

Heath had talked about it at breakfast. Mr. Sampson was worse off than either of them had realized.

"Keep trying, I guess. It seems like that's all you can do. Assess the situation and make decisions based on what you learn."

Her gaze cut back to me. "I spent so many years away and I missed him being himself, and now he's . . . not. I feel like I should've been here the whole time. I can't leave again. It's like I'd be abandoning my family, which I guess I already did."

Her expression was so crestfallen that I wanted to wrap

her in a hug. Instead, I reached out and twined my fingers with hers.

"If anyone at this table should feel guilty about abandoning family, it's me. I walked when it came out that my dad was a dirty cop. I didn't answer the phone when he called for an entire fucking year. That was being a shitty son. You were out living your life and making your mark. You have nothing to feel guilty about."

I kept the *but I sure as fuck do* to myself. It went without saying that I'd fucked up in a big way, and that was something I'd have to live with for the rest of my life.

Ari threaded her fingers through mine. "You were dealing the best way you knew how. I couldn't imagine how it felt to find out that everything you thought was . . . wrong. He betrayed *you,* Rhett. Betrayed everything he taught you to hold sacred. You reacted. I understand wanting a chance to go back, but you can't crucify yourself for what you did for the rest of your life. I know your dad wouldn't want that."

I heard the logic in her words, but that didn't mean I believed it. I flipped it back on her anyway. "And your dad wouldn't want you to feel guilty for living. He's always been so damn proud of you. I feel like I haven't missed out on many of your accomplishments because your dad was always bragging to Heath and me about how you were kicking ass."

A wobbly smile formed on her lips. "Really?"

"Really. He wanted the best for you, and you went out and made the best life you could. There's nothing to feel bad about."

"I'll believe it if you will."

I was saved from having to respond when our server

returned with our whiskey and menus. The restaurant offered Creole and Irish fare, and Ari picked the shrimp and I went for the oysters.

After the server retreated, Ari picked up her whiskey and sniffed. Before she could lift it to her lips, I raised my glass.

"To a long overdue date."

A smile flitted over her features. "I can drink to that."

TWENTY-THREE
ARIEL

Be cool, Ari. Act like an adult who has it all together. Because you are. Don't think about that toast . . .

"What exactly have you been doing for the last year?" I lowered my whiskey glass to the table.

Rhett sipped his, and if the abrupt change in subject threw him, he didn't let it show. "PI work. Mostly surveillance on spouses suspected of cheating."

"Wow. That has to be a little depressing." I picked up my drink again and tipped some back, the heat from the liquor warming a path down my throat.

Rhett shrugged. "Yes and no. What's depressing is the fact that there's no trust between them, and they get to the point where they feel like hiring someone is all they can do. Honestly, they could save themselves a lot of grief by just asking the other person where the hell they're going."

It sounded like there was a story there. "What do you mean?"

Rhett picked up his drink again. "I had one client who swore up and down her husband had to be cheating on her because he was gone the same time every week and withdrawing cash from the ATM on the same day. She told me it had to be a hooker, but she wasn't going to file for divorce without proof."

"Oh my God. That's terrible." After the way things ended with Carlos, I never wanted to deal with a situation like that ever again, and we hadn't had anywhere near that level of commitment between us.

Rhett tilted his head. "Only if you don't trust your husband enough to ask him where he's going."

"What was he doing?" My curiosity piqued, I leaned back in my chair, my glass poised to take another sip.

"Laser hair removal on his back. Technician I talked to after I got the pictures said he felt self-conscious when his wife called him a wooly mammoth on the beach, so he wanted to be ready for summer."

I laughed, choking on my drink and practically spitting it onto the table. "Oh my God. You're joking."

"No, definitely not joking. She cried a lot and apologized. They booked a cruise to the Bahamas as a second honeymoon."

"Wow. That's better than the alternative."

He nodded. "For sure. Plenty of the cases end up using my photos for evidence in divorce proceedings, which is depressing as hell. The best cases are the ones where I'm able to prove that they're *not* doing anything wrong. Like the guy sneaking away to play bingo to try to win his wife a new car."

"Seriously?"

"Dead serious. I can't make this stuff up, and these aren't even the crazier stories."

"Tell me the crazy."

Rhett studied me for a moment. "You sure you want to hear this?"

"Of course. It's fascinating. I've never understood people, but I still find them interesting."

He took another sip and settled back in his chair. "My favorite client was a guy who joined the military when he was eighteen. He went off to boot camp and ended up going to war, and didn't make it home to find his girl for almost twenty years."

"Oh my God." Sympathy washed through me, rivaling the heat of the alcohol.

"Yeah. Vietnam POW. The kind of thing you'd see movies about. He was messed up when he got out, and it took him a long time to pull himself together to the point where he felt he even had the right to go looking for her."

I shook my head, unable to imagine what it would have been like. "What happened?"

"He looked for her but the trail was cold. She'd left town and disappeared. No one knew where she went. He called in favors, and someone led him to me."

"You found her?"

Rhett's lips tugged up in a smile. "Are you going to let me tell the story? You're just as impatient as you've always been."

I grinned sheepishly. Impatience was a fault I'd openly own and would probably never overcome, and I was perfectly okay with that. "Tell your story."

He took a sip and then continued. "I had a hell of a time finding leads, until one day it occurred to me why someone would disappear in that day and age." He looked pointedly at me. "Go ahead. I know you want to guess."

Rhett knew me well. "She was pregnant, wasn't she?"

He nodded. “Yeah, she was. The reason he couldn’t find her was because she changed her last name—to his. Said she was a soldier’s widow so her son wouldn’t bear the burden of being raised by an unwed mother. When I tracked them down, I found the son first. He could’ve passed as his dad when he was younger. When I showed the surveillance pictures of him to my client, he broke down and cried in front of me. Couldn’t believe he had a son he’d never known, but was so damn happy she’d raised him as his.”

I was practically bouncing in my seat to know what happened next, but I was exercising a modicum of patience.

“When I told him she’d never remarried, never dated, and still wore her POW/MIA bracelet with his name on it every day, he was stunned. It devastated him that she’d been alone for so long, but at the same time, he was amazed at her loyalty to his memory.”

My patience dried up. “What happened next?”

“I contacted her and told her that he was alive. She bawled in my arms and begged to see him. When I told her he was waiting in a car out front, you would’ve thought I told her the house was on fire. She barely looked at me before she ran. She threw herself into his arms, and he caught her and held her tight. They stood in her little front yard for an hour, not saying anything.”

Unable to hold them in, I felt tears slip down my cheeks. The image was too powerful. “That’s amazing.”

“It was. I’m not too proud to admit I shed a few tears watching them together. It was absolutely incredible. Made me believe that things can last, even after all the cheating and bullshit I had to deal with on a daily basis.”

For someone like Rhett who prized honor and loyalty, the

job sounded horrible. I was glad he'd had some cases that restored his faith in humanity. "Did he meet his son?"

Rhett nodded. "I wasn't there for that reunion, but the client wrote me a letter a couple days later telling me he didn't get his life back when they released him from captivity. He got his life back when I found his world. I framed it. Reminded me that what I did mattered."

I snuffled and lifted my cloth napkin to my eyes to dab the tears away. "Wow. You gave him his happily-ever-after. That's huge."

Rhett's smile wobbled, as if recalling what the letter said. "Sometimes it's the little things that make it all worth it."

"I'd say that was a big thing."

"Yeah, I guess you're right."

As I dealt with my tears, trying to pull myself together after his emotional story, our server arrived with our entrées.

"Ma'am, are you okay?"

"Totally fine. Don't mind me."

She settled our beautifully plated food in front of us and disappeared just as quickly. Before I picked up my fork, I had to ask the question hovering on my tongue.

"What do you want to do? I mean, after you find out what happened with your dad. Do you want to join the police force again, or keep doing PI work?"

Rhett got quiet and his hand stilled before closing around his fork. I could have kicked myself for the abrupt question and the change in mood it caused.

"Haven't thought about it. Taking it one day at a time."

The concept was foreign to me because I planned by weeks, months, quarters, and years. I had a five-year plan and accompanying goals, along with a ten-year plan.

When I didn't respond, he added, "I'm just a guy trying

to make a living after the rug got pulled out from under him. I don't have grand plans of building an empire like you do."

I tried to put myself in his shoes and imagine what it would have been like. For as long as I'd known Rhett Hennessy, which was all my life, he'd wanted to be a cop. Nothing more. Nothing less. That was his identity, and he'd lost it all in an instant. How did someone recover from that and forge a new life?

I thought about the company I'd built and how many directions it had taken. If it were all gone tomorrow, I'd be completely adrift. I had to have purpose in my life, and Rhett was the same.

That was when it dawned on me—all these years, I'd kept Rhett Hennessy on a pedestal, untouchable and unattainable. And now, he was *real* to me. He was a man, flesh and blood with hopes and fears, victories and disappointments. The shift in perspective was groundbreaking and rocked my world. This Rhett, the *real* Rhett, was better than I'd imagined.

I was self-aware enough to know that this was huge. And what's more, I had something I could offer him—a willing ear to listen and a creative mind to help him figure out what he could do next.

TWENTY-FOUR
RHETT

I dug into my oysters, wishing I had all the answers. Or hell, at least something that would make me sound like less of a loser when it came to my plans. Ari was smart, successful, and knew exactly what she was doing with her future.

"If you could do anything, no limits, what would you do?"

The question was so completely Ari, it was almost predictable. Even so, it took me off guard. I had no frigging clue what I wanted to do next, and that ate at me. I lowered my fork and thought for a minute.

I was taking this day by day.

"Right now, I want one thing—answers. I need to know the truth about what happened with my father, and I'm not going to let it go until I figure it out."

Ari nodded sagely, obviously no longer a girl in awe of every word coming out of my mouth. She was the one who had it all together and I was the mess, but there was no judgment on her face. She was unapologetic about knowing what she wanted, methodical and driven in going about achieving it. I'd never realized before how sexy that could be or how much I envied it.

"When you find those answers, will they affect what your future looks like?"

Another logical question I hadn't taken the time to consider before. I bought myself time to think by taking a bite of my dinner and she did the same, although I could tell she was eagerly awaiting my response.

Would the truth about my dad affect my next steps? If it came out that he was framed and was exonerated, would I want to rejoin the force?

I had my answer before I even finished chewing. I'd never go back to the department. Something in me had changed irrevocably. I couldn't carry a badge anymore, because it didn't stand for what I thought it did before. And if I couldn't believe in it, I didn't deserve one.

"I'm done being a cop."

"I wondered. I can't say I'm completely surprised either. It would be hard to go back now. I couldn't imagine going to work for anyone else now that I've been working for myself for so long."

When she said that, it occurred to me that she understood something that I hadn't consciously realized yet. I'd gotten a taste of freedom, and I didn't have the patience for department politics anymore.

"How did you know I'd feel like that?"

Ari finished chewing a bite and swallowed. "You're a leader, Rhett, not a foot soldier. I can only imagine that you'd be happier with complete autonomy."

Her insight hit me like a round to a bulletproof vest, slamming into me with shattering force.

I never thought I'd be this glad to be off the pedestal Ari had put me on because *she saw me clearly.* Maybe even more clearly than I saw myself.

I grinned at her in awe. "You're right."

One side of her mouth tilted up in a quirky smile. "Don't sound so surprised. I am a genius." She winked, and it broke a laugh free from my chest.

"Smartass too."

She shrugged. "Never said I wasn't."

There it was again, the confidence I always thought might be hovering beneath the surface, but she'd never shown before. And it was hot. My sexy little genius. Before I could go further down that line of thought, she picked up with the questions again, forcing me back to the subject I'd been avoiding.

"What does that leave? PI work? Do you enjoy it?"

Did I? I let myself answer honestly. "I don't want to follow cheating spouses around ever again. I've had enough. Sure, it pays the bills, but it blows."

She abandoned her fork on her plate and leaned her elbows on the table, dropping her chin on her hands to study me. "But you liked tracking down that guy's family. That meant something to you."

Hell yes, it had. Absolutely. That had given me just as much satisfaction, if not more, than closing a case as a detective ever did.

I nodded.

"Have you considered focusing on missing persons? You have the skills, and you're building the independent résumé on top of the experience you had at the department."

It was like a light bulb going off in my head, and Ari had flipped the switch.

Help people locate the loved ones they refused to let go of, and get them answers? The work could be just as hard as chasing down cheating spouses, just in a different way. But when the outcome was positive, it was a hell of a lot more rewarding. The more I turned the suggestion over in my mind, the more I liked it.

"That's a damn good idea."

Ari's face lit up with a wide smile. "I'm glad you think so. Finding something you enjoy makes all the difference. I wouldn't work as much as I do if I didn't love it. You could change lives by helping people in a way that only you can."

I soaked up her enthusiasm. "It's something to think about. But first, I have to figure out . . ." I stopped short because we both knew where I was going.

"Is there any way I can help? I have skills, you know. Maybe not perfectly legal ones, but they're helpful in the right situation."

My gaze sharpened on her. "You're talking about hacking into the department, aren't you?"

With her chin still perched on her hands, she lifted her shoulders to her ears and dropped them. "It's not like it would be hard. I got into Heath's work computer in about twelve seconds, but that's only because he's not creative with his passwords. If there's information on the inside that they're not being up front about, you need to know. You deserve to know."

I thought about what she was saying. Not so very long ago, my perspective on the world was very black and white. Things were either right or wrong, and I didn't spend much time considering shades of gray. But that was before. Now I realized that life was more blurry gray lines than anything at all.

The department *was* holding something back. There was a lot more to the story than they were saying, and Heath's position in IA meant that he should know what it was. Or he would if he hadn't requested to be removed from the case due to a conflict of interest.

"What exactly are you proposing, Red?"

Her brain was wired differently than mine, so I couldn't help but wonder what she planned. I could swear excitement lit her eyes at the question.

"Just some snooping around. See if maybe there are files they've tried to bury. Digital footprints are everywhere, even when you think you've erased them."

"You don't think they know how to cover their tracks?"

She lifted her chin and tapped her index fingers together with a sly smile. "I don't think you realize how good I am at what I do."

That smile. That confidence. This woman. She was the full package, and beyond intoxicating with that light shining in her eyes. And her loyalty—willing to do whatever it took to help me find answers—that was even sweeter.

"What do you need?"

"Only your permission."

My grip tightened on my empty glass. "Do it."

It was as if those words unleashed something in the universe, because at that moment, Ari's phone rang.

TWENTY-FIVE
ARIEL

"I'm a little busy, Heath."

"We have a big fucking problem."

The panic sharpening my brother's tone put me on edge. "What's going on?"

"Dad's gone. I can't find him."

I tensed as dread crawled through me. "What do you mean?"

Rhett's eyes locked on mine as Heath explained.

"He wanted pizza from that place he loves that doesn't deliver, so I ran out to get it. When I came back, the door was open and he was gone."

I didn't know that a disappearing parent could be my worst nightmare, but tonight, it was. "Oh my God. What are we going to do?"

Rhett tugged the phone from my nerveless fingers. "Hey, it's Hennessy. What the hell's going on? Your sister's as white as a sheet."

My stomach knotted as Heath filled Rhett in, talking loudly enough that I could hear every word. Frozen in place,

I didn't know what to do. Crisis mode required emotional separation and a rational, cool head. Business was business. No one was going to die regardless of the outcome of those decisions, and I could handle them with proper processing and analysis. But the thought of my dad wandering alone on the street, lost and confused, destroyed me.

There was nothing rational going through my head right now.

Not my daddy, please.

"We'll be there in fifteen. Call the department. Call in every favor you have. Get everyone on the streets. Make a list of places he might go, or where he liked to go—his favorite bars, restaurants, hell, even your mom's grave—and give it to everyone. We're on our way."

Rhett ended the call and yanked out his wallet. He tossed a handful of cash down on the table, rose, and grabbed my hand. "Let's go."

Like a robot, I followed him, thinking through every worst-case scenario. I couldn't even form the words until we stepped outside. "What are we going to do?"

With his face set in a determined mask and his voice strong with conviction, he answered. "We're going to find him." He pulled me across the street to the parking lot and stopped beside my door.

"He's . . . you saw at lunch. There's something—"

He unlocked the Jeep and urged me inside. "I know. We got this. We're going to find him. I swear we won't sleep until he's safe."

Before I could reply, he shut the door and rounded the hood.

His vow dulled my terror in a way I didn't expect. While I was crumpling inside, he was calm, collected, and determined. His confidence and unwillingness to accept any other alternative shored up my strength, and I took a deep breath.

"We got this," I repeated to myself.

Rhett jumped in the Jeep and with a roar of the engine, we pulled away.

TWENTY-SIX
RHETT

Watching Ari's face go white with terror was something I wouldn't forget for a long time and never wanted to see again. I swore I had a direct line to the fear ripping through her system when that call came through.

My first instinct was to strangle Heath for letting this happen, but I knew that wasn't fair. Neither Ari nor her brother had realized how bad their dad was until recently, and this had to be the last thing they expected. Up until a few days ago, he'd been living alone. According to Heath, there hadn't been many warning signs except a sprained wrist from a fall.

I'd been on the hunt for more than one elderly person who had wandered away from home, but this was personal. I would do whatever it took to make sure Mr. Sampson was safe as soon as fucking possible.

Breaking every speed limit, I made my way to Heath's house as fast as I could. When we got there, three black-and-whites were parked out front with their lights on. I wasn't sure how I would be received by my former colleagues, but I didn't give a damn. This was more important than bad blood.

Heath was outside, poring over a map spread across the hood of a squad car. Good, that meant they were working out the search parameters.

Ari jumped out of the Jeep before I could open her door and rushed to her brother. He caught her in a hug, looking just as panicked as she did. As I got closer, I heard him whisper "I'm sorry" to her over and over.

An officer I didn't recognize spoke up. "We're gonna get more units out, and we'll notify all the news and radio stations. If you have any other friends and family that can help search, call them too."

Ari's expression crumpled. "It's just us. We don't have more family. Dad is all we have." The pain in her voice jabbed me in the chest.

"It's gonna be okay, Flounder. We're gonna find him," Heath promised. He finally looked up and noticed me. "Thanks for getting here so quick."

The officers around the hood of the car glanced my way as well. Flashes of recognition streaked across their faces, but I wasn't about to waste time with introductions.

"Put me to work. I can help."

All business, the officer in charge handed out assignments and copies of the list Heath had made of all his dad's favorite places, and we moved out.

Ari was selected to stay at Heath's house in case her father returned. Everyone had her cell phone number to notify her as soon as someone located him.

Before I jumped in my Jeep, I stopped in front of her and gripped the back of her neck, turning her face up to mine. I pressed a hard, quick kiss to her lips.

"We'll find him."

"Thank you," she whispered.

"You don't need to thank me."

Tears filled her eyes, and I released my hold on her neck to wipe away one that tipped over her lid. "We got this. It's gonna be okay."

"It's just . . . he's all we have left."

"I know, Red. Hold it together."

She swallowed and straightened her shoulders, visibly collecting herself as Heath and the units pulled away from the curb to start the search.

"I'm good. Go. Find him."

TWENTY-SEVEN
ARIEL

It had been an hour with no leads. I sat in my brother's house on his beat-up leather sofa, staring at the wood-paneled wall as I waited for my phone to ring again. Each time someone called, my hopes soared. And each time, it had been the same story.

"Nothing yet. We're still looking."

The TV flickered with a rerun I'd muted because I couldn't focus on the banter. Instead, my gaze drifted to the few pictures Heath had on his entertainment center in dusty frames.

One of him and me as kids. His arm was wrapped around my shoulder, squeezing me tight to his side against his Saints T-shirt. I must have been about six years old. Dad had decided I was due to see my first game, and I still remembered how safe I felt between them in a wild stadium packed with people yelling *Who dat?*

I'd give anything to feel the press of both their shoulders against me again right now. Grabbing my phone off the table for the seventh time, I stared at the screen, checking for missed calls.

Obviously, there weren't any. The volume on my ringer was turned all the way up.

I sent up another prayer to the man upstairs. *Please help them find my daddy. Please let him be okay. He's a good man. He doesn't deserve this. Please.*

Tears spilled onto my cheeks as I stood and paced the room, finally stopping in front of the only complete family picture my brother had. It was taken the day my parents had brought me home from the hospital. Mom held a pink, red-faced bundle down for Heath to see, and my dad beamed at her.

She'd died less than three months later from cancer, sacrificing herself so I could live. If she'd terminated her pregnancy, she could have undergone treatments and might have survived. But on the rare occasion Dad would talk about it, he said that she wouldn't even consider it.

Tears flowed more freely as I reached out to trail a fingertip along her face behind the glass. "Watch over him, please. Keep him safe, angel mama."

I was convinced she'd done just that on plenty of occasions before, or maybe it was just my way of dealing with the sense of loss that ached in my chest.

Dad and Heath had both had more close calls than I wanted to think about, but somehow, they'd always come home safely at the end of their shifts. When I was young, I would wait at the Hennessys' kitchen table while Mrs. Hennessy fed me dinner. One night, not long after the first department funeral I ever attended, I remembered asking her, "What would happen to me if my daddy didn't come home?"

She'd rushed to my side and hugged me. "Oh, child, your

daddy will always come home to you. Your mama wouldn't let anything happen to him. She knows you need him more than she does right now."

That night, Dad had missed being grazed by a bullet, and he and Mr. Hennessy were still talking about it when they walked in the door. At least, they were talking about it until Mrs. Hennessy had given them both the evil eye with a glance toward me.

I'd burst into tears and ran toward him, wrapping my arms around his waist and telling him he couldn't ever get hurt. Dad had extracted himself from my wild grip, picked me up, and crushed me in his arms.

"You know I've got a guardian angel riding on my shoulder, Ariel. She's going to make sure I get home to you no matter what."

Please make sure he gets home to me, I pleaded silently again to the woman in the picture I'd never had a chance to know.

I backed away from the entertainment center and my phone blared to life, scaring the ever-loving crap out of me. I looked down at the screen at my brother's name and froze before answering.

"Did you find him?" I answered it the same way I had before.

"Not yet. Still looking. Nothing on your end?"

My shoulders hunched, and I found myself crumpling into the couch again. "No. Nothing. Jesus, Heath. Where could he have gone? We have to find him." My voice broke on the last part, and Heath's breathing roughened.

"I know. We will. We have the whole friggin' department, including the retirees, on the streets. Everyone is looking. We'll bring him home. We will."

I noticed he didn't say *safe*, and I cringed.

I didn't know if it was to make myself feel better or to remind Heath, but I whispered, "Mama's watching him, and she's going to make sure he comes home to us no matter what."

"I know, Flounder. I know. I gotta go. Call me if he shows."

"I will. Call me the second you or anyone else find him."

"Of course. Love you, little sis."

"Love you too."

Heath ended the call, and it felt like my stomach had developed a new gaping hole. Helplessness wasn't something I could handle. I needed to be doing something, or I was going to lose my mind.

My fingers itched for a computer, but my laptops were all at my place.

Heath has to have something here. I would have felt bad poking around, but I told myself it was to save my father and my sanity, so I forgave myself for the invasion of privacy, and I knew Heath would too.

It didn't take me long to find his department-issued laptop tucked in its black case near the door.

A less desperate daughter would probably not consider breaking into a laptop that was technically the property of the police department, but I didn't care. If he got in trouble for anything I did, I would take the blame and they could try to send me to jail. My lawyers would undoubtedly come up with a creative defense. I paid a big enough retainer to ensure it.

I pulled the machine out of the bag and set it up on the kitchen table. Already, just having the smooth keys beneath my fingertips made me feel more in control. As I turned on the power, I mentally sorted through the options of what would be most helpful, and decided on traffic cameras.

Was it a massive long shot? Absolutely. Without facial-recognition software, especially my proprietary version, the odds were like finding a needle in a haystack, but at least I was doing *something*.

I thought about the pet project I'd been working on for the last several months because I knew that people like Heath faced ridiculous danger daily just because they carried a badge. I was still working out how to give them the best defensive weapon I could. *Information*.

If the police had cameras on their cars or clothing that could automatically run every face they saw through a database and identify all threats, they would be better prepared for whatever was coming their way. I was still working out the bugs, as well as the legal and ethical issues.

If I were able to perfect it, it wouldn't be a product I would sell. I would donate the technology to police departments nationwide.

Getting into Heath's computer didn't even take real hacking. His username and password were a variation on the same thing he'd always used—Chester16. It was our childhood dog's name and his football number.

Come on, Heath. Time to step it up in the password arena.

But then again, it saved me valuable time.

Once I was logged in, it didn't take me long to tap into the city's traffic-camera system, being careful enough not to get caught but not so careful as to slow myself down. The number of options was overwhelming, but I went through the feeds methodically, choosing the ones closest to our house and working outward in a grid pattern, similar to what the cops were doing right now.

Where are you, Daddy?

Settling in, I finally felt less like I was going to throw up because I was doing something to help instead of wringing my hands and staring at the door.

We will find you.

TWENTY-EIGHT
RHETT

Two hours after I left Ari at Heath's house, I was beginning to lose hope when no one had spotted him yet. I'd called in every favor I was owed, and checked in with all my old informants. It was full dark, and wandering the streets wasn't safe for anyone right now.

And with the darkness, the chances of randomly spotting him went down dramatically.

My phone rang with a call from an old CI who worked security at the cemetery on Frenchman Street.

"Otis? You got something for me?"

"What was this dude wearing? Gray shirt and navy sweatpants? 'Cause I just ran off some guys with my truck who were kicking the shit out of an old man in the cemetery."

"Fuck. Yeah, that could be him. He okay?" I yanked my steering wheel in the other direction, heading for Otis.

"No, man. He looks like he got the shit kicked out of him. You want me to call 911? I'm on the northeast corner.

Remember the place those punks tagged my tombs? Close to that."

"Yes. Fuck. Call 911. I'll be there in two minutes."

For a moment, I debated whether to call Ari, but I wanted to be sure first. If it wasn't her dad, I didn't want her hopes up. I'd know if it was the right decision soon enough.

I turned two more corners, and finally my headlights cut across the gray tombs of the cemetery. A flashlight beam waved in the air.

Otis.

I bolted out of the Jeep and ran toward him, not bothering to turn off the car or shut the door behind me. When I skidded to a stop next to the dark human-shaped lump on the ground, Otis was still on the phone with 911, giving them the situation.

I snatched the flashlight out of Otis's hand and flashed it over the man's face. It was smeared with blood, but there was no doubt it was Ari's dad.

Thank fuck.

I dropped to my knees at his side. "Mr. Sampson. This is Rhett Hennessy. I'm here to get you help. Okay, sir?"

He tried to roll to his side, but groaned instead.

"Mr. Sampson. Stay with me. We're getting help. Can you hear me?"

His glasses were smashed and both eyes were swelling shut. Otis hadn't exaggerated in the slightest. If anything, he'd understated the situation.

Jesus Christ.

I checked for immediate life-threatening injuries, my first-responder training coming back quickly. One of his legs was bent funny. *Shit. Shit. Shit.*

"Heath?" His voice shook, but the fact that he was talking was a good sign in my book.

"No, sir. Rhett. We had lunch together yesterday."

"You broke my window with a baseball."

"Yes, sir. That was me. I'm really sorry about that. Can you tell where else you're hurt?"

"My ribs hurt. They kicked me. Fucking assholes." He pushed on the ground like he was trying to get up, but his leg buckled.

"Hold still a second, sir. We need to get you looked at before you try to move."

"Something ain't right. Think I'm gonna be sick."

I reached out and laid a hand over his, not wanting to squeeze in case his fingers were jacked up. "Ambulance is on the way. We'll get you to a hospital so they can check you out."

I expected him to protest, but he just grunted. *Shit*, they must have worked him over real good for him not to argue about that. The man I knew was stubborn to a fault, just like his son and daughter.

Otis held the phone away from his ear. "They're coming. They want me to stay on the line."

"Good. Do that."

"They made me go with them," Mr. Sampson mumbled. My instincts told me to ask him what he meant, but his fingers curled around mine as he groaned in pain. "Wanna talk to Ariel."

"Yes, sir. I can make that happen."

I yanked my phone from my pocket and called Ari. "I got him. Ambulance is on the way. He wants to talk to you."

She broke down in sobs that shredded my heart. "Oh my

God. What happened? Is he okay? No, of course he's not okay if you called an ambulance. Can I talk to him?"

"Hold on." I extended the phone toward Mr. Sampson, flipping it to speaker. "Mr. Sampson, I have your daughter on the phone."

"Ari? Heath's getting pizza for dinner. You want some?"

She choked on her tears. "Yeah, Daddy. I'd love that."

"Good girl. Missed you."

"I love you, Dad. Missed you too."

I took the phone off speaker as Ari's voice cracked on the last words. "Hold it together. Where's Carver? Get him to drive you to the ER."

"How bad is it? Tell me the truth."

I glanced at the broken old man on the ground beside me. "It's pretty bad, but he's gonna be fine." I prayed I was telling her the truth.

She hauled in a breath. "I'm getting Carver. We'll meet you there. Which hospital?"

I calculated the nearest one from where I was and gave her the name.

"I'm on my way. And, Rhett? Thank you."

I hung up the phone as sirens and flashing lights pierced the night. "Mr. Sampson, help is here. We're gonna get you all fixed up."

TWENTY-NINE
ARIEL

I rushed into the emergency room while Carver found a place to park. Police cruisers were pulled up near the ambulance bay, so I hoped Heath was already there. I'd called him as soon as I'd hung up with Rhett.

A uniformed officer that had been at the house was in the waiting room.

"Is my dad here?" I asked him. "Where is he? Can I see him?"

"Yes, ma'am. Your brother asked me to wait for you. I'll take you back."

"What happened?"

"I didn't get all the details. I'm sure your brother will fill you in."

I didn't bother asking any more questions as we hustled back through the doors that led to the exam rooms. Rhett stood outside the third one and I ran to him, throwing myself into his arms. "Thank you. Thank you so much." Tears spilled down my face, and he hugged me hard.

"He's gonna be okay, Red. I promise."

I snuffled. "I hope so."

"No hoping. He will be. They're running tests."

I forced myself to let Rhett go and reached for the door handle, but he stopped me with a hand on my arm.

"He's a little banged up, so make sure you're ready. Don't freak out. He's gonna be just fine."

"Are you coming in?"

He shook his head. "I'll be right here. It's getting a little crowded in there."

The dread that had been thrumming through my veins curdled in my stomach as I took a fortifying breath and pushed open the door. When I stepped inside, I was glad Rhett had warned me. My dad's face was swollen and bruised. Tears burned behind my eyes, and it took everything I had not to let them fall.

"Daddy?"

My brother was at his side, talking to him as the doctor attended to his hands. Both Heath and my dad looked up when I spoke.

"Ari? When did you get here?"

I didn't know if Dad was asking whether I'd just gotten here from California or when I'd gotten to the hospital. "Just now. How are you doing?" I kept my answer generic, not wanting to confuse him further.

"I got a little banged up. I'll be fine." His voice sounded strong and sure, which was a good sign.

I swallowed back the tears and chose my words carefully. "You've looked better, but you're still the most handsome man I know."

He tried to smile, but the tug on his split lip stopped him.

I cringed at the flash of pain and crossed the room to get closer. I desperately wanted to ask who the hell had done this, but a warning look on Heath's face stopped me. Instinctively, I knew that keeping the atmosphere light in the room was paramount.

"You've been working too much," Dad said. "Gotta take time off now and again to spend with your old man."

His words almost knocked my tears loose, but I held them in and cleared my throat. "I was just thinking the same thing. I think I'm going to be spending a lot more time in New Orleans from here on out."

My dad gave me a half smile, probably the biggest one he could without pain. "I like the sound of that."

To see that joy on my father's face, there wasn't much I wouldn't do. "You got it, Daddy." I looked to the doctor standing near the wall. "Sorry to interrupt. I just—"

He waved me off. "Don't worry about it. As I was telling your brother and father, they'll be here shortly to get him down for a CT scan, and we'll go from there."

The panic that was just starting to fade kicked up again. "CT scan?" I jerked to look at Heath and my dad.

Dad answered. "They're worried about me knocking my head and jacking my hip up."

"What?"

When no one elaborated further, a tense silence hung in the room. The doctor excused himself, and I drilled Heath with a stare. His look again carried enough warning that I couldn't miss it. Now wasn't the time to ask questions. We made small talk with Dad until someone knocked on the door and it opened to reveal a woman dressed in scrubs.

"Mr. Sampson, we're ready for you."

I backed away, hating that they were wheeling him out of sight. The door shut, leaving Heath and me alone in the room.

"What the hell happened?" I asked as soon as the door shut.

"He wandered down into a bad neighborhood and got jumped."

"He got jumped? They could've killed him!" I hadn't been a New Orleans resident in a long time, but even I knew the city had a dark side that couldn't be hidden.

Heath crossed the room and dragged me into a hug. "But they didn't. He's okay. We'll make sure this never happens again."

My mind raced through the possibilities. "We can get him twenty-four-hour care if he doesn't want to leave his house. I can afford the best, and you know damn well I'll make sure he gets it."

My brother kissed the top of my head. "I know. We'll figure it out. You know he's stubborn as hell, and he's still a little out of it. This isn't going to be easy for any of us."

I squeezed him harder. "I meant what I said. I'll stay as long as I need to. He needs both of us."

"Yeah, he does." Heath loosened his grip and I looked up. "I'm glad you're staying."

"Do you want to try to move him into the place I'm renting? Maybe it would be easier?"

"I don't think a lot of change is a good idea right now. Let's see what they say about his hip first. Then we'll decide."

"Okay. We'll do whatever we have to."

The door opened and Rhett stepped inside.

Heath released me. "There's our hero. He found him. Who knows how long we would've been out there without his help."

I didn't care that my brother was watching. I crossed the room and threw my arms around Rhett.

"Thank you," I whispered to him again.

"I didn't do anything you wouldn't have done for me," he said as he gently wrapped an arm around my shoulders and pressed my face into his chest.

"Whatever you say," Heath said, "but I'm damn glad you were here. We owe you."

"He's right. We do."

Rhett held me tighter. "None of that owing shit. This is what we do."

Fifteen minutes later, Dad and his hospital bed were returned to their previous position. Conscious of all the eyes on us, I stepped out of Rhett's arms.

"I wondered how long it would take him to make a move on my girl. Took him long enough, but I'm glad to see he finally figured it out."

My face heated, and I was sure it had turned red at my dad's words.

My instinct was to inch away from Rhett, but he looped an arm around my waist and pulled me in front of him.

"Glad we've got your blessing, sir."

"Take good care of my girl."

"Of course, sir. Understood."

"Good."

I took the clarity in my father's words as a good sign, even though a few moments of awkward silence followed. We waited another hour before the results of the CT scan were delivered. Dad had a hip fracture, but nothing that would require surgery. They weren't able to determine the cause of his altered mental state.

"He's lucky it's not worse," the doctor explained. "We'll keep him overnight to run a series of tests, make sure he's stable, and get a neuro consult. Depending on what we find, it might be a good idea to look into rehab facilities for the hip fracture."

Dad protested, but Heath and I overruled him. When I volunteered to stay with Dad and sleep on the pull-out chair, Heath overruled *me*.

"I'm pulling rank on this one. Go home. I need to stay with him to make myself feel better about letting him wander off. This was on me."

I argued and told him it wasn't his fault, but he wouldn't listen. As we left the room, two uniformed officers waited outside, ready to take Dad's statement despite the late hour.

I paused in the hallway. "I don't know how much he'll be able to tell you."

The young officer shrugged. "Any little bit helps. We want to get out there and find whoever did this. Do you want us to wait?"

"No, now's fine. It'll be a while before they move him to a room," Heath said to the officer. When I opened my mouth to volunteer to stay again, he shot a pointed look at me. "Go get some sleep, Ari. I got this."

That was how I found myself back in Hennessy's Jeep at four o'clock in the morning, heading back to my place. I'd sent Carver home earlier, knowing it would be a long wait and there was no reason to keep him.

When we pulled up to the gate, Rhett punched in the code that he clearly remembered. After he parked the Jeep in the driveway, I shared my decision.

"I told my dad I would stay as long as he wanted, and I meant it."

Rhett turned slowly to look at me. "You can run your business from here?"

I nodded. "I can run it from anywhere, provided I can travel on occasion for in-person meetings." I hesitated before continuing.

"What?" Rhett asked, reading me too effectively.

"How long are you staying? Are you going back to wherever you were?"

His gaze left mine for a moment before returning. "I'm not going anywhere until I find out the truth about what happened with my dad. I owe him that."

"And then?"

"And then we need to figure out if you're gonna give me a reason to stay longer than that."

"Wait, you mean—"

"You figure into this decision, Red. I'm not gonna lie and pretend you don't."

THIRTY
RHETT

You would have thought I told her I had the nuclear codes. That's how dumbstruck Ari looked when I told her she played a role in my decision.

I knew she wasn't dense. She was a goddamned genius, after all, but sometimes she missed the simple things right in front of her face. I probably should have been insulted that she didn't think I realized just how amazing she was and wanted to see where this could go. I'd have to be a moron to miss this opportunity.

Which, apparently, I was for years.

But no longer.

Maybe there was some truth to the idea that things happen when and how they're supposed to. I never would have believed any good could come out of the fucked-up events of this week, but I was willing to admit when I was wrong.

Figure out what you want and go after it.

That's exactly what I was doing. My life was in ashes, so

this was the time to rebuild. Something new. Something good. With Ari.

And right now, I needed some of that good.

I cupped her jaw and lowered my lips to hers. What surprised me the most was how fast and how hard she threw herself into the kiss. It had to be crazy spikes in adrenaline that we'd been running on throughout this roller coaster of a night.

Ari slid to the edge of the seat so quickly, I wondered if she might climb right onto my lap, which for the record, I wouldn't have had a problem with at all. One hand went behind my neck and the other dived into my hair. I groaned against her mouth, adjusting my grip to pull her closer.

Fuck it. I dragged her over the center console of the Jeep. She straddled me, leaning up higher and pressing down.

My dick, which I would have sworn would be dormant for days after tonight, went rock hard.

She kissed me like she needed it more than air. Like this was all that was holding her together. I let it go on for another long minute, because I couldn't find it in me to push her away, but I knew I had to stop it soon. If I didn't, the first time I'd have Ariel Sampson under me would be in the front seat of my car after an exhausting, emotional night.

I pulled back. "Ari, sweetheart."

"Shut up," she whispered, going after my lips again.

That's when I finally understood. She needed this, and that meant I was going to give it to her . . . to a point.

That point being the one I was about to hit in five . . . four . . . three . . .

My countdown didn't make it any further because someone knocked on the window and Ari jerked away and screamed.

I yanked her against my chest and reached for the gun hidden between my seat and the center console. I had it pointed at the form beyond the window before conscious thought kicked in.

Carver.

Releasing my grip on Ari, I tucked the gun away and reached for the button to roll the window down.

"Oh. I'm sorry. I didn't mean—"

"You need something?"

I had to give the guy credit. He kept his eyes off Ari, which was the exact right thing to do.

"I just wanted to make sure there were no issues and that Mr. Sampson was doing well."

Ari shifted in my lap, brushing my half-hard dick as she straightened. I suppressed a groan as she replied.

"He was banged up and has a hip fracture, but it won't need surgery, just rehab. Thank you for asking."

Carver nodded. "That's good news." He paused for a moment, not turning away like I expected. "Um, Ms. Sampson. One more question."

"Yes, Carver?"

"Will Mr. Hennessy be staying? For security measures, it would help me to know."

Ari stiffened in my lap, clearly taken off guard by the question, but I didn't hesitate.

"I'm staying."

Her grip tightened on me as Carver's gaze jumped from my face to hers, and she nodded, repeating my answer. "Yes. Rhett will be staying."

"Sir. Ma'am. I'll leave you to it." He backed away and disappeared into the side door of the massive garage.

Ari's head jerked toward me, and I wondered if she was

going to comment on my jumping in and saying I was staying without consulting her, but she didn't. Her fingers threaded into my hair again and her lips found mine. This time the kiss was desperate and wild, like she'd lost all inhibitions. Like she was afraid this was the only moment she'd get with me.

It wasn't. I was going to make damn sure we'd have a hell of a lot more.

I reached for the door handle with one hand and kept the other wrapped around her ass.

"Wait—"

"Done waiting, Ari. Tonight, we're taking."

Any other protest died on her lips. She freed me from my seat belt, shifting as I climbed out of the car and hefted her up.

"Wrap your legs around me." The command wasn't even out before her skirt was pushing further up her thighs and her legs gripped my hips.

It took extreme willpower to walk to the front door rather than lay her out across the hood of my Jeep and shove the skirt the rest of the way up her legs so I could find out what she was wearing beneath it.

Ari's lips sucked at my jaw, my neck, and my ear as I took measured steps toward the door. My fingers curled into her ass when we reached it, that willpower losing strength.

I pressed her back against it, using the leverage to pin her to the massive wood panel. "Jesus Christ, woman."

My words stopped her movements long enough for me to return the favor, scraping my teeth over her jaw and down the tendon of her neck. Husky moans filled my ears and my cock pulsed in my pants. If I didn't get her inside now, we weren't going to make it there at all.

Tearing my mouth away, I cupped her jaw. "The first time I sink inside you isn't going to be up against your front door."

Her gray eyes hazy, Ari nodded in agreement. "Okay. But maybe the second?"

"I'll consider it. Keys?"

"Should be open. Carver was here. He would've swept the house."

I didn't like that answer, but at this moment, I didn't care because the unlocked door meant there was one less barrier to getting what I wanted. "Hold on."

Ari gripped my shoulders, and I stepped away from the door and tugged open the handle.

"Down the hall," she said as she pointed, and I wasted no time striding toward the massive master suite.

Even though I was determined that this wasn't going to be a one-shot deal, I was going to treat it like my only chance to show her exactly what it was like to be my woman. Prove to her that I could give her something no one else could.

When I strode into her bedroom, Ari's lips were on me again, making it harder and harder to concentrate, but I found the bed in the middle of the giant space and laid her down on it.

She reached for me, but I stepped away. I needed light. I wanted to see her face. This wasn't happening in the dark.

I switched on one nightstand lamp and a soft glow filled the room. She was beautiful. She'd always been beautiful, but I'd never let myself appreciate her until now.

"You're gorgeous."

A blush crept up her cheeks.

"Don't believe me? Because you are. And I'm gonna bet

that applies to every damned inch of you, even the ones I haven't seen yet."

The blush deepened and I stepped closer to her again, this time reaching out to pull her to her feet.

"What—"

"Time to take this sexy dress off."

THIRTY-ONE
ARIEL

I'd been through the emotional wringer tonight, but my body buzzed with the high that came from too much adrenaline and too little sleep. Logically, I knew we both needed rest, but there was something else I needed more.

Rhett.

My heart hammered so hard, I thought it might be in danger of exploding. *Wham-bam, wham-bam, wham-bam.* The rhythm pounded in my chest as Rhett turned me around, found the zipper tab at the top of my dress, and slid it down. The cool air hit my overheated skin with each inch he uncovered, and when Rhett pressed his lips to the top of my spine, I thought I was going to trip right out of my shoes.

But he didn't stop there. He took his time, kissing a path down my back until he was kneeling behind me, my dress pooled in a puddle at my feet, and his lips just above the lace band of my thong.

I thought he'd yank it down and keep going, but the man kept me guessing.

I didn't know why *that* surprised me most of all. Probably because I'd envisioned what this moment would be like hundreds of times, and I couldn't have been more wrong. This wasn't the crazed tearing at clothes like it was when it started in his Jeep. No, Rhett was savoring every moment, tasting every inch. *Worshipping me.* That's what he was doing.

Rhett kissed a trail around my hip, guiding me with his hands until I spun to face him and his lips were pressed just below my belly button. He leaned his forehead against my stomach and breathed me in.

"I'm gonna devour you." His husky voice sent shivers zinging to my clit and hardened my nipples. "I want you to know what my lips feel like on every inch of your skin."

He lifted his head, and I regretted the loss of contact for a moment before his eyes met mine with a swift emotional punch. "This isn't a one-time thing, Ari. This is just the beginning."

"I don't expect promises from you." I didn't recognize my own voice.

"You're getting one anyway."

The heat burning in his eyes wasn't just arousal, it was a vow. Everything building between us had led to this moment.

He scraped his teeth from my belly button to the top of my panties and reached up with both hands to drag them down my legs, his mouth following every inch he uncovered until he skimmed over my bare lips.

"Red, you're soaked."

I didn't know what possessed me to say it, but I blurted, "Didn't you know everything's better when it's wetter?"

A moment of silence followed before Rhett's entire body shook with laughter. His piercing green gaze met mine.

"You're priceless, and I swear I'll always treat you like it. But right now, I'm going to eat this pussy until you scream."

One hand pressed to my stomach as he pushed me back onto the bed, where I landed with a bounce. Before I could say anything, he was between my legs, his tongue sliding through my wetness.

I couldn't tell who moaned louder, me or him. My hands fisted the covers as I pressed up against Rhett's mouth. Whatever he was doing—

"Oh my God." I couldn't possibly already be coming. It was impossible. Wasn't it?

But sure enough, the orgasm built and my cries grew louder and louder, until he slid a single finger inside and my climax slammed into me.

"That's right. Come hard for me, Red. Grip my finger like you're gonna grip my cock."

Who knew Rhett was a dirty talker? It turned me on like I never would have guessed.

His lips circled my clit as he pumped his finger in and out, sucking and nipping and tugging until the first orgasm stretched into two. If I'd been capable of rational thought, I would have worried about the wet spot I was surely going to leave on the bed.

Rhett lifted his head, and my eyes took a few seconds to focus on him. "You come just like you do everything else. You don't hold back."

My mouth was moving before I'd even consciously decided what to say. "Probably because you eat pussy like you do everything else—perfectly."

The grin. Oh sweet Jesus, that grin. It stretched across Rhett's face and tugged at my heart. I was in serious danger here, and it didn't scare me at all.

"I'm just getting started." He pushed in a second finger, cutting off any response I might have made with a harsh intake of breath. "You're so damn tight."

"Uh . . . thank you?" I didn't know if that was a compliment, but I was going to consider it one.

Rhett's laugh told me it was the right response. "That's going to be what I say when I slide into your sweet pussy and you wreck me."

Having his magic fingers working me over and his hot eyes on mine while he said those things sent waves of heat up my cheeks.

His eyes glinted as his grin turned lopsided. "It makes you even wetter when I talk dirty."

It wasn't a question. He was stating a fact, and it occurred to me that he could tell.

"I didn't know—"

"It's sexy as fuck." He pulled his fingers free and lifted them to my lips. "You ever taste yourself, naughty girl? Because I can tell you that it's tart and sweet and spicy, just like you."

My eyes probably bugged out of my head comically. "Taste myself?"

He painted his fingers along my lips, and I imagined him painting something else along them. My nipples hardened even further, pushing out the lace of my bra.

Rhett missed nothing. "What's that thought?"

I swiped my tongue out to taste, and he was right. It wasn't bad. It was different. "Could be worse."

"That's not what you were thinking when those little nipples peaked."

I sharpened my gaze on him. "How do you know?"

Rhett rose to his feet, the bulge in his pants becoming

obscene. "Because I know you, Ari. Now tell me, what were you thinking?"

He reached for the first button on his shirt and unfastened it. One after another, he released the buttons until he pulled the shirt off and dropped it on the floor. Then he reached for his belt.

Oh God.

"You were thinking of me rubbing something else against those plump lips, weren't you, Red?"

How does he know this stuff?

As if I'd voiced my question, Rhett twitched his lips into a smile. "Yeah, you keep forgetting those detective skills I still have. Number one? Reading people, especially the beautiful woman who's lying on the bed, legs spread, wet pussy waiting for me, when she's thinking about what it'd be like to have her lips around my cock."

The flood of moisture between my thighs would have given me away if he'd still had his fingers inside me.

"Don't worry, Red, you'll have your chance as soon as you admit it. I see it all over your face."

Leather hissed against the fabric as he pulled his belt through the loops.

Oh sweet Jesus. How did I admit that I'd imagined this moment more times than I could count? The moment when I finally learned if the rumors I'd heard in high school were true? That Rhett Hennessy was *hung*?

My breathing quickened and I was probably in danger of hyperventilating when he dropped the belt, thumbed open the button, and slid down the zipper. His thick bulge strained against the black boxer briefs and all the saliva in my mouth dried up.

He might be even bigger than I thought.

Rhett released his grip on his pants and they fell to the floor. After he stepped out of them, I levered up on my elbows and stared. He didn't look like he had in high school. Nope.

Rhett was built like a brawler, not a boxer. He was around six feet tall with broad, heavily muscled shoulders and a carved chest that tapered down into a narrow waist gripped by the band of the boxer briefs. His thighs stretched the fabric to the limits, just like his erection.

And those tattoos . . .

I was a goner.

"You should probably put your dick in my mouth." I slammed said mouth shut, unable to believe what had just come out of it. It was a good thing I didn't close my eyes too, because I would have missed Rhett's jaw drop before he recovered and shot me a wicked grin.

"I can honestly say those aren't words I ever expected you to say."

My cheeks burned. *I shouldn't be allowed to talk. I'm totally screwing this up.*

"Umm . . ."

"Do you know what the sexiest thing about you is, Ari?"

I was naked except for my bra, laid out on a bed, and I wasn't about to start guessing. "No."

"Your mind. Sometimes, it works so fast you don't have time to filter it, and I get the pure, unvarnished parts of you. Smart, funny, sweet, sexy. You check all the boxes. You're the ultimate package. The fact that you're here, with me, shows me that sometimes life does work out the way it's supposed to."

I didn't know what to say to that, but any other rational thought disappeared from my super-smart genius brain when he hooked his fingers in the sides of his briefs and tugged them down.

Oh. My. God.

Big, thick, and built just as solid as the rest of him, Rhett's cock bobbed free. If it hadn't been weighed down by its own bulk, it probably would have reached up to his navel.

My mouth formed into an *O* as he stepped forward. I scrambled up from the bed and did the only thing I could think of.

I threw myself at him.

THIRTY-TWO
RHETT

Realistically, there's not a damn thing a guy can do about his dick size. It's either big or it isn't. I'd never spent much time worrying about mine, but apparently, it's impressive enough for Ari to launch herself off the bed and slam into my chest.

I'd take it.

I reached out to steady her. "Whoa, Red."

"No whoa. Whoa means slow and we're done with that. Moving on now."

Her lips pressed against my neck, my shoulder, my chest . . . and trailed down to the promised land.

If I'd thought I was going to find a shy, uncertain girl on the bed before me, I would have been dead wrong. Ari was ravenous. Before she could wrap her lips around my dick, I gripped her shoulders and stopped her from dropping to her knees.

"What?"

"You gonna admit it?"

Her eyes smoldered, and I knew she was aware of what I was asking.

"Yes. I pictured you taking the head of your cock." She gripped the shaft, tearing a groan from me. "And dragging it —" My fingers faltered as she leaned forward, her mouth an inch away. "Across my lips."

She tried to close the distance, but I had other plans. With a tug, I plucked her up and tossed her on the bed.

"What—"

I pressed a knee on either side of her hips and worked my way up her body until my dick bobbed over her mouth. Ari's tongue swiped out to wet her lips, just missing me. I gripped my shaft as pre-cum beaded on the head.

With one hand bracing me on the bed, I leaned down and painted her lips with it. "Like this?"

Her moan vibrated up my shaft, and then her tongue darted out again, swiping along her lower lip. "Mmm."

I groaned, wishing she was laving the head of my cock.

"You want my mouth on you, Rhett? Have you ever pictured that?"

Somehow she turned the tables on me, and hearing the dirty questions on her lips kicked the intensity of the situation up another notch. Filterless Ari was perfect in the bedroom.

My dick jerked, giving away the answer.

Her eyes lit with heat. "You did, didn't you? You wanted to push your cock between my lips?"

"Fuck yes, I did." I stroked my cock as it bumped against her. "I'd come in my hand, wishing it was your mouth."

The blush on her cheeks deepened. I knew we were both pushing her boundaries, despite her bold words, but damned if I didn't like it.

"Then do it." Her voice came out on a husky whisper as she lifted herself to suck my dick between her lips.

It took every ounce of restraint I had to keep it slow and steady as I pressed further inside the wet heat. "Fuck, Ari. *Fuck.*"

Her gaze was on mine, and I read the triumph in it. She was getting off on this, and that made it infinitely hotter.

Stroke after stroke, she sucked me down and I regulated the depth, not wanting to bottom out in her throat, even though it would feel amazing. No, we'd work up to that.

When my balls tightened, I had to stop or I'd come before I was ready. I pulled free and her lips turned into an instant pout.

"Where—"

"I'm not coming anywhere but inside you the first time." I pushed off the bed and snagged my pants to find a condom. Within moments, I had my dick sheathed and my hips between her thighs, the head lined up at her entrance.

Her nipples puckered against the sheer lace of her bra. That had to go. I wanted every inch of her naked, and swore to myself that I'd take the time to learn every freckle later tonight.

"Take it off."

Ari twisted to unclasp her bra, and as soon as her tits spilled free, I planted a hand on either side of her head and thrust home.

Holy fuck, so tight.

A hoarse cry spilled from her lips, and a gruff sound tore from my throat.

Ari's hands flew out to grip my shoulders. Her eyes met mine, and she said exactly what I was thinking. "More."

"I'll give you everything you can take."

I pulled back and buried myself balls deep, stroke after stroke, until her body clenched around mine. I reached between us and found her clit, pressing hard until she screamed and grasped at the covers beneath us, arching her hips and gripping my dick with an orgasm like nothing else I'd ever felt.

I powered through, pumping over and over until I couldn't hold back any longer. I threw back my head and my climax tore through me.

Absolute and complete perfection. Better than anything I could have imagined.

THIRTY-THREE
ARIEL

I might have blacked out. I definitely saw stars. Possibly fireworks. Maybe even the Madonna. Sex with Rhett Hennessy was an almost religious experience, and it left me in a state of semi-shock.

Sweat beaded on my forehead, and Rhett's chest heaved as he sucked in breath after breath. Where was that wheezing sound coming from? Oh, wait, that was me.

"You okay, Red?"

I nodded. Or maybe my head just lolled to the side.

"You sure?"

This time I managed a nod. I wasn't sure words were possible at this point. Besides, what could I say? I'd imagined this moment so many times, and not a single variation had come remotely close to being as awe-inspiring as the reality. My fantasies had been shattered, and I wasn't sure how to deal with the aftermath. *Need to process.*

Rhett lowered his head and pressed his lips to mine when I didn't answer.

I found my voice after a few more centering breaths. "I'm good. Really good."

"Glad to hear it."

His deep voice did something to me, sent shock waves through my body, and my inner muscles clenched, turning the chuckle into a groan.

"Damn, Red."

I bit my lip as I realized how I affected him. "Sorry. Kinda. Okay, not really at all."

His lips quirked into a grin. "Don't ever apologize for having a perfectly tight pussy."

I slapped a hand over my eyes. "I'm not sure I'm ready for you to say things like that when we're not . . . you know, in the heat of the moment."

One of his eyebrows went up, clearly taking my statement as a challenge. "Guess you're going to have to use that genius brain of yours to adapt and deal."

My brain was the problem. It was having a hard time catching up to this new reality. "I may never be able to look you in the eye again," I mumbled, finding the ceiling very appealing.

Rhett's fingers gripped my jaw and he forced my gaze to meet his. "Never be embarrassed about anything that happens when we're together. This is as raw and honest as two people can get, and there's nothing to be worried about. I love that you let go, that you don't think too much and stop yourself from doing and saying what you want. It's sexy as hell, Ari. Be you, because you're amazing."

I just barely kept in the *awww* that wanted to escape. I had to change the subject. "Thank you for that."

"It's the truth."

Then he rolled off the bed and lifted me into his arms. "Come on, Red. Time for a shower."

Wet and naked?

My mind flipped back into dirty mode. "What else is happening in that shower?"

Rhett looked down at me, his eyes flashing in the early signs of sunrise cutting through the high windows. "Whatever I want."

Annnnd, I'm a goner.

THIRTY-FOUR
ARIEL

My eyes flew open as I rolled over and a hand slipped off my hip. The morning sun blazed through the blinds, but it wasn't the sun that was new today. No, it was the large source of body heat to my right.

For the first time in my life, I didn't *imagine* waking up next to Rhett Hennessy. I *actually* woke up next to him. Which meant the vivid scenes playing through my head were memories, not fantasies.

I lay there, my eyes darting back and forth as though they couldn't believe what they were seeing. Rhett's dark blond hair was truly on the pillow next to mine.

Even though last night I'd convinced myself he was no longer some figure of mythical proportions staring down from me on his pedestal, it was still overwhelming to comprehend.

My body ached in places I wasn't sure it had ever ached before. I bit down on my lip to keep the hysterical giggle trapped inside.

Real Rhett beat the dream Rhett every day of the week, and apparently three times on Sunday. Even in the *shower.*

My gaze stroked over his thick biceps as I recalled the way he'd held me pinned against the wall. He was just as strong as he looked.

But if last night with Rhett actually happened, that means . . . My thoughts took a dark turn as I recalled standing in the emergency room as my father was wheeled in and out for a CT scan.

Last night was both a dream and a nightmare. My hopes and fears collided all at once. I'd felt helpless, but Rhett had given me his strength.

And his dick.

I choked on a breath. My brain apparently didn't understand the solemnity of certain thoughts right now. In fact, as the synapses started firing, chaos reigned and there was only one way to corral it back into order. *Coffee.*

Even though I loathed the thought of leaving the bed, I had to move. Had to push forward, or I'd find myself curled up next to Rhett, covers over my head, refusing to ever get up because I didn't want to face the day, and that wasn't how I operated. I took things, good and bad, head on.

When I slipped out from under the covers, he didn't move. Halfway around the bed, I found his dress shirt from last night and shrugged it on, buttoning it as I walked toward the door.

The scent of coffee was absent as I hit the hallway leading to the kitchen because I hadn't set the coffeemaker timer. Every day I'd been in New Orleans, Carver had woken up before me and had it brewed and waiting. Given last night, I doubted Carver would set foot inside the house unless there was some kind of crisis.

I got the coffee going and stared out the window over the lake, watching as the sun rose higher in the sky. *Dad's waking up in a hospital bed this morning because we couldn't keep him safe.*

Last night had scared the hell out of me. I wasn't used to worrying about my father this way. He'd always been the most capable, larger-than-life man I knew.

I can't lose him too. My shoulders drooped as I wrapped my arms around my body and squeezed tight.

Lost in my depressed thoughts, I missed the sound of footsteps coming toward me, and didn't feel his presence until Rhett closed his arms over mine.

"It kills me to see you like this, Ari. I promise we're going to make everything right again. As right as I can possibly make it."

His chest pressed against my back and warmed my entire body. I wished I could soak up his strength and confidence as easily as I soaked up his body heat.

"We have to make sure this never happens again with Dad . . . and I have no idea how to protect him if he won't let me."

"We'll figure it out together. Your brother too. We've got this. Everyone wants to make sure your dad stays safe."

The certainty in Rhett's voice helped me center myself and focus on the right attitude. *We will figure this out. Dad is going to be fine. I won't let anyone or anything steal the remaining time I have left with my father. Once I find out who did this, I'm going to ruin their lives.*

Seemed like a fair and logical solution to me.

I turned in Rhett's arms to find him staring down at me, sincerity radiating in his gaze. He meant every word he said.

He might have been the one person, other than my brother, who cared about my family as much as I did.

"Thank you for staying."

He cupped my cheek, stroking with his thumb. "That's not something you need to thank me for, Ari. I should be thanking you."

The cheek he touched heated. "Um, nope. If there's anyone deserving thanks, praise, accolades, and possibly Olympic medals, it would be you." My gaze darted up to his before focusing on his chin again.

One corner of his mouth tugged upward, and I could picture the devastating smile in my head without seeing it.

"Olympic medals? Then I guess it means I didn't disappoint."

My eyes cut to his. "You thought I was disappointed? Are you deluded?"

Rhett's eyes crinkled at the corners as he laughed. "I wouldn't go so far as to call myself deluded, but I had some pretty big expectations to exceed, and I wanted to make sure I didn't fall short."

"Again, the scientific answer to that question would be a solid *no way in hell.*"

Rhett chuckled again. "Good. I mean, apparently it wasn't groundbreaking or life-changing, but that gives me things to work up to. I've still got room to impress you."

I pressed a hand to his chest. "If you impressed me any more, I might find out what cardiac arrest is like."

He leaned down and slid his lips along my temple. "We can't have that. I liked waking up beside you too much. It was almost like I could hear your brain flip on and the gears start turning."

I froze. "You were awake?"

"While you were watching me sleep? Yeah, I was."

My face heated. "I swear I'm not a creepy stalker. I left that in high school."

Silently, I amended, *Okay, maybe it was really college after I first hacked into his life to see what was going on. And maybe there was that alert I set up to see if he ever applied for a marriage license . . .* But Rhett didn't need to know about any of that. Clearly.

He shook his head. "I watched you after you fell asleep, so I consider it fair."

My chin jerked. "You did?"

"I finally had you where I'd wanted you for a long time, and I didn't want to miss a minute of it."

THIRTY-FIVE
RHETT

Ari melted against me, and I knew in that moment that I would do whatever it took to find who hurt her father and make sure they paid. Anyone who would beat up a confused old man deserved the same ass-kicking they'd handed out. Even my black-and-white sense of justice would have agreed with that.

I looked down at her face and had no qualms about being the man to deliver that ass-kicking. Whatever she needed, I'd find a way to be that.

"You want to break out one of your fancy computers and see if your dad was able to give them anything helpful last night?"

Ari straightened in my arms. "Do you think they would've filed a report already?"

I considered her question. "Not normally, but given that your dad is who he is and with your brother being on the force, I bet they filed it right away."

"On it." With a practiced hand, she poured herself a mug

of coffee and scooped a laptop off the counter before making her way to the table with it under her arm.

Her fingers flew as soon as she laid them on the keyboard. A tiny concentration line appeared between her brows as she worked, her attention focused on the screen.

Once I had my own cup of coffee in hand, I walked around the table to watch. Lines of gibberish appeared on a black screen as her hands worked some kind of magic spell I would never understand.

Until . . . I did.

The police department's internal search screen popped up in a window.

"Wait a minute. You just hacked into the system in less than five minutes?"

A huff escaped her lips. "Less than two. Five would be sad. It didn't even take me that long the first time."

I blinked twice, and my gaze darted between her still-flying fingers and the screen. When she said she was good, she was telling the truth.

"Shouldn't it be harder? Do they have any idea that people can do that? It seems *wrong*."

Ari shrugged. "What's *wrong* is the fact that the government won't spend the money to secure its own sites, even though it knows about the vulnerabilities. A baby hacker could get in, although they might not be as good at covering their tracks as I am."

The implications of what she was doing settled like lead in my gut. "You're sure no one can trace this back to you?"

"It all leads back to an IP address in Bangladesh this time. I never use the same one twice," she replied absently as she scanned the screen.

Her body was sexy. Her face was beautiful. But her brain blew me away.

"You're incredible."

She shrugged off the compliment. "We'll see. I haven't found anything useful yet." She returned her attention to the keyboard. "But I will."

Within moments, she had a police report on the screen that was filed in the early hours of the morning by the detective in charge of her father's case, and I read over her shoulder.

"Your father reported that there were two assailants. Hispanic. In their twenties. Both speaking Spanish. Distinctive tattoos that have surfaced as being associated with a certain Mexican drug cartel in the last several years." They'd also stolen his Saint Michael medallion, and I remembered Ari saying he'd never taken it off for as long as she remembered. Her mom had given it to him the day he'd graduated from the academy.

I could tell when she got to that part of the report by the tensing of her body. Silence hung between us as we both processed the details.

"I don't get it. Was it random? Or are they trying to say there's a connection to a prior case?"

I reread it. The report was incomplete, which wasn't surprising given the time it was filed. "He was homicide and retired before the cartel became the issue it is today."

"So it was random," she concluded.

"It could've been."

I didn't tell her the rest of what I was thinking because I didn't understand how all the pieces fit together yet, but my gut said this wasn't random. These guys didn't just go around beating up retired cops. They might have been arrogant, but they weren't stupid.

My brother was killed in a cartel drug raid gone wrong, and my dad died while the cops were on their way to arrest him for being on the cartel payroll. This connection hit way too close to home, even if it didn't make sense yet.

I read through the description Mr. Sampson had given again and committed everything to memory.

Ari finally lifted her hands from the keyboard. "This doesn't make any sense, does it? Maybe they were just out and saw him as an easy target?"

"Maybe."

Again, the answer didn't sit right in my gut. Heath was IA, and his department was investigating my father's cartel connection. He'd taken himself off the case, but maybe they thought he was involved and getting too close?

Ari turned to look at me, her eyes narrowed. "What aren't you telling me?"

"I don't know anything for sure, but something here isn't making sense."

She crossed her arms. "Tell me. We're a team in this, right?" Her eyebrow rose, and I had a feeling this was a test.

"Yeah, we are. But this team keeps Ari safe and lets Rhett do the stuff that could be dangerous. If we're talking about Mexican drug cartels, there's nothing that's safe about this, which means half our team is on the bench until I figure out exactly what the hell is going on."

"But—"

"But nothing. This isn't a game." I met her gaze. "You have to promise me that you won't go trying to hack into the cartel's networks. Imagine the biggest, most lethal and ruthless corporation in the world, twist it up so it's worse than even your nightmares can imagine, and then maybe you've come a tenth of the way toward understanding how friggin' dangerous these people are. You don't fuck with them. You do *nothing.* I don't want them knowing you exist."

"But if I can find a connection—"

I shook my head. "Absolutely fucking not. What they did to your dad would be nothing compared to what they'd do to you if you got caught snooping around. This isn't a challenge, Ari. It would be a suicide mission, and I'm not letting you put yourself in danger like that. We'll find another way."

My seriousness finally sank in, and she nodded. "Okay, so no trying to hack the Mexican drug cartels. Got it."

"Promise me." I needed to hear her say it.

"I promise." She paused. "But how are we going to find out who did this to Dad?"

I squeezed her shoulder. "You let me do what I'm good at—investigate."

With the threat of a cartel connection, there was no way I wanted to leave Ari alone, and I wouldn't have if Carver hadn't been there.

Something was off in a big way, and my gut said things were going to get worse before I figured this out. I was determined not to let it touch Ari, though.

As I climbed in my Jeep and drove away, my mind spun with possibilities.

First, I didn't think my dad killed himself by wiring and blowing up their house. He loved my mom too much to be that stupid. That meant that someone else did.

Who had the most to lose if Dad were formally arrested

and possibly given the opportunity to make a deal? The cartel insiders he had information on, and possibly anyone else in the police department who was dirty.

Any of those people could have done it.

I put myself into the mind of the sick fucks I was dealing with. If I were trying to keep someone on a leash, keep them from talking, I'd find some way to threaten them, and wiring their house with explosives was pretty damn effective. But why wouldn't they have taken Dad out to begin with? Why let him live once the investigation started?

He must have had some sort of leverage on them. That was the only answer I could come up with.

So, how did any of this tie to the Sampsons? They lived next door. Heath was IA, but not on the case. The connections were tenuous, at best—unless I was missing something. Now I had to figure out what.

I only knew one person who'd taken on a faction of the cartel successfully, so it made sense to start there. When Rix didn't reply to my text, I turned my Jeep toward the French Quarter and someone he would always answer.

Fifteen minutes later, I parked my Jeep along the side street a block over and crossed the uneven sidewalks to Noble Art. A familiar face was wiping down the glass windows of the door where the sign was turned to CLOSED. She unlocked the door and held it open.

"Well, well, Detective. Didn't expect you to pop up around here. It's been a while. You know my boss is thoroughly and completely taken by now, I assume?"

"It's not detective any more, but I got that. Trinity, right?"

She nodded.

"Your boss around?"

"Not yet. She should be here any minute." Trinity's eyes narrowed. "Thought you said you weren't sniffing around?"

"I'm not. I'm hoping she can tell me where to find Rix."

"They had an appointment this morning. Should be here anytime."

Ten minutes later, Rix hadn't replied to my text, and I saw why. He parked on the side of the street and hopped out to help Valentina from her seat.

How the hell had I missed it before? Valentina wore a formfitting dress and she was clearly pregnant.

Neither of them saw me when they swept into the shop.

"Go to work," Valentina said. "I'll be fine."

"The doc said you needed to take it easy."

"And I will. But it's not like I'm on bed rest, and Trinity won't let me lift a finger anyway."

"But when she has to leave for class—"

"I'll tell anyone who needs a piece crated they can pick it up later. You don't work here, so you're not staying. Go do your job, and I'll do mine the same way I did before your super-sperm knocked me up."

I stepped away from the statue blocking me from their view. "Congratulations."

Both of them whirled on me, but it was Rix who spoke.

"What the hell are you doing here?"

"Came looking for you, but I didn't realize you had a lot more important things happening. I'll find another way." I wasn't going to drag Rix into this after learning they were expecting a kid. I wasn't that much of an asshole.

"Oh no, not you too. Whatever you need from him isn't changing just because I've got a bun in the oven."

"Duchess—"

When Valentina raised an eyebrow, Rix released a frustrated breath. "Fine. But I'm bringing you lunch at noon to make sure you eat, and you're leaving on time today. No working late."

"Deal." She leaned forward and kissed him before turning toward me. "You get him into any trouble, Rhett, I expect you to get him out of it."

"You got it."

"Good. Now both of you, shoo. I have things to do."

Rix took one last look at his wife before she disappeared into the back room, and then turned to me. "You must need something awful bad to be tracking me down here."

"It wasn't my first choice."

He led me out of the shop. "Don't do it again. I got my reasons, and now you know 'em."

"Sorry, man. I wouldn't have come here if I'd known."

"Crazy to think I'm gonna be a dad in a few months."

"Definitely crazy."

I followed him to a blacked-out SUV and the lights blinked.

He nodded toward the passenger side. "Get in."

After I climbed inside, Rix pulled away from Noble Art. "You wanted to find me, and you found me. What's going on?"

I glanced around the interior. "You sweep lately?"

Rix nodded, and it was good to know some things didn't change.

"Did you hear about what happened last night?"

"To Skip Sampson? Yeah."

"You read the report?"

Rix shook his head. "Haven't been to the station yet. Didn't plan to at all today. Once I get a look at the report, I can fill you in, though."

"Already read it, and from the descriptions he gave, it sounds like the cartel was involved."

Rix's eyes narrowed. "Do I want to know how you got your hands on that report?"

"Does it matter?"

"Guess not. But back up. Why the hell would the cartel have any interest in jumping a retired cop? Doesn't make any sense. It had to be wrong place, wrong time."

"Do you really believe in coincidences like that?"

Rix shot me a sidelong glance. "Fine. I agree it doesn't seem random. But still, it could've been some low-level guys bored off their asses."

"Which is why I need to find them. Need to interview them."

"You're not a cop anymore, Hennessy. This ain't your case."

My hands clenched into fists. "You think I don't know I'm not carrying a badge? It's not something I fucking forget. Ever."

"Then why—"

"If Judge Noble were found jumped in a parking lot, would you let someone else handle it? Even if you didn't have a badge?"

"I take your point."

"So are you going to listen to me? Because I need your help tracking these assholes down, and I'm not about to let Ari get involved. If her dad somehow got mixed up with all this cartel shit, I need to know."

Rix slowed for another stop sign and looked over at me. "So that's how you got the report. Heath mentioned his little sister has mad computer skills."

"We're not talking about that."

He laughed. "Got it. She doesn't hack into police departments and pull up reports. Check."

"You really want to go there? Your girl was cool with dating the head of a gang."

The laughter faded and his expression sharpened. "Shut the fuck up."

"Glad to see you take my point there too. So, you gonna help me or what?"

"Tell me what you know."

It took me all of three minutes to give him everything I had, because there wasn't much. Other than the fact they'd beat the hell out of Mr. Sampson and stolen his medallion, he'd only been able to give some crappy generic descriptions, except for the tattoos that were associated with one particular cartel.

"I got an idea," Rix said when I was done.

Ten minutes later, we turned down a familiar street. If I'd been thinking straight, I would have come back here too.

Chains, the pawnshop Lord Robichaux owned. It was a better place to start than Voodoo Ink because Con had banned all gang ink from his shop long ago.

If these were low-level guys out for kicks, there was a chance they'd try to sell the medallion for a little quick cash. Lord saw plenty of commerce on a daily basis, and all sorts of stuff came across his counter.

Rix and I climbed out of the SUV and headed inside.

Elle, Lord's woman, looked up from the display case where she was reorganizing jewelry as Rix leaned on the glass.

"You leave fingerprints on that, they might be your last."

"Didn't you hear you aren't supposed to threaten a cop?" Rix said.

She laughed. "You know I'll always think of you as the scary mofo who convinced me *way* too well with your bad-guy facade." She paused and tapped a finger on her lips. "I can't decide if I liked you better then."

"You harassing the customers again, sweet thing? Pretty sure we had that discussion a few dozen times," Lord said as he stepped out from his office, closing the door behind him.

"It's not like they're here to buy anything. I mean, I could *maybe* guilt Rix into buying this super-sweet stained glass pendant that came in last week because Valentina would lose her shit over it, but I know that's not why he came."

"What do you guys need?" Lord asked.

"Information," I said, finally joining the conversation.

Lord's expression didn't change, nor did he seem surprised to see me here. I guessed word had already gotten around that I was back in town. "What kind?"

"I'm looking for a Saint Michael medallion that got stolen last night. Gold, probably about forty years old."

"Whose was it?"

"Skip Sampson. He got jumped by two guys who might've been with the cartel."

One of Lord's eyebrows rose when I mentioned the word *cartel*. "You know I stay away from that. Don't need that in my shop. They use Hector's shop to fence their shit. They know better than to come here."

"It was a worth a shot," Rix said with a shrug. "Let's hit Hector's next."

Lord leaned a hip on the counter. "You sure you know what you're doing? Fucking with those guys would be a bad move. They fuck back with a whole lot of firepower . . . if they get permission first."

"Who gives permission to the cartel?" Elle asked. "I thought they were a law unto themselves."

Lord shot her a pointed look. "No one you need to know about, because he doesn't exist for you."

"Who?" she demanded with a glare.

Lord didn't have to say his name. Rix and I knew who he was talking about. Everyone did, but they didn't talk about him . . . a man who lived in the shadows but had his hands in everything that happened in this city. I knew exactly where I needed to go next.

"We'll get out of your way. See you around, Lord."

"I heard you've got a girlfriend now. Word on the street is you took Heath Sampson's sister on a date last night to the Distillery. Your old partner, Mac, was in here this morning on another case, and mentioned his wife was there last night with her sister and saw you both."

I had to suppress a sigh. *I swear, men gossip way more than women.*

Rix turned to me. "You're dating Sampson's sister? For real?"

It wasn't like I was keeping it a secret. "Yeah. You'll be seeing more of her." To Elle, I added, "She doesn't have a lot of friends in town, but I don't know if I trust your crew not to scare her away."

"Oh, hush. We don't scare anyone away. We welcome them into the fold. What's her number? When can we meet her? How long is she staying? Does she like Thai food? We're going later this week."

Lord wrapped an arm around her chest and pulled her back against him. "Let the man talk and maybe you'll get a few more answers." He dropped a kiss on her red hair like he couldn't resist, and he sure as fuck didn't care who was watching.

"She'll be around a while. I don't know if she likes Thai, but I'll ask."

The declaration was enough for the men, but clearly not enough for Elle. She opened her mouth again, but Lord squeezed her.

"I'll get your number to her. She's good people."

Elle clapped her hands. "I can't wait. Fresh meat!"

I was a little worried I'd unleashed a tidal wave that would be uncontrollable, but helping Ari make friends wouldn't be a bad thing.

Being back and seeing familiar faces after staying away for a year made me realize how much I missed home. Maybe it was selfish of me, but I wanted to give her even more reason to stay too. Also, unless things had changed, she'd never been the kind of girl to have a posse of girlfriends, and from what I knew of Elle, Vanessa, Yve, Valentina, Charlie, and Delilah, they'd be good to her.

As we walked out, Rix mumbled to me, "You sure you know what the hell you're doing?"

He could be talking about either me going to see Lachlan Mount, the man whose name no one spoke, or about unleashing the girls on Ari. The answer was the same in both cases.

"Probably not."

"You know I can't go with you if you're heading back into the Quarter," Rix said, talking about Mount now.

"Don't need you to. Don't want you to."

"If he doesn't like what you have to say, you might not walk out of that building."

The cartel didn't acknowledge the authority of anyone in this city except Lachlan Mount, and no one knew exactly how he held that sway over them. But if he could help me put all these pieces together and get answers, it was a risk I was willing to take. Maybe a stupid one, but at least it was calculated.

"I'll come out," I said, hoping I was right. At this point, I didn't have many other options.

"Good luck."

I nodded at Rix as I headed to the corner to catch a cab.

THIRTY-SIX
ARIEL

I shut my laptop and stared out at the water. Esme was tasked with researching the top cognitive specialists in the New Orleans area so I could select one for Dad. My instinct was to find the best in the world, but I knew Dad couldn't just hop on a plane and fly somewhere for a doctor's appointment. They were still running tests at the hospital, and Heath had asked me to wait to stop by because all the commotion had upset Dad, and he was trying to keep him settled. It frustrated me to no end that he didn't want me there, but I didn't argue.

I felt helpless. My fingers itched to dig through more department files, but Rhett had made me give my word that I wouldn't do it without him.

There were a million and one other things I could do for work, but my mind was too chaotic. I was a scatterbrained mess, and that wasn't going to help anyone. I needed to center myself and find some calm so I could kick ass when it was my turn.

My gaze drifted from the lake to the pool—a completely

over-the-top, ostentatious, resort-style swimming pool with a grotto and waterfall that was sitting there unused. I couldn't remember the last time I'd put on a bathing suit. Maybe an hour of relaxing would give me what I needed to be able to keep charging forward at my normal pace? I'd learned the hard way a few years ago that I couldn't work 24/7 without taking a few hours to just breathe now and then.

So maybe that was what I'd do, and I'd be more effective when the time came.

Fifteen minutes later, slathered in sunblock and clad in a bikini from my suitcase that I didn't remember asking to have packed, I made my way down and snagged a towel from a neat stack in the pool house. The thickly padded lounge chair called my name, and I opted to soak up a little much-needed vitamin D.

I lasted a whole five minutes before I drifted off.

The realistic dream sucked me in. I was walking down a beach hand in hand with Rhett, my gauzy white dress billowing in the breeze, when he stopped to pick me up and spin me around. Once I was dizzy, he laid me down on the sand and knelt beside me to whisper in my ear.

"You'll never get away from him. He's the only one who ends things."

Wait, what?

The menacing voice hissed in my ear, jerking me from sleep as Rhett's face morphed into someone dark, a black ski mask covering everything but his mouth. I blinked to try to change the image in front of my face, but it stayed. It was *real*.

"You hear me, bitch?"

Oh my God.

I froze.

"Yeah, that's right. You see me. You hear me. Don't fucking forget it. You can hide in a fortress all you want, but he can get to you. *He* says when you're done. Not you."

Paralyzed by fear, I remained completely motionless except for my blinking eyes. I watched while the man rose to his feet with a malicious smile and bolted toward the lake.

It took me a minute to process what had just happened and yell for help. The sound of a boat ripping away from the shore drowned out the sound.

I snatched up my phone, poised to tap in my code to unlock it, but a text message notification popped onto the lock screen.

Unknown Number: I told you to be on a plane. That means you get on a plane. You do not let another man touch you.

My brain spun back to the text I'd gotten from Carlos yesterday, followed by his email with the plane ticket. After I'd confronted him about the pictures of him screwing another woman, I thought the plane ticket was some ridiculously misguided last-ditch effort to return things to the status quo. I couldn't understand what planet he must be living on for him to think I'd respond, let alone use it. Apparently, his expectations had been different.

A shiver ripped through me as I wrapped myself in my towel and ran for the house.

Who the hell was that guy? Carlos wouldn't have sent someone, would he? How did he get in without setting off the security? Where was Carver?

The voice echoed in my head. *"He can get to you.* He *says when you're done. Not you."*

I swallowed the bile rising in my throat as I threw open the sliding glass door and locked it behind me. Once inside, I forced myself to think rationally.

This was *Carlos*. The nice guy who liked to go out for dinner when our schedules meshed and was my on-again, off-again boyfriend who clearly didn't limit himself to being exclusive. He wasn't a crazy psycho with possessive tendencies. He just *wasn't.*

My brain, logical to a fault more often than not, couldn't connect this type of behavior to the man I knew. This was stalker-crazy, and I was too smart to ever get involved with a guy like that. Wasn't I?

I leaned back against the door, my first instinct to run to Carver and tell him what had happened, but something stopped me.

I'm capable. I can handle this. Carlos isn't crazy.

I picked up my phone and stared at the text for another second. Part of my mind told me not to engage, but the other part wanted this done and over with, without anyone else having to know what kind of man I might have gotten myself involved with. It was one thing when a security threat came from some rogue ex-employee, but this was a guy I'd dated. I'd slept with. I'd shared things with.

Before I could talk myself out of it, I punched in a text.

ARIEL: *We're done.*

His reply was instant.

UNKNOWN NUMBER: We will discuss your temper tantrum and poor decision-making when you return to California today. The date on your ticket has been changed. Don't make me come collect you myself.

WHAT. THE. HELL.

I flipped open my email and, sure enough, there was a new first-class return ticket leaving New Orleans in a few hours.

ARIEL: Don't contact me again. I'll be calling the police to report the person who broke in and threatened me, along with screenshots of these texts.

The unknown number popped up on the screen as my phone came to life with a call.

I hit IGNORE and pulled up the security screen to block this number as well. My hand shook, knowing it would only be a temporary measure.

Now I had to decide—

Another text popped up. It was from a different unknown number, and chills racked my body at how quickly he could skirt my security.

Unknown Number: If you tell anyone about my visit today, I'll make sure they die. Think carefully, because I always follow through.

This wasn't Carlos. This was. . . This was the guy who was just here.

Icy fear, completely at odds with the bead of sweat rolling down my face, locked me in place.

Think logically, Ari. They want you to be afraid. They want to use your fear to control you. You can't give in to emotional and psychological terrorism. They can't hurt you.

But they could hurt me.

That man had stood not two feet away from me while I was completely unaware, not tripping any security measures, otherwise Carver would have been on him. He could have killed me instead of delivering a warning.

What do I do?

I'd never run to my brother for help. That wasn't my MO. But I knew the right answer was to get a larger security team in place and tell Carver, Rhett, and Heath what happened.

But what if his threat is real? What if telling them puts them in danger? I couldn't live with that.

Rhett's parents' house *exploded* last week, for Christ's sake, which was all the proof I needed to know that life was unpredictably terrifying sometimes.

But I couldn't do nothing. I had to take action. Forcing myself to my feet, I clasped my hands together and squeezed until they stopped shaking.

Security footage. The house came equipped with a full

video-surveillance system that was only accessible from within the secured network.

With deep, calming breaths, I grabbed my computer, took it to a landline where I knew I'd be one hundred percent safe, and plugged it in to access the network. Within moments, I found the most advantageous camera angle and rewound the footage by ten minutes.

"You've got to be kidding me," I whispered as I stared at the black screen. I bumped it up to five times the normal speed and flew through two minutes of nothing. When the picture finally returned, the lounger where I'd lain was empty. Rewinding it further, I found the cameras hadn't caught a single frame of me heading out to the pool or sleeping in the sun.

Nothing. Like it had never even happened.

Apprehension skittered down my spine like scattering spiders.

That's how they didn't alert Carver. They must have shut down the security system completely. But how?

No one could hack into this network without leaving a trail for me to find them. And I would. They might have been good, but I was better. I would track them down and not let them scare me into submission.

No one threatened the people I cared about and got away with it. And no one was allowed to dictate to me.

Carlos can take that airline ticket and shove it up his ass.

I needed to get my shit together and work out a game plan.

Step one: Figure out how the hell I was going to tell Rhett without him going to California to rip Carlos to shreds with his bare hands.

THIRTY-SEVEN
RHETT

The cab dropped me off at an intersection, and I walked the rest of the way to the building where I knew Mount kept an office. He didn't have to hide where he operated because no one was dumb enough to try to fuck with him. The man was virtually untouchable. Any evidence that could lead to charges was guaranteed to disappear, not that the DA would have had the balls to prosecute anyway.

I walked into the bar, already open because this was New Orleans. The bartender dusted bottles with a rag and met my gaze in the mirror.

"Can I help you?"

"I'm here to see Mount."

She turned around. "I'm sorry, I don't know who you're talking about."

She told the lie with a straight face, I'd give her that.

"Guaranteed he already knows I'm here. Hell, he probably already knows why I'm here." I glanced up at the camera in the upper left corner behind the bar. "I've got a deal for him."

I swore I could feel the man's eyes on me through the camera.

The phone behind the bar rang, and the bartender turned to pick it up. She said nothing, just listened and hung up before turning around.

That's right, even bored kings of the underworld get curious sometimes.

"Come with me." She walked out from behind the bar and led me to the back of the room and into an office with a desk, a bookcase, a chair, and a couch. There was no Mount.

"What the fuck?" I reached for my piece, but someone stepped out from behind the door and snatched it from the back of my jeans before I could pull it. I threw an elbow, but the guy behind me caught it.

"Mount, if you—"

"Shut the fuck up. Boss ain't gonna see you if you're armed, ex-cop or not. You think he's stupid?"

I stilled and let the owner of the voice pat me down. He pulled my backup from the ankle holster and the knife I'd strapped there as well.

"You got it all. I'm clean."

The bartender surveyed me from the door. "Like he'd let an ex-cop take him out." She laughed and left the office, and I turned toward the goon who'd stripped me of my weapons.

He glared in my direction. "I'll kill you. Don't fucking care who you are. Don't make me do it. I hate going to confession."

I couldn't imagine what this man's priest had heard, but that wasn't my problem. "I'm not here to cause trouble. I just want information, and I'm willing to trade for it."

"Don't know why he agreed to see you, but you step out of line and you'll be going out the back door."

"Got it. Dead. Check. We good now?" My tone was annoyed. I'd been in enough tough situations over the years that I wasn't about to let this guy rattle me.

"You got brass balls." As soon as he said the words, the bookcase slid open and revealed a set of stairs. "Follow me."

He plodded up the dimly lit stairs like a mule, and it took all the patience I had not to hurry him up. At the top was a wood-paneled hallway with multiple doors, all closed. Brass sconces lined the walls with bulbs flickering like gaslights, casting shadows across the old wooden floor.

The man led me toward the last door, his pace like molasses, at best. Was he under orders from Mount to move this frigging slow? I had to wonder.

When we reached the door at the end of the hall, he pushed it open to reveal a library. Floor-to-ceiling shelves covered almost every inch of the walls, overflowing with books. Two empty chairs sat in front of an empty fireplace.

No Mount.

While I was surveying the room, my escort triggered yet another hidden door and led me behind the fireplace. I followed him through a maze of rooms, stairs, and secret doors until I stepped into another room carrying the scent of cigar smoke and leather.

The man himself sat behind a massive wooden desk, but this room was totally different from the others. A glass ceiling supported by an intricate design of oxidized copper let in shafts of light from outdoors. The walls were white. No decoration. Two chairs sat in front of the desk, and I wondered how many missing men had sat there before they were never seen again.

It wasn't what I expected, but for some reason, it was

completely fitting for the self-proclaimed king of New Orleans.

"Detective Hennessy. Although that's not right. It's Mr. Hennessy now." His rough, deep voice delivered the dig with precision.

"That's right. No badge. No gun."

Mount nodded at the goon behind me. "You can wait outside, Z." The door opened and closed on silent hinges, and when we were alone, he nodded toward one of the leather chairs in front of his desk. "Sit."

I didn't take commands well, but I wasn't going to fuck up my one shot at getting the information I needed from the only person who might be able to get it for me. So I sat.

Mount leaned back in his chair, already looking bored. "What the hell do you want?"

Straight to the point. I could handle that.

"Information about the cartel. Who's running what in this town. Who the fuck blew up my parents' house. Who targeted an ex-cop last night."

One of Mount's dark eyebrows rose, and he cut through what I delivered to stab at the heart of the matter. "So sure it wasn't your father who did it?"

His question confirmed that he really did know what was going on in this town.

"He wouldn't."

"You think."

"I *know*."

Mount reached for the cigar smoldering in the ashtray and lifted it to his lips to take a puff before replying. "And if I had the information you wanted or could get it, why would I give it to you?"

"Because I can give you closure."

His hand barely paused as he returned the cigar to its previous position. "Explain yourself." His gaze narrowed on me, and I hoped I'd tapped into his curiosity.

"Your mother abandoned you, according to the rumors. Don't you want to know what really happened?"

His nostrils flared with the first sign of emotion. "I wouldn't waste a dime to find out what happened to that bitch."

"You won't have to."

With burning intensity, the man studied me, and I didn't flinch.

"You misjudged, Hennessy. I don't care what happened. I am what I am. What the streets made me. What I made myself. Now, get the hell out of my office."

Fuck. I had misjudged. Completely. Offering to find his mother was my bargain, and since he clearly didn't want anything to do with her, I'd pissed him off.

Frustrated that I'd wasted my one chance, I stood. It had been a long shot anyway.

My phone went off in my pocket before I could turn to leave, and I pulled it out. If the man was kicking me out, what the fuck did it matter if I was rude?

ARIEL: I think I'm in trouble something happened. Something bad.

I stilled as I stared at the screen.

"Something wrong, Hennessy?"

Interest edged his tone, but all I could hear was the blood roaring in my ears.

“I’m getting out of your office, just like you wanted.” I went for the wall I’d entered through and pushed, hoping to trigger the mechanism so I could get the hell out.

“In a hurry all of a sudden.”

I spun around as Mount stood, knowing I’d made a mistake. I’d exposed a weakness in front of a man who wouldn’t hesitate to take advantage of it. But to get to Ari, I didn’t fucking care.

“Let me the fuck out of here.”

He shook his head, his eyes alight with interest. “No.”

I scanned the room, ready to grab the nearest blunt object as a weapon, but there was nothing. Maybe for that exact reason.

“It’s a woman, isn’t it? Not your friend’s woman, either. What’s her name, Hennessy? What would make you stupid enough to consider attacking me?”

The fact that he knew about Valentina shouldn’t have surprised me, but it did. “What the fuck does it matter?”

“Because I deal in information. And this piece is too good to pass up.”

I’d never give him Ari’s name. Fuck that. This piece of shit didn’t deserve to know she existed. “Fuck you, Mount.”

His smile was pure predator. “Willing to risk it all for her?”

My hands curled into fists of rage. “I’d fucking die for her.”

He slipped his hands into the pockets of his suit pants. “Then I hope she’s worthy. So few are.”

I turned around again and reached for the next book, but the wall slid open before I could touch it. I jerked my head around to look back at Mount as he spoke.

"Look closer to home, Hennessy. You're missing something."

With those cryptic words, he turned his back on me, and I bolted out into the maze.

I'm coming, Ari.

THIRTY-EIGHT
RHETT

I had my phone to my ear the second I hit the front door, bolting down the sidewalk toward the street where I'd parked my Jeep near Noble Art.

"Rhett?" Ari's voice sounded scratchier than normal, like the connection was fuzzy.

"Are you okay?"

"Don't freak out," she whispered.

Normally it took a hell of a lot to shake me, but where Ari was concerned, all my reactions shifted. Keeping my cool if she was in trouble wasn't possible.

"Too late. Tell me what's going on." I dodged a crowd of pedestrians and almost took out a street performer's dog wearing a tuxedo. My heart hammered, not because of the exertion, but because of a memory.

Heath and I had been playing football in the front yard as Ari came walking down the street, one arm hanging limply and the other pushing her bike alongside her. Blood had dripped down one leg, and when we'd noticed her as she turned her bike up the driveway, the first thing she'd told us was *don't freak out*.

"I'm in the panic room. I'm safe."

I didn't even know she had a panic room in that place, but the thought of what could have happened to make her lock herself inside made me want to kill someone. "What the hell is going on?"

"I'll explain when you get here. I just . . . I got spooked and I don't know who to trust anymore, so I'm taking precautions."

Only Ari could sound so calm while locked in a fucking panic room. I finally saw my Jeep up ahead. The day she'd broken her arm, she hadn't even cried, even though her bone was sticking through the skin. My parents and her dad had gone to Baton Rouge for the day, and they'd left Mr. Sampson's patrol car at home. Heath and I had hustled Ari into the car, and I'd broken so many frigging laws when I jumped into the driver's seat, flipped on the siren, and hauled ass to the hospital, driving through red lights and cutting off traffic.

Something about her being hurt had taken my hardened sense of right and wrong and thrown it out the window until she was safe again.

"But you're okay? You're not injured?"

"I'm fine, Rhett. I swear. I'm just . . . being careful."

I could tell there was a hell of a lot that she wasn't saying, but I'd get there as soon as I could. I dug my keys out of my pocket and hopped in the Jeep, putting my phone on speaker and dropping it on the passenger seat before I fired up the engine.

"Does Carver know you're in there?" I checked the rearview mirror and backed up to get out of my parallel parking spot.

"Not exactly."

My hands gripped the steering wheel harder than necessary. "Did he do something?"

"I don't know, but I'm trying to figure it out, I swear. I disabled the sensor that would've notified him when I engaged the door. He was out in the garage, last I knew."

I tried to keep my voice calm as I floored the gas pedal and roared down the street. "None of this makes any sense, Ari. He's there to protect you—"

She cut me off, and the fear in her tone finally came through. "It's not safe to talk about on the phone. Please. Just get here."

I softened my voice. "Hold tight, Red. I'm on my way."

THIRTY-NINE
ARIEL

Dramatics weren't my thing. Being capable was. But when my fingers went to work and I couldn't figure out how someone could have deleted the security footage, I went down another path. *Carlos.* The things I found chilled my blood, and it didn't take long before I knew I was in way over my head.

I was a realist. Bad people were everywhere. Evil existed. And even knowing this, I was still a naive, trusting idiot, and I'd stumbled into the crosshairs of something I wasn't equipped to handle on my own.

Cyber threats? No problem.

Cocky hackers? I could handle that.

A man standing over me close enough to kill me while inside a secured estate? Um, *nope*. It turned out I couldn't handle that all by myself once I figured out who had sent him.

I might have been naive, but I wasn't stupid. As soon as I discovered what I'd walked into, I knew I had to tell Rhett. I probably could have worded my text better so as not to send him into a panic, but I needed to get him here as quickly as possible, and apparently, that worked.

I looked around the safe room, thankful it was well-appointed. It had been another huge draw when I'd selected this house from Erik and Esme's list. Whoever had built it must have been a security nut. It was a dream setup, and the price of the rental had reflected that.

The room was upscale—white plaster walls covering eighteen-inch concrete walls reinforced with thick steel sheets. If someone just stumbled into it through the master bedroom closet, it would be easy to assume it was a luxurious dressing room, given the ornate cabinets lining two walls, the island in the center topped with a slab of fancy granite, and the massive leather sofas.

That was, until you locked the door and engaged the hydraulics, and the whole place gave itself a little makeover. The cabinets pulled away to reveal a security center with dedicated landlines separate from the rest of the house, and a cell-signal amplifier strong enough to penetrate the walls.

This was the second main access point to the security system, with the first being in the garage with Carver. I'd hooked up my laptop and gotten to work. Instead of using my cell, which I wasn't entirely sure was safe, I set my number to work through a secured VOIP connection.

I'd texted Rhett through another secure channel, and decided to keep Carver unaware until I knew whether he could be trusted.

Now, I was set up with my laptop on the luxurious queen-sized bed that had transformed from one sofa when the hydraulics kicked on. I'd helped myself to a bottle of water from the fridge and a package of Oreos from the pantry—both stocked for the apocalypse.

As I twisted the cookies apart and ate the creamy filling, I focused on what I knew as I waited for Rhett.

The things I thought were true, weren't. Which made me an idiot for not digging deeper into Carlos's background from the beginning. But he'd given me no reason to. A fellow tech-lover, he'd talked about rebelling against his family's expectations when he'd gone to Berkeley and graduated a few years before me.

It hadn't occurred to me that I should have checked his records to make sure he'd really gone there. Brace for the spoiler—he hadn't. No, Carlos had had an education of a very different sort.

Part of me hated getting Rhett involved in this, especially if it put him in danger, but I didn't see that I had any choice in the matter. Besides, if they touched a single hair on his head, I would use every skill and resource I had to burn them to the ground.

I wouldn't let Rhett suffer for my bad judgment.

I wouldn't.

FORTY
RHETT

The ride in the patrol car to the hospital kept playing through my head as I hauled ass to Ari's place, my knuckles white as I clutched the steering wheel. When I finally pulled up to the gate, I punched in the code and my vision turned red at the sight of Carver washing the car in the driveway. I wanted to rip into him for whatever had Ari spooked and locked in a goddamned panic room, but she'd obviously made the decision not to tell him, so I did the same.

He gave me a nod as I jumped out of the Jeep. "She knows you're coming? She's been quiet all day. I've been staying out of her way."

"She asked me to come by. We'd appreciate some privacy."

He schooled his reaction, but I knew what he was thinking. *He's here to get some.*

No, motherfucker, I was here to handle whatever scared her enough to go into lock-down mode.

I jogged up to the front door, closing and locking it

behind me before charging toward the master suite closet. I had no frigging clue where the panic room door was as I scanned the mostly empty white racks and shelves. I'd just found my way out of a maze at Mount's place, and now I was faced with another hidden entrance.

Turning toward a shelf, I pushed on the side, hoping something would move but knowing it was a long shot. When it didn't budge, I pulled my phone from my pocket and tapped her number.

"I'm here."

"Oh, good. Hold on, let me hit the lock."

"I don't see a damned door or where it's hidden."

"Give me a second. Wait, should I have you answer a question first? To make sure you're not being held at gunpoint or something?"

"Ari . . ." My patience was wearing thin, but her tone had lost a little of the fear from earlier, which reassured me.

"Who was your favorite comic book hero?"

Why did this question not surprise me? "Superman."

"Because you wanted to save the world and everyone in it, right?"

"Open the damn door, Ari."

"Okeydoke."

I ended the call as soon as the shelf I'd tried to push out of the way started moving. *Fucking hidden doors*.

As soon as the opening was wide enough, I saw Ari's deep red hair and I charged toward her, wrapping her in my arms. She reached out and slapped a button, and the door slid closed behind me.

"You scared the shit out of me, Red." As much as I wanted to demand an explanation right then, there was something else I needed more. I cradled both sides of her face in my hands and crushed my mouth against hers, letting my tongue sweep inside.

When I finally pulled back, I checked her for injuries, my hands roaming her bikini-clad body. She stood motionless and let me.

"I told you I was okay."

"And I need to make sure for myself."

Her gray gaze met mine, and I asked the question that was burning on my tongue. "What the hell happened?"

Her expression changed in a single moment, all lightness leaving it. She swallowed as though she didn't want to tell me, but dug up the courage to do it anyway. "I fucked up. Big time."

My first thought was that she'd hacked the NSA, and Feds were going to be bearing down any minute.

"Tell me. Everything." From my tone, I was pretty sure she got that I was seconds away from shaking the answer out of her.

After she took a deep breath, she dropped a bomb. "I think I'm the reason your dad was killed."

FORTY-ONE
ARIEL

D*eep breaths. I can tell him without losing it. I can.*

"My boyfriend—"

"Ex-boyfriend," Rhett said, correcting me, and I nodded.

"Ex-boyfriend. Carlos Herrera is really Carlos Alberto Moreno Herrera." Rhett showed no sign of recognition at the name, so I continued. "He's essentially the crown prince of one of Mexico's deadliest drug cartels."

Rhett stilled, every muscle in his body tense and ready to spring into action. "You had no idea?"

I shook my head. "No clue. Until now, when he started displaying latent possessive tendencies."

His eyes narrowed. "Tell me what the hell you mean by that? Break it down in simple terms."

Sucking in another deep breath, I braced myself to tell him the truth. "He thinks he owns me."

Rhett's hands curled into fists. "No man fucking owns you. And he will never touch you again, I swear it."

"I know, but he seems to have other ideas. He sent his

goon here to threaten me when I didn't use the plane ticket he sent me yesterday to go home to California."

Rhett's expression darkened to something deadly. "Someone came here? Threatened you? In person? And you didn't think you should tell me that on the goddamned phone?"

I explained about the cameras and the missing footage, and my concern about my phone being tapped.

"The resources they have are insane. I don't know who we can trust, and I wasn't taking a chance. They said if I told anyone, they'd die. I'm not risking you. He sent a second plane ticket. Told me I'd better use it this afternoon—"

Rhett took two steps forward. Instinctively, I stepped back, my knees dropping out from under me as I hit the edge of the bed.

"You don't belong to him. You don't go to him. No one orders you around. Ever. You get me?"

"But he said—"

Rhett reached out to cup my chin. "He'll have to bring an army to get through me. No one touches you. Over my dead body."

There was no way I was going to use Rhett as a human shield. He wasn't going to suffer for this. I refused.

"But—"

"No buts. He doesn't touch you. Ever again. In any way. You belong to *you* and no one else."

For a moment, it shocked me that he didn't throw out the caveman phrase that I belonged to *him*. By recognizing I belonged to *myself*, he wasn't marginalizing how hard I'd worked to become independent and self-sufficient. He recognized that it was a massively important part of my identity that I couldn't and wouldn't surrender. Something surged in my chest with the realization.

Rhett didn't just see me—he saw me *clearly.* He understood me in a way no one else had before. And that meant everything.

I wanted him. Now. This man came rushing to my rescue only to find out that I'd gotten myself into a horrible position, and yet he didn't judge me for it. Instead, he vowed to protect me in any way he could.

His presence gave me strength because I was able to lean on him without worrying that I was sacrificing any of my autonomy.

No one else could make me feel the way Rhett could. He wasn't my childhood crush anymore; he was a man who could handle life at my side. I'd never had that. Ever. And the possibility intoxicated me.

"You scared the hell out of me." His words came out roughened with emotion.

"I'm okay." I took his hand and pressed it to my chest. "I promise."

My heart hammered beneath his palm, and I swallowed as I slid it so he could feel my hardened nipple. His gaze burned into mine, and I knew I would have to ask because he wouldn't push. Not right now.

"I want you."

He didn't make me repeat myself. His fingers closed around my breast, catching my nipple between his thumb and forefinger. Shivers of arousal shot to my clit, and his mouth covered mine again and our tongues collided.

Rhett tore his mouth away and tugged my wrap away from my hips. "I'm going to touch every inch of you. Memorize you. Drive every other thought from your head except how perfect you are. How much you matter to me."

I melted. "Okay."

Rhett tossed the wrap aside and I reached for his shirt. He let me drag it up and over his broad shoulders. I pressed my lips over his heart.

"You matter to me too."

My words unleashed him. His nostrils flared as he yanked at the tie to my bikini top and it fell, revealing my breasts. He lowered his head, capturing a nipple between his lips as he pushed me onto my back and braced himself to kneel over me.

Heat sizzled through me as he nipped with his teeth and tugged before switching to my other nipple, leaving the first one hard and aching. I wrapped my hands around his shoulders, at least until Rhett lifted and caught me under the armpits to haul me further up the bed while he stayed braced over my thighs. With his eyes on mine, he moved a knee between my legs, and I slid them wider apart to make room.

Oh God. I knew what was coming, and my body was already aching for it. Rhett's gaze never left my face as he untied my bikini bottoms and pulled them from my body.

"You belong to you, but this is my pussy. *Mine.* No one else touches it. Tastes it. Fucking thinks about it. I don't care if that makes me a dick. I don't share."

Hearing that declaration come from Rhett sent a shock wave of heat through me that ended with a hard thump of my heart. "No one else."

Rhett reached down and spread me wide with his big hands, stroking from bottom to top with his thumb. "Already wet for me, Red."

"I can't help it."

"I wouldn't want you to."

His thumb circled my clit, and pleasure mounted until I was writhing beneath him, on the edge of coming, and he'd barely touched me yet.

Rhett bent down and replaced his fingers with his mouth, ripping a moan from my throat. With each lick and nip and then the thrust of a finger inside me, I tumbled closer and closer to shattering.

"I'm going to—" My words broke off as he plunged a second finger inside, and an orgasm burst over me.

I twisted on the bed, bucking against his mouth as he continued to drag out the waves of pleasure until I didn't know when they stopped or began again.

When Rhett finally rose, I was a boneless mess.

He produced a condom from the pocket of his jeans before he kicked them off. My eyes fixed on the bulge in his boxer briefs, and how much I wanted to return the favor.

When I tried to sit up, Rhett held me down with a hand on my chest. "You put that mouth on me, and I'll be coming in a second. Right now, I need to be inside you."

I understood. I needed the connection too.

Sheathed and rock hard, he notched the head of his cock against my entrance and powered inside. I gripped his shoulders and lifted my hips to take him deeper. With each thrust, the connection intensified until we moved together in a perfect rhythm, and when I screamed his name, he roared mine. I let go of everything, and the orgasm swamped me as Rhett's cock pulsed inside. When he collapsed on top of me, our ragged breathing merged into a single pattern.

I wrapped my arms around his neck and held him tight, feeling like I could face anything with him by my side.

I was right. He was so much more. He was a gift, and he was mine.

FORTY-TWO
ARIEL

Once our skin started to cool, Rhett pressed a kiss to my forehead and levered off me to take care of the condom. When he came out of the attached bathroom, I rewrapped my sarong to fit like a dress.

He planted a swift kiss on my lips before surveying the interior of the safe room. When he'd arrived, he was wholly focused on me, so I supposed it wasn't surprising that he was taking in the details.

"Do you want to hear all of it?"

He nodded. "Absolutely. Lay it on me. Don't leave anything out."

I proceeded to tell him everything I knew and everything I didn't. By the time I got to the end of it, I didn't feel like I had a better handle on the situation.

"I don't know why he targeted me. I really don't. It doesn't make sense, unless he was after my technology."

Rhett's expression darkened. "What kind of technology do you have that the cartel would be interested in?"

I shrugged and considered my pipeline. "I have a few pet projects that I mess with when I have time."

"Like?"

"Facial-recognition software that works with wearable cameras and can be synced to any database. Information about the subjects recognized by the software can be relayed through an earbud. It's not ready for use, but it's not far off. I was playing with stuff I thought could make cops safer on the streets. You know, for people like you and my brother."

Rhett closed his eyes for a beat before opening them. "Who knows you've been working on this?"

"A few people. I haven't made a big deal about it, but R&D knows because several of them contributed ideas when I got stuck, and they helped me get unstuck."

"It could be valuable to the good guys and the bad, so that's a possibility. What else?"

"Some other products that don't seem to have much useful commercial application, except maybe the advanced scent-blocking technology. It's better than what's available now. Even drug dogs can't sniff . . ."

Rhett's eyes lit up. "That could be it too. I know the cartels have advanced tech, but something that could help them move more product over the border with fewer seizures would be of interest."

"You think so? It doesn't explain why they'd blow up your parents' house."

Rhett's shoulders stiffened and his mouth pinched tight. He shook his head. "That doesn't have any connection to you. My dad got involved with them somehow, and I don't have the answers about why and how. But it started a long time ago, before my brother was killed. Just because there's cartel involved on two different ends doesn't mean it's the same people or even related."

It seemed unlikely that there was no relation at all, but I wouldn't push it because I'd been trying to find a correlation all afternoon and I'd come up empty. God, I hated this. Hated bringing up what I knew was incredibly painful for Rhett, especially because he didn't have any more answers than I did.

"Then what do we do? How do we handle this?" I asked.

"First, we figure out how the security footage was wiped. Could someone else have been on the property at the same time as the guy who threatened you?"

I shrugged. "I don't know. I guess."

"You have to realize that they have resources you can't even imagine. If they're able to get in here, they're able to do just about any damn thing."

"So you don't think Carver would've done it?"

"I'm not saying that. I'm saying there's more than one possibility, and we need to look at all of them."

"Occam's razor says when you hear hoofbeats—"

"Think horses, not zebras. Yeah, I know. But guess what, Red? The cartel is a zebra, not a horse. They don't play by the rules of simple logic."

I let that sink in. "Okay, so throw out logic. How do we confirm it? I'm never going to feel safe with Carver around until I know he wasn't involved."

Rhett was quiet for several long moments before his lips curved up in a smile. "We go old-school."

FORTY-THREE
RHETT

All the information Ari relayed churned through my brain. I tried to put the pieces together as she got dressed so we could find answers.

Her ex-boyfriend was a top cartel member, and even though I told her there couldn't be any connection, something was eating at me. Maybe there was. It was possible.

They'd been working their way into New Orleans for years, and the fact that they'd latched onto her was too convenient. If there was one thing I'd learned from all my years on the force, it was that coincidences *did* happen. You could go looking for meaning and connections, and all you'd find was lack of causation. Just because A and B happened around the same time didn't mean they had jack shit to do with each other.

I wasn't going to drop the possibility until I had more information, though.

But the last thing I wanted was Ari thinking there was a connection between her and what had happened to my dad.

Those events were set into motion years before she'd ever met this guy.

Years before I knew the cartel was in New Orleans. Years before I had any power to stop it.

A little of my guilt evaporated with those realizations. My dad had hidden it from us all, had covered his tracks well. He didn't want me to know there was anything going on, and he'd done a damn good job of it. If he'd been getting paid, I had no idea what he did with the money. My parents hadn't lived a flashy life. The occasional new car and vacation was it.

I'd tried to talk Ari into staying in the safe room, but she refused. As much as I wanted to lock her inside until I had an answer about Carver, I couldn't. I would never try to put her in a box and expect her to stay there. Ari was her own boss and would always make her own choices.

Which was why she followed me out to my Jeep, and I unearthed the crime-scene kit I rarely ever took out. I'd used it a few times for my PI cases. Fingerprint powder was messy and old-school, but it worked.

Carver had finished washing the car and had his gun apart for cleaning on the coffee table in the garage lounge area. Obviously, the guy was bored out of his mind, which worked out perfectly for me.

I pulled my pistol and turned it on him. No point in being subtle.

"What the fuck?" His expression darkened and he reached for his empty holster.

"You know about the guy who was here earlier? The one who threatened to kill Ari?"

His eyes widened, shooting from me to Ari as she stood

behind me, my backup pistol held loosely in her hand. "No. What the fuck? Why didn't you tell me? Scream for help?"

"I did yell, but the boat driving away drowned it out," she replied.

"But—"

I interrupted because we didn't have time for the question-and-answer game. "Security footage is missing for that span of time, Carver, and from what I understand from the boss here, this is a closed system, which means you could've been the one to erase it."

His eyes got even bigger. "I didn't do shit. I swear it."

I lifted my shoulder, and his gaze shifted to the bag. "That's what we're going to find out when we fingerprint the keyboard."

"But my hands have been all over it. That's not going to tell you anything."

Ari finally cut in. "Actually, that's where you're wrong. The series of commands necessary to disable the system or delete footage requires keys you have no reason to use under other circumstances."

Carver sat back on the couch and crossed his arms over his chest. "That's so damn comforting."

"It should be, because we might be able to exonerate you without any issue. All you gotta do is sit here and not move while I check. Ari will keep you company." I looked at Ari, who hadn't lifted her gun, but I felt confident she would if it were necessary. "Shoot him if he moves."

She nodded solemnly, and I glanced back to Carver. "She might not aim to kill, but she'll wound. Her dad and brother taught her how to handle a gun, and she's a damn good shot."

"Then do your thing. I'll wait for your apology when you're done."

"We're just taking the only precautions that make sense, Carver. It's not personal," Ari said, her voice cool, calm, and collected. Yeah, my girl was a badass.

I pressed my lips to her temple. "You good?"

She nodded. "Yep. Do your thing. Remember what I told you."

I turned my back and headed to the security terminal with my kit. Ari had pulled a printout of Carver's file she'd been given when she hired him, and now we were hopefully going to use it to rule him out.

Ten minutes later, I had my answer.

"So?" Carver asked as I walked back toward them.

"You're right—your fingerprints are all over that keyboard." Ari shot me a look, so I spared them the dramatic pauses. "But F1 and F10, along with a whole hell of a lot of other keys, were smudged like someone used the keyboard with gloves on. Now, I'm not saying you didn't do that, but I'll give you ten seconds to explain why you weren't watching the cameras when she was out in the open."

Carver tilted his head back, his eyes going to the ceiling for a beat before looking back at me and Ari. "Because I felt like a perv, okay? My job is to keep her safe, not stare at her while she sunbathes. The pool is fenced, and so are the outer edges of the property. I figured it was safe to give her an hour of privacy instead of feeling like a creep."

"Where were you?"

"Walking the front perimeter." He paused and added, "On the phone with my mom. I don't expect you to take her word for it or mine, but you can ask her."

Ari lowered the gun. "I believe him."

I did too, but I was still calling his mom and checking his phone records. It took five minutes to prove that he was telling the truth. When I hung up with his mom, we told him what was going on.

His first reaction? Anger. “FuckJesus fuckJesusFuck,” he shouted. “How can I protect her if she doesn’t tell me what the hell is going on? I’ve never let a threat get near a subject. Ever.”

“First, don’t talk about me like I’m not here. Second . . .” Ari paused and flipped up her middle finger as number two. “I made a calculated decision to determine whether you were involved before informing you. Given the nature of the threat, it was the intelligent choice, regardless of what you have to say about it. I’m the boss. You work for *me*.”

I couldn’t argue with her. It was the truth.

Carver finally nodded. “Fine, but I need to make a report to the agency.”

“No, this goes nowhere. Not yet. Call them and get files on more guys so we can bring in more help. Only people you know and trust. We’ll have them vetted ourselves as well, but you say nothing else.”

Carver looked like he wanted to argue, but I didn’t care.

“You got a problem with that?”

“No. No problem. I’ll tell them the threat level has increased and additional security is needed. No one will question it.”

“Good.” Then I looked at Ari. “Now we have to tell your brother.”

FORTY-FOUR
ARIEL

"He doesn't need to know," I argued. "This will get him all riled up for nothing."

My hands twisted the hem of my T-shirt because I *really* didn't want to tell Heath any of this. My brother had always seen me as his head-in-the-clouds little sister who was better at being a geek than navigating real life. For the record, I was good at both, *thank you very much.*

Rhett shot me a look. "Have you forgotten that your brother is a cop? He kept tabs on you in California. He knows about the employee who kidnapped you. He told me so himself."

Self-righteous anger swept through me like a firestorm. "Are you kidding? He told you that?"

"Yeah. He did."

"Shouldn't he have known who Carlos really was then if he was keeping such close tabs?"

"How many layers of shit did you have to hack through to find out the truth?"

Rhett's question reminded me of just how carefully Carlos's identity had been hidden. "A lot," I mumbled.

"And who else has the skills to uncover that information?"

"No one he knows."

"So, all those times your brother warned you off Carlos, it was his gut talking, a gut that you should have listened to because he knows his shit. He's got good instincts."

I didn't have to come up with a response because Heath pulled up to the gate and Carver hit the button to let him in. We waited in the driveway in silence.

Heath was out of his car and coming toward us in seconds. "What the hell is going on? I finally got Dad settled after they finished all the tests, and I thought you'd be able to come out and take a turn and sit with him."

Rhett held up a hand before Heath could rip into me like he clearly wanted to. "She locked herself in the safe room. There was a breach."

All color drained from Heath's face, along with any remaining righteous indignation. "Tell me everything."

Rhett filled him in, and when he got to the part about Carlos's real identity, Heath finally looked at me again.

"Told you I never liked that fucker. He's dead. Fucking dead."

Rhett stepped forward. "You're gonna have to get in line."

"Stop. Both of you." I pushed myself between them. "We need a plan. A solid one. I don't know what to do. I've gotten us all into a big old mess, and I'd like to get us out in one piece."

Heath glanced at Carver. "You sure he's solid?"

Rhett nodded. "Yeah, and he's getting a bigger team

together to keep Ari safe. Now we need to figure out the offensive strategy. How do we take Carlos out so he backs off? You have connections in Cali, obviously."

Heath exhaled a long breath. "Yeah, I got a couple buddies with the Feds. No one knows who this guy is for real, otherwise there'd probably be a *do not touch* slapped over him, like so many of those other assholes we can't take down without permission. But this guy, his ass is swinging. It might take me a couple days, but he'll make a wrong move and I'll have them bring him in. I don't care if it's a taillight out or a failure to yield. All they need is a legit reason to make contact, and then his ass is in for questioning."

Even though I'd grown up in the world of cops and their strategies, it didn't make sense to me. "Why can't they just go to his door and arrest him for threatening me?"

Both men looked at me before Heath spoke.

"We don't want your name coming up in the questioning. You're staying as far out of this as possible."

"But I'm already involved."

"Not anymore," they replied in unison.

"And you think this will work?"

Heath and Rhett had a silent conversation I couldn't interpret before Heath turned back to me.

"Yeah. It'll work. You lay low, and I'll handle this my way. Rhett stays on you like white on rice. Don't leave the compound. Get your extra security and make sure they're solid. You stay safe inside the walls, and I'll deal with what's happening outside."

"And Dad?"

Heath smiled. "I'll take care of him. Don't worry."

"You sure you're okay with this, Rhett?" It seemed so

out of character for him to agree to let someone else take the lead, but he squeezed my hand.

"Keeping you safe is my number-one priority." To Heath, he said, "We'll be here. Keep us updated."

We said our good-byes and watched from the front steps as Heath drove out the gate.

"So we're on lockdown . . ."

Rhett winked. "I'll make sure it doesn't suck."

I raised both eyebrows. "What if I want to?"

FORTY-FIVE
RHETT

"Do you think this is the right decision?" Ari asked when we walked back in the house, all joking aside.

I thought of how Heath had hugged her, shooting me a look while he did it.

The look said, *Don't let anything happen to my baby sister, motherfucker*. It was because of my respect for Heath and my need to keep Ari safe at all costs that I didn't demand to be out there running down leads.

I wasn't used to letting someone else take charge. I was always the guy in the field, chasing the bad guys, finding the answers, and making shit happen. But with one decision, I found myself locked down. It should piss me off. Make me itchy. Make me want to get out of this house. Because not only did it limit my ability to help Ari, it pushed my own case to the back burner.

But none of that mattered in comparison to her safety.

I wouldn't do it for anyone else, but it was becoming clear that I'd do anything for Ari. I thought about what I'd said to Mount in a moment of pissed-off frustration. *I'd die for her.*

It was the truth. No second-guessing. No take-backs.

Ari was *good*. She was smart and funny and sweet, and deserved the best life could offer her. She made me want to be a better man for her.

"Rhett?"

I pulled myself back into the conversation. "This isn't how I normally work, but I can hang back and let you take point."

Ari's bottom lip went sideways, and I knew from watching her that she was biting the inside of it. "You're only saying that because you know if you were out there, I would be too."

I couldn't lie to her. She was too smart, and it wouldn't get me anywhere. Only barefaced honesty would.

"If staying locked in this house with an army of security around us keeps you safe, then we're staying here and not leaving until this is over."

Her lips settled into a flat line. "But what about your dad? Are you going to be able to figure out what happened to him without being out there and investigating in person?"

I rounded the table to pull her into my arms.

"We'll attack it all from your domain and dig for the information no one wants us to find. One way or another, we're gonna take these motherfuckers down."

FORTY-SIX
ARIEL

The curtains were drawn and empty take-out containers littered the table. The scent of mint and cilantro hung in the air from the Thai food we'd just devoured. Part of me had expected Rhett to be the meat-and-potatoes guy I'd always thought he was, but he surprised me by suggesting Thai and then ordering like a pro.

The surprises were refreshing. For years, I thought I knew everything there was to know about Rhett Hennessy, but it turned out there were so many more layers than I ever realized. The pedestal I'd put him on for all those years was firmly crushed when we started talking football and I realized he didn't root for the Saints.

"How can you be from New Orleans and not be a Saints fan?" My tone was aghast as Who Dat Nation ran in my blood.

Rhett shrugged. "I grew up watching the Cowboys with my dad. His dad raised him on them too."

I shot up from the table. "I feel like I don't even know

you anymore." I grabbed the take-out containers and whirled around to take them to the trash, playing up the moment.

He followed me into the kitchen and trapped me against the island. "You need me to reintroduce myself? Because I'd be happy to."

"Is that right?"

He stroked a finger down my chin. "Hey, beautiful. Couldn't help but notice you eating dinner earlier. My name's Rhett, and I'm the guy who's taking you to bed tonight."

I leaned up on my toes and skimmed my lips along his jaw. "Lucky for you, I like a cocky guy." With my free hand, I reached out and palmed his dick through his jeans. "And you seem to be *plenty* cocky."

Rhett groaned and buried his hand in my hair before covering my lips with his. His cock stiffened, and I reached for the button of his jeans.

He pulled away and shook his head. "Nah. I know exactly how this is going down. I've been dying to fuck you bent over this island since the morning you made me breakfast after I kissed you for the first time."

"I wish you would've."

His grin was wicked, but I only caught a glimpse before he spun me around and yanked up my skirt, baring my thong to the empty room.

Rhett's hand cupped my ass and squeezed. "Every time you walk away from me, I can't get enough of this sweetness. Makes me wonder what my handprint would look like on it."

A shiver rippled through me. Spanking was definitely on my *must try* list.

"Possibly even better than your cock in my mouth."

A growl filled the kitchen before his palm landed on my cheek with a sharp smack. The burn stung, but morphed into heat when he massaged it.

"You like that, Red? Because it's turning the prettiest pink, just like your cheeks when you blush."

My panties were officially toast. "Then you better make them match."

He released his grip and his hand swung again, his palm connecting with my other cheek in a delicious burn. I moaned and arched into his touch.

He landed two more sharp strikes and then tucked a finger under the back of my thong. He pulled it away from my crack, sliding a finger all the way down until . . .

"Fuck, you're soaked." His finger dipped inside me, teasing me with shallow thrusts.

Was that moan bouncing off the walls mine? Why, yes. Yes, it was.

I parted my legs and Rhett plunged a second finger inside, dragging me closer to the edge. He moved behind me, and the hiss of his zipper met my ears.

He reached for the waistband of my thong and tugged it down my legs before stepping between them, his powerful thighs spreading mine further. I turned my head to the side, intending to lift and look back at him, but Rhett stopped me by snatching the pen from my bun and grasping my messy tresses in a strong grip.

"You're going to take everything I give you, aren't you, Red?"

Oh sweet Jesus. The feel of his fingers digging into my scalp sent me soaring as he notched his cock against me from behind.

When I didn't respond verbally, he clutched my hair tighter. "Tell me you want this as fucking bad as I do, Ari."

"I want it all." I meant every word of it. I wanted this man, this flesh-and-blood imperfect man who was perfect for me.

He plunged inside, pinning me to the counter. Something about his dominant hold on me lit every nerve aflame, and I was consumed.

As he powered into me over and over, he kept his fingers buried in my hair, sending shock waves of sensation through every cell. When he reached around and strummed my clit, I detonated. Writhing against the kitchen island, I let out a harsh sob as I came over and over. Rhett fucked me like I'd always wanted to be taken, but had never known what to ask for.

Reality *rocked*.

FORTY-SEVEN
RHETT

We moved our laptops to the bedroom and set up on the king-sized bed to keep working the next day. The way that Ari shifted seamlessly between sex kitten and determined partner was refreshing and amazing. I could imagine doing this for years to come and never getting bored.

I thought more about her idea about finding missing people when this was all over, and it felt right. But first, I needed closure.

I looked over at Ari, her fingers moving so damned fast, I didn't know how she hit the right keys half the time. "What are you digging into now? Do we need to discuss not breaking federal law?"

She smiled my way. "Don't worry your pretty head about it, Rhett. I swear it's for a good cause."

Anyone else who'd said something along those lines would earn a killing glare, but coming from Ari, it made me laugh. "That means you're seven layers deep in NASA, doesn't it?"

Her face twisted into a moue of annoyance. "NASA's pointless. And no, I decided to go back to the beginning to figure out how all the pieces fit together."

The humor seeped out of my body like water through a handful of sand. "Back to the beginning of what?"

She looked at me again. "Everything. There's gotta be a connection somewhere. I met Carlos a year and a half ago at a cocktail party that Esme made me go to with a bunch of Silicon Valley CEO types. Basically, a *revenge of the filthy-rich nerds* get-together."

As much as I didn't want to hear about the guy, I was curious about her life. "And how did it start?"

"That's what I was thinking about. We were introduced by another CEO I was friends with. He was into nanotechnology, and I was trying to find worthy startups to take equity stakes in while I messed around with my facial-recognition project."

For some reason, listening to her talk business was sexy as hell.

"I thought that's why he was bringing Carlos over, because he was a protégé who needed capital."

"But he wasn't?"

She shook her head. "No. He was a very random introduction that night, and I couldn't figure out why he was there. He clearly had money, but he wasn't a geek who'd made good like the rest of us. We talked for a bit and that was it. He didn't hit on me or anything. Actually, he left with my friend to have another round of drinks elsewhere, and I passed and went home to work some more."

I pictured the scenario playing out in my head. "When did you see him again?"

She looked at the ceiling for a minute, as if sorting

through that filing cabinet in her head. "A week or so later. I was leaving the gym and literally bumped into him on the sidewalk on the way to my car. I dropped my protein shake and it splattered everywhere."

Textbook move. "So he'd been doing his recon and figured out where you would be to stage a casual second meeting."

She stiffened. "You think?"

"Did he take you somewhere to replace your protein shake as an apology, then strike up a conversation and leave after having secured a date?"

Ari's eyes went big. "Yeah. That's exactly what he did."

I finally said what I'd been thinking. "Textbook. If I'd been in his shoes and trying to infiltrate your life, that's exactly what I would've done."

"Infiltrate? That sounds so deliberate. You think it was planned from the beginning?"

I threaded my fingers through hers. "You were a target. He followed a set MO that worked the way it was supposed to. None of that is something you could have foreseen." I paused, something else occurring to me. "Did your nanotechnology friend know about the facial-rec software project?"

Ari bit her lip as she considered. "Yeah, he did. We'd talked about applications and how to create an interface that could be used for public safety." She turned toward me. "How did I not see this? He must have told someone, and Carlos swooped in and played me like a complete idiot."

I plucked her laptop off her lap and pulled her into my side. "It's not your fault. This isn't something you should've or would've seen coming. There's too much good in you to recognize motives like that in people who come across as straightforward."

She craned her neck to look at me. "Says the former cop to the hacker. Don't you think I should've suspected?"

"No. Why would you?"

"Because I didn't have a lot of guys coming around trying to take me out on dates. After the first one, he got a little more aggressive, making sure he could fit into my schedule." She shook her head. "I thought it was just the cultural difference, but now I realize it was all motivated by something completely different. And then he'd disappear for a while and pop back in, checking on my progress by casually bringing it up on another date. Gah, it makes me feel so stupid."

I pressed a kiss to her forehead. "There's no reason to feel stupid. None."

She stiffened. "I wonder if he's behind the hacking attempts? It would be logical. *Shit.* What if he was trying to get his hands on the software before I figured it out?"

"Were the attempts successful?"

Ari shook her head. "No, but they were aggressive, smart, and targeted. God, it makes total sense now." She grabbed her laptop and resettled into her position, her fingers flying. "Now I'm even more determined to figure out what this asshole is up to. He's not going to take my technology and turn it against the people I created it to help. No way in hell."

For Ari's sake, I hoped he didn't have the chance, but there was no telling what the cartel could accomplish in that short time.

With her lost down the rabbit hole of cyberspace, I thought back to when everything happened with my brother

Robin. He was killed in the line of duty, and when the department said he was dirty, my father retired from the force rather than fight to find out what really happened.

Then I went digging, even though they wanted me gone. That's when I found out, just over a year ago, that my father had let Robin take the fall for *his* actions.

Or so I'd thought. *Could Robin have been dirty too?*

It seemed like a twisted and knotted mess that was impossible to untangle. What was the truth? Why did they do it? With both Robin and Dad gone, I couldn't ask them.

When I pushed off the bed, Ari glanced up. "What are you doing?"

"Going to call my mom on the secure line in the panic room. See how she's doing."

She smiled. "Tell her I said hi."

I smiled back, but it didn't remove the rock from the pit of my stomach. *What does Mom know?*

I left the bedroom and headed for the closet where the panic room door remained open. I picked up the landline and dialed my mom's cell number, kicking myself for not thinking ahead and giving her a burner phone.

She answered on the third ring.

"Hey, Ma."

"While I live and breathe, it's my son calling."

"How's Vail treating you?"

"Oh, you know, just staring at the mountains and contemplating the meaning of life while I drink coffee and wish I had some answers."

I huffed out a forced chuckle. "Sounds a little like what I'm doing."

"Any news? What should I do with the house?"

"I've already got a line on a cleanup crew to remove the rubble soon. There wasn't much that could be salvaged."

"I figured as much." Her tone was quiet and resigned.

"I know, but at least insurance is taking care of that part of things so you don't have to worry about the cost."

"That's a relief at least." She paused. "How are you doing, Rhett? I know being back there can't be easy after . . ."

Some things moms just know. "It's not bad. I'm . . . dealing with things."

"You know, when you left, part of me was happy that you were getting out. Breaking the mold. I didn't want to take the chance that I'd lose another son."

It surprised me to hear her say it, especially when I didn't just leave, I cut my family out of my life for a solid year.

"I'm sorry, Mom. I shouldn't have turned my back on you and Dad. I couldn't—"

"You don't have to say it. I understand. Your father had to know that by going down that path, it would cost him, even if he didn't see it when he started."

My mother's words made me wonder again if she knew more than what she was saying. "What happened? Do you know? Did he tell you?"

Her end of the line went quiet for several moments. "I don't know much. He shielded me, or at least he tried. But there were things that didn't make sense. Money that would magically show up and I was expected not to ask questions, so I didn't. Rhett, as much as I wish you could uncover evidence showing this was all a setup, I think the further you dig into this, the more you're going to find that isn't true."

I attempted to swallow over the lump in my throat. My father's image had already been tarnished by the evidence, but hearing it come from my mother was a sucker punch to the gut. "What money?"

"I know I should've told you, but . . . we were having some hard conversations. How he was going to be able to afford to retire with the pensions getting sliced to practically nothing. Then a downturn in the market took out half our retirement savings. We weren't smart, Rhett. We didn't plan right. Your father was angry, furious that he'd worked for years for promises that kept changing. I worried that he would do something rash, but I didn't ask questions. I didn't want to know. That was my fault. I should've gotten a job, or—"

"Mom, stop. It's okay. You didn't do this. He did."

Bile rose in my throat as my mother confirmed my worst fears. My father had a motive. *Resentment.* I understood it, but I hated to think that it could have been something so simple that would have caused him to betray everything he stood for. Everything he'd raised my brothers and me to stand for.

"It's not okay. If I'd stopped him, maybe we wouldn't have lost you for a year. Maybe he could've found some way to make it right."

"You didn't lose me. I'm right here. And we're going to figure this out and make sure you have everything you need so you can come home as soon as I get your place rebuilt."

She laughed, but it was without humor. "I'm not coming back to Louisiana, Rhett. I can't. I'm notorious there. I don't want to be an old lady who can't face her neighbors because of the shame. Here, I'm someone completely different. No one knows my past. No one looks down on me with judgment. I'll be able to make friends, start a new life. Maybe you should think about doing the same."

Her words ripped through me with a force I didn't expect. "Are you sure?"

"Positive. In fact, if you'll help me, I'd like to take the insurance payout without rebuilding. I'll sell the lot. Someone else can build something good over all this bad, and maybe, just maybe, the Lord will forgive us all someday."

Resignation settled in my bones. "If that's what you want, Mom, I'll make sure it happens."

"You've always been a good boy, Rhett. You need to let go of the past and focus on the future. Find your own happiness. Have you taken my advice? Are you going after the life you want?"

"I'm working on it." I glanced toward the bedroom. "And Ari says hi as well."

"Tell her I'm sending my love all the way from Colorado. I always adored that girl. She's something special, Rhett. You could do worse than to keep her by your side for the rest of your life."

And . . . that was my mother. Jumping to forever in a single sentence. But if I had a choice, forever was on the table as an option. "I know, Mom. We're testing the waters."

"Make sure you treat her right. She's a grown woman. Wine and dine her. If you need any suggestions—"

"Thanks, but I got this."

"I'm sure you do. Take care, and don't forget about me all the way up here in the mountains."

"Never. Talk to you soon, Mom."

I hung up the phone with mixed emotions, but the primary one was despair.

Mom knew something was going on and she never said anything. Did that make her guilty? No, I refused to believe that. But her admissions were a crushing blow to the last shred of hope I had that this could have been a setup. Now, I had to face the fact that things were, at least to a certain extent, exactly what they'd seemed.

My dad was a dirty cop, and someone took him out before he could go down for good and possibly talk.

There were so many more questions I wish I would have asked my mom, but I wasn't going to drag her down that path again.

I made my way back to the bedroom and glanced through the doorway at Ari braiding her red hair around the side of her neck. She tilted her head one way and then the other as she read what was on her screen, and then looked up at me with a smile on her face.

"How's your mama? Did you tell her that Team Awesome is going to get to the bottom of this mess, and she'll never have to worry about anything ever again?"

Team Awesome.

A smile fought through the darkness in my head and tugged at my lips. I thought about what Mom had said about Ari. *You could do worse . . .*

She missed the mark there.

I would never find anyone better.

FORTY-EIGHT
ARIEL

Rhett was quiet for a while after he got off the phone with his mom, and then he disappeared outside to talk to the new security team Carver had been able to put together in a matter of hours.

I'd met the linebacker-sized guys, but in the craziness, their names hadn't stuck with me. I never wanted to be that asshole client who didn't think of service providers by their names, but I thought I deserved a pass on this one. Besides, Rhett was covering that side of things. After I jokingly called us Team Awesome, I decided I wasn't kidding. We could be a powerhouse duo. Before I could let my imagination wander, my cell rang through a secure phone line app that I'd gone back to using.

Esme and Erik.

"Hey, what's going on?"

"We're holding down the fort. So far, so good." This came from Erik.

"That's good. No sign of the zero?" I asked. Erik had

taken to calling Carlos "the zero" because he was on a World War II kick right now.

"Nope. Nothing. We've upped security protocol, and the critical team has been alerted that all precautions should be taken. The building isn't admitting anyone who isn't on the employee roster without heavy advanced screening."

I didn't like the idea of my company running like a prison, but in this case, I was happy to take the *better safe than sorry* route. After all, it wasn't every day I got on the wrong side of a Mexican drug cartel.

"Anything else new?"

"Not much. We were more calling to get an update on how it's going in lockdown land with the sexy Rhett Hennessy. Did ya get some?" Esme was shameless.

"As your boss, I'm going to pretend you didn't ask that question."

"Ohhh, you know that means she did! Score, girl!"

Erik's enthusiasm had my cheeks turning pink and doubly glad this line was untappable and untraceable. "We are not discussing this."

"Sure, boss. Whatever you say. Not discussing the fact that you finally banged the guy you've been lusting after your whole life."

They didn't realize what was happening between Rhett and me was so much more, but I wasn't about to lay it out for them right now.

"And moving on . . . Is there anything else we need to discuss?"

Both Erik and Esme morphed into the super-capable employees I knew they were and gave me a rundown on everything I'd missed. Basically, despite the increased security measures, things were running smoothly.

"There's only one thing that was a little weird," Esme said. "I wasn't going to mention it, but given the situation . . ."

"What?"

"Jan Hofer called in sick three days in a row after having nearly perfect attendance since her appendix was removed a few years ago."

Jan Hofer was an R&D scientist who was part of the facial-recognition project.

"Have you called her? Checked on her? Found out if she's really sick or if she's missing?"

"We're on it. We're going to have security check out her place to make sure everything's okay. HR called her twice, but got her voice mail both times."

A creepy sense of uneasiness swept over me. "Tell them to be careful. Let me know what they say ASAP."

"No problem. We'll report back," Esme promised.

When we hung up, I logged into my company's intranet and dug up Jan's notes from her research the last few weeks. Nothing was out of the ordinary, but still . . . I didn't like the coincidence.

I didn't want to jump to conclusions, but I wouldn't feel settled about it until Esme and Erik called back with more information. *She can just be sick*, I told myself.

In the meantime, I needed a distraction.

Rhett opened the door to the bedroom. "Hey, Red. You in a good place to take a break for a couple hours?"

Exactly the distraction I needed.

My stomach growled, and I realized it had been almost six hours since we'd eaten last. "I could be talked into that."

He nodded. "Good. Then meet me down in the pool room when you're finished. We've got a date."

"A date?"

"Yeah. And if you wanted to put on a dress and no panties, I wouldn't argue with you." With a wink, Rhett closed the door before I could respond.

A dress with no panties?

I looked around the room as though someone else could confirm what I'd just heard, but there was no one.

What does he have planned? I rose from the bed and stretched my arms and kinked muscles before moving to the closet where my limited wardrobe hung. My gaze locked on a navy-blue T-shirt dress with a V-neck that I wouldn't look out of place walking around in at home.

I stripped off my shorts and panties, and pulled it on.

Ask and you shall receive, Rhett Hennessy.

FORTY-NINE
ARIEL

When I entered the pool room after primping for ten minutes, candlelight flickered off the walls and the surface of the water from votive candles scattered across the stamped concrete decking surrounding the indoor pool. Through the tinted glass sliders, the sun was setting outside, showing me just how much I'd lost track of time.

Who really needed two pools anyway? I wondered at the motivation of whoever had built this place.

Then I pushed the thought out of my head and focused on how deliciously naughty I felt wearing a dress with no panties. I'd never done that before, and found it was something worth repeating.

Rhett stood by a table as he lit two taller candles in the middle. He'd managed to find a button-down shirt and paired it with worn jeans but no shoes. It was a *very* good look on him with his messy dark blond hair and the scruff on his jaw.

"Wow. Someone decided to go all out."

"My mama told me to wine and dine you, and I always try to listen to what she tells me."

I smiled. "Is that so?"

He nodded and pulled out a chair. "Sure is. Would you like to have a seat so I can tell you what we're eating tonight?"

I crossed the concrete toward him, also barefoot because nothing else had felt right, and stopped next to the table. "Thank you for doing this. It's really sweet."

Rhett's gaze dropped to my red-painted toenails and dragged up my body to my hair, pulled halfway up in a messy casual style. "You look beautiful."

My cheeks heated. Not at the compliment, but at what I was about to say. "I decided to honor your request."

Hunger blazed in his green eyes. "Is that right?"

I nodded.

"Show me."

My heart skipped a beat. "What?"

"Show me," he said again.

I swallowed. *Oh hell, what did I get myself into?*

I reached down and caught the hem of my dress on my left side and dragged the fabric up until it hit my hip and the lack of any panties was visible.

Rhett didn't move. Didn't touch. But his stare was enough to raise goose bumps all over my skin. "That's so fucking sexy."

I dropped the fabric and it slid down my thigh, but Rhett's eyes lifted to mine.

"You're wet right now, aren't you?"

"Maybe."

He reached out a hand like he was offering to seat me for dinner, but that wasn't his purpose at all. "Show me."

My heart thundered in my chest. "What do you mean?"

Rhett stepped forward, reached for my hand, and wrapped my fingers around his wrist. "I want you to show me."

My thighs clenched when I put together exactly what he meant. He wanted me to put his hand . . . *oh sweet Jesus*.

With my fingers trembling, I directed his hand under my dress and up between my legs. I sucked in a breath when the pads of his wide fingers skimmed my leg and then ghosted over my lips.

"Spread your legs, Red."

My teeth caught my bottom lip as I scooted my feet further apart, making room for his hand.

Rhett kept his fingers completely motionless as his skin slid through my wetness. His nostrils flared, and my hips pushed forward almost of their own accord. Back and forth, I dragged his hand through my heat, touching lightly enough to drive us both crazy.

"Touch me. Please. I can't take it."

Something lit his gaze, and I didn't care what it was, but Rhett's fingers curled upward and one plunged inside me. I released a broken moan at the same time his groan echoed through the room.

With the look of a starving man on his face, Rhett pulled his hand away from my grip and brought his finger to his mouth and sucked it clean.

"Delicious."

FIFTY
ARIEL

Dinner was cold by the time we got around to eating it, but neither of us cared. Once we were finished, Rhett stood and looked at the rectangular pool beside us, and then out the windows at the massive outdoor pool with waterfalls, fountains, and the rock grotto with its lazy river that went through it.

He looked at me, and then back out the window before stripping off his shirt and tossing it on the chair.

"What exactly are you doing?"

"What does it look like?" He reached for the top button of his jeans.

"Oh my God, you want to skinny-dip in here?"

Rhett shook his head. "Out there."

My gaze snapped to the pool outside, lit by only a few romantic underwater lights. It looked completely different than it had yesterday, when I'd been frozen in terror on a lounger. And with Rhett there . . . he would never let anything happen to me.

There was also one other consideration. "What about security?"

"You afraid to get caught?"

I probably shouldn't admit that a wave of heat slammed between my legs, but I didn't know whether that was due to the idea of getting caught or because of Rhett dropping his jeans and the decadent bulge fighting against his boxer briefs.

I needed that in my mouth.

"You're not the rule-follower here, Ari. We both know that."

He was right. I was the *rules are flexible, so just bend them to fit your purpose* girl.

I reached for the hem of my dress, my thighs squeezing together. I had nothing on under it. Not a single stitch.

"What happened to the *follow the rules* guy you've always been?"

Rhett kicked off the jeans and tucked his thumbs in the waistband of his briefs. "Maybe you've been a bad influence on me."

With a single move, he shoved them down his hips and his cock sprang free. Whatever I was going to say flew right out of my brain as I stared.

I hadn't had nearly enough time to study it. Touch it. Taste it. I wanted to do all those things right now.

When I took a step forward, Rhett moved toward the slider that led to the outdoor pool. "Show me how daring you are, Red. I want to see it."

And then he was out the door and in three long strides, diving into the water outside.

I knew Carver and his cohorts were out there. Did I care

if they caught a glimpse of me naked? It wouldn't be the end of the world.

Screw it.

I yanked my dress up and over my head, dropped it on the chair, and raced after him. I didn't think. I just jumped.

When my body hit the water and my head finally resurfaced, Rhett was right there.

"I knew you would."

"How?"

He pressed a kiss to the tip of my nose. "Because I know you. It could be fifteen years or fifty, and I'd still know you."

He ducked underwater and tugged at my ankle before disappearing beneath the waterfall.

Apparently, we were playing hide-and-seek. That was cool because I was good at games. Usually they were logic-based puzzles that other people used to study for things like the LSAT, but I found them entertaining. It didn't take a genius to realize naked games with Rhett were way more fun, though.

I swam after him, letting the warm waterfall pummel my body as I stroked beneath it. Rhett had his arms spread out along the concrete hiding behind it, and I knew right then what I wanted to do.

With a new boldness charging through me, I looked him in the eye. "What would you say are the odds of us getting caught?"

Interest sparked in his gaze. "No idea. Why, what did you have in mind?"

"Hop out of the water and I'll show you."

He raised a brow, and my boldness grew as he pressed both hands to the edge and lifted himself out of the pool. His shoulders, chest, and arms flexed, and a shiver worked through me at the power contained in his body. When he settled on the concrete, his cock rose in front of me. I hadn't totally figured out the logistics of how to do this, but I knew one thing—I was getting him in my mouth.

When I reached out and wrapped a hand around his thick shaft, Rhett sucked in a breath. "What do you think you're doing, Ariel?"

"If you call me by my full name, you might never find out what I'm planning."

He laughed quietly. "But it's too damn perfect. The turquoise water lit up around you, and that gorgeous mass of red hair floating in the water . . . Sexy as hell, Red."

"Okay, maybe you get a pass."

I found the underwater ledge along the side and stood on it, putting me at the perfect angle to hopefully make this a night Rhett wouldn't soon forget.

When my lips moved closer to the tip, he slid a big hand around the back of my neck. "You gonna suck my cock? Out here in the open where they might see me buried in your throat?"

A shiver worked through me at the thought of getting caught. Why did that make this even hotter?

"Does that bother you?"

"Another guy getting an eyeful of my girl getting me off?" He paused as though to consider. "I might take offense to them seeing your gorgeous naked ass, but your mouth on my cock sure says you're taken."

My girl. Taken.

Warmth spread through my veins at the words. I gripped his shaft tightly and wrapped my lips around the head, pulling the first grateful groan from his lips as I sucked.

Rhett's other hand grasped my soaking wet tresses in a fist, but didn't tug.

I wanted him to tug. I wanted him to direct me how he liked it when he was close to coming. With that goal in mind, I took him deeper, using my tongue and lips to drag unintelligible words from him as he shifted his hips and I swallowed him deeper.

"Goddamn. That mouth of yours is heaven."

I took as much as I could, but my hand was still closed around the base. I was going to have to practice to get him to fit all the way. Rhett's gaze flashed a brilliant green as he gripped my hair, pulling me deeper into the water.

"You want me to show you how to take me? Want me to fuck your face?"

Oh God. Something about those words had me ready to beg for it.

I slid my lips away with a pop and answered. "Show me what you like. I want to know."

His lips curled up into a sensual smile. "I fucking love that you want to know." Rhett angled his hips and skimmed the back of two fingers across my chin. "Ready?"

I nodded, taking the head in my mouth again.

"When you feel like it's too much, swallow."

Stroke after stroke, he fucked my mouth, getting me used to the length, until he bumped the back of my throat and I fought the urge to gag.

He gave my hair a squeeze and my gaze shot up to his. "Next time, swallow."

I could do this. I *wanted* to do this. It became a personal mission.

Rhett slowly worked me up again, and instead of gagging when he hit the point of no return, I swallowed and breathed. He paused to make sure I was okay, and I gave him another nod.

Holy shit, I'm deep throating. I'm officially a sexual rock star. I gave a mental fist pump as Rhett's features twisted into a mask of pleasure. He might have been trying to hold out, but it didn't work.

"Fuck, I'm gonna come. You taking it?"

I didn't pull back, so he let loose, the salty heat bursting into my mouth and down my throat.

As soon as he moved away, footsteps pounded toward us.

"You okay? We heard a noise!" someone called, and I thought it sounded like Carver.

Rhett slid back into the water and used his body to block mine. "We're all good. Give us five minutes to get back inside, and we'll be locked down for the night."

I didn't need a mirror to know my face was on fire.

"Yes, sir."

As the footsteps receded, Rhett turned to me. "You almost gave me a heart attack."

"And somehow I'm not even sorry about it." I winked, and he laughed before wrapping his arms around me and dunking us both.

FIFTY-ONE
RHETT

After I enfolded Ari in a towel, I carried her back into the house and to the shower. As water poured down on us from the massive spouts, the chlorine washed away but something else remained.

Guilt.

I was here, getting a glimpse of the future I wanted, and none of this would have happened if my dad hadn't been killed.

Ari finished rinsing her hair and caught my stare. She read me easily. "What's wrong?"

"If my dad was still alive, I'd probably be sitting in my Jeep, waiting to catch a picture of a cheating spouse and ignoring his call. He gets murdered, and all of a sudden I'm getting everything I wanted."

She watched me with sad eyes before reaching out to place a hand on my arm and squeeze. "I'm sorry. So damned sorry that it happened this way."

"Me too." I looked up at the ceiling. "You know he

called four times in the two days before he died, and I never answered?"

She bit her lip but said nothing.

"What kind of son does that? What kind of *person* does that?"

"Rhett—"

I shook my head and kept talking. "When I talked to my mom, she basically told me that digging for evidence to prove him innocent was a waste of time. She thinks he did it. She said money would magically appear." I closed my eyes as the truth crashed down on me once more. "Maybe he wanted to come clean. Maybe he knew they were coming after him and wanted my help. But I'll never fucking know because I was too damned angry to listen to him."

"You couldn't have known it was your last chance."

My eyes snapped open and fixed on her. "What if I could've stopped it? Changed things? Instead, I did *nothing*. I'll never know the entire truth. Ever. And now I have to live with that for the rest of my life."

Ari wrapped her arms around me and laid her cheek against my chest. "I wish I could change it for you. I wish I had the ability to turn back time and give this back to you. But I can't." She snuffled. "None of us can. We make choices and we have to live with them. There was no way you could know."

"If I hadn't been so stubborn, I wouldn't have lost the only chance I had to make peace with this."

"What would you have said to him?"

I dropped my chin to rest on her head and thought of how the conversation might have gone if my dad had admitted what he'd done. "I probably would've hung up . . . at least at first."

"And then what?"

Imagining the conversation was like shredding my insides with dull knives. "I would've asked him why he did it. I would've wanted to know if he realized what he'd done."

Ari hugged me tighter. "And if he said he regretted it? Wished he'd never done it? Could you have forgiven him?"

I thought of my father's remorse. How much he probably regretted putting my mom in danger. The more I thought about it, the more I could see why he didn't come forward sooner. When you were dealing with the cartel, talking meant not only were you risking your life, but your family's as well. Maybe my dad had a weak moment and got into something too big to get out from under.

Could I have given him my forgiveness?

Water droplets slid down my cheeks, and I didn't know if it was from the spray or another source.

"He was my dad. The best man I'd ever known until—" I broke off, not wanting to say it.

"He was *human*, Rhett. People make mistakes. I thought my dad was invincible too, but he's not."

"But he didn't betray everyone who believed in him!" My shoulders shook.

Ari pressed her lips to my chest. "No, but you have to give him grace anyway. Holding on to the anger isn't going to change what happened. Someday, you're going to have to forgive him—and yourself. You won't be able to move on until you do."

Intellectually, I knew she was right, but it wasn't easy. The tight grip that held my anger and feelings of betrayal loosened a little.

He was human.

My father was only a man. An imperfect man. A man who believed he deserved more than he was being given, so he found a way to get it—and paid the ultimate price.

There was nothing I could do to change what happened. He'd already suffered for the sins he'd committed.

I'm sorry, Dad. I'm sorry you felt like you had to do this. I'm sorry I wasn't there to help you find your way free. I'm so fucking sorry.

The words echoed in my head and tore open the wounds festering inside me. Ari never loosened her grip, and I lost track of time as I let go.

FIFTY-TWO
RHETT

The next morning, Ari's phone woke us both up from a dead sleep. She snatched it up and hit the button to answer.

"Hello?"

Even without it being on speaker, Esme's voice came through loud and clear. "Security hasn't been able to find Jan. There's no sign of her."

"Shit," I muttered, my brain roaring to life.

"But that's not why I'm freaking the fuck out. Erik didn't show up for our Soul Cycle class. He *never* misses. He's not answering his phone either. I'm heading to his apartment right now."

"Wait, what?" Ari sputtered. "No. If you're—"

I snatched the phone out of her hand. "Esme?"

"Yeah? Who the hell is this?"

"Hennessy."

"Oh my God, if I weren't losing my shit right now, I'd be freaking out over the fact that you're clearly in bed together."

"Not important. What's important is that you stay the fuck away from Erik's apartment. Is there a manager you can call? Someone who can check on him?"

"I already called and they didn't answer. I have to go check myself."

Ari rubbed her eyes, turning them red. "Don't let her—"

I held up a hand. "Esme, listen to me. If something happened to Erik, what matters most is making sure nothing happens to you."

"You can't stop me from going. He's my best friend, dammit!"

I knew from her determined tone that nothing I could say would change her mind, so I had to secure her safety another way. "If you're going to his place, don't go near his door without the manager. Wait for someone to walk up there with you. If there's any sign of tampering with the lock or door, get back in your car and call the cops. I'll check on things from my end and call you back."

"But—"

"Call the manager."

"Tell her I said she better not go up there by herself," Ari said, her tone panicked.

"Your boss forbids you to do this by yourself, and she doesn't care if you have a key." I was guessing about the last part, but it was a safe assumption.

"Okay. Fine. But I'm going. I'll call as soon as I get there."

"Good. We'll be waiting."

When I ended the call, Ari clutched the covers to her chest. "Oh my God. Do you think . . ."

Snatching my phone from the nightstand, I dialed Heath.

"I don't know, but your brother better have an update, because this shit ain't cool."

Heath answered on the first ring. "What's happening?"

"Two of Ari's employees are missing. Where are things at on your end? The Feds bringing Carlos in?"

A moment of heavy silence stretched for too long before he answered. "Not yet. They're trying to do this smart because they want him to flip, and—"

"You've gotta be fucking kidding me. The Feds really think he's going to betray his whole family? And for what? Fucking idiots."

"I can't make them bring him in. You know that."

"Yeah, well, if something happens to your sister's employees, it's gonna be on them for not getting off their asses."

"I know it's frustrating. We're making progress. The gears just turn slow with all the red tape. You get how it is."

"Tell them to move faster. They might have more to investigate than just him if they don't hurry the fuck up."

"I'll relay the message. Anything else? Ari okay?"

I met her stare. "She's safe, and that's what matters."

"Good deal, brother. Take care of her."

"You know I will."

I hung up and grabbed Ari's hand. "They haven't brought him in."

She cleared her throat. "I gathered that. What are we going to do if something happened to Erik or Jan? I can't . . ." She trailed off as if the words got caught in her throat.

I reached out to loop an arm around her and pulled her against my chest. "Don't borrow trouble. We'll take it as it comes."

"Okay." When I finally released her, she rolled to the

side of the bed. "I need my computer. I need to dig. I have to feel like I'm doing something instead of just waiting and hoping."

"You do that, and I'll call Esme."

She nodded and left the room. I used her phone to call her employee back.

"Did you find out something?" Esme asked in lieu of a greeting.

"Carlos Herrera is still walking free. You need to be careful."

"This is my best friend we're talking about. I would do anything for him."

"And he would want you to stay safe."

"I'll call you back as soon as I get there. Give me five minutes."

I paced the room while I waited, and finally, the phone rang.

"He's not here, but his door was unlocked! Erik wouldn't do that. Ever."

"Don't go inside. Call the cops."

"They won't take a missing-person report for forty-eight hours. I saw him eighteen hours ago."

Fuck. I knew that all too well.

"We'll call in a favor and have someone come check it out. Lock the door, keep your key, and go to the office. Stay there until you hear from me."

"Okay. But if something happened to Erik . . ."

"I'm going to tell you the same thing I just told your boss —don't borrow trouble."

We said good-bye and I hung up. I yanked on jeans and followed the scent of coffee to the kitchen where Ari was standing on one leg, the other foot pressed against her inner thigh like she was attempting a yoga pose, her fingers flying over the keyboard.

"Do I want to ask what you're doing?"

"Probably not."

"How many felonies?"

"None, if I don't get caught."

It was amazing how little her absolute lack of remorse for breaking the law bothered me. In this situation, if one of my friends were missing, I'd feel the same way.

I stepped up behind her, dropping a palm on each shoulder. "Don't get caught."

"Don't worry. It's the Feds. They're not that good at back tracing."

I looked over her shoulder. "What are you looking for?"

"I wanted to see what kind of surveillance they were running, and what they were planning to bring Carlos in for, but there's not a single mention of his name anywhere. Not even a basic file. Didn't Heath say they were investigating him? There should be *something*."

"Maybe they're keeping it off the books."

"Or maybe they're not doing jack shit," Ari countered. "No warrants. No reports. No surveillance. Nada. Who the hell is Heath having look into this anyway?"

"He didn't give me a name. I'll find out."

Her fingers kept flying. "If he weren't my brother, I'd wonder if he was lying about having someone look into it, because there's literally nothing. It doesn't make any sense."

"They have to be keeping it off the books then. I wouldn't be surprised if they were. I'll get in touch with him again."

I fired off a text to Heath asking for a name. His response came just as quickly.

HEATH: Tell Ari to quit doing her thing. I'm working on it.

When I relayed his message to her, her face screwed up into an angry expression and she grabbed her own phone.

ARI: I have two employees missing, and one of them is Erik. His apartment was unlocked. Don't tell me not to do anything about it.
HEATH: I'll call in a favor and have them check on him. Probably nothing.
ARI: Cops are already involved. Do better.

Ari released a growl of frustration. "He knows Erik and Esme are basically my family!"

"I know. We're going to figure it out. Let's brainstorm."

FIFTY-THREE
ARIEL

Esme called back two hours later, and this time the panic in her voice had morphed into hysteria.

"The cops won't do anything. His car is here but his bike is missing, so they said he must be out for a long ride." She paused. "But I hacked into his search-engine history, and before we left work last night, he looked up Jan Hofer's address. What if . . . what if he went to find her and something bad happened? What if he never even made it home last night? He's back on that stupid *ride your bike to work* kick again, and Jan's place isn't that far from his."

Dread curdled in my belly. "Shit," I whispered.

"I'm hacking all the camera feeds around his and Jan's places. If the cops won't do anything, I'll find him my damn self," Esme vowed.

"Good. I've got part of the security team looking for Carlos, and I'm running down any properties he could be at."

"If you find an address—"

"No, Esme. You go nowhere by yourself. Promise me."

"Fine, but if that asshole did something to him—"

"It'll be on me, and I'll make sure he gets what's coming to him, I swear it." I wished I could hug her, because both of us needed it. "Stay safe, and call me if you find anything."

"You too."

We hung up, and I turned into Rhett's arms. I didn't realize I was shaking until he tightened his hold on me.

"I don't like this, Rhett. I really, really don't like this." I swallowed back the urge to cry, but tears burned behind my eyes.

He pulled back and lifted my chin. "Your ex knew how close Erik and Esme were to you?"

I nodded. "I talked about them both all the time. I swear to God, if he touches one hair on Erik's head . . ."

He pressed a kiss to my forehead. "We'll make sure he pays."

I stepped out of his embrace and grabbed my laptop, ready to tear Carlos's life to shreds.

Rhett paced the kitchen. "Something doesn't feel right. I know I said having cartel connections in California and New Orleans didn't mean they were related, but this seems like too much coincidence to me. We need to know if they're related. The same cartel. The same people."

The knot in my stomach grew. "How? Why? What's the common link?"

"I keep turning it over and over, and I keep coming up with the same answer."

"What?"

He met my gaze. "You are."

FIFTY-FOUR
ARIEL

Two hours later, the pounding behind my eyes reached migraine proportions. I'd sent a list of properties to my security team to search, and then I started on another angle. One I never expected to be considering.

Something was wrong here. *Very* wrong.

Rhett was outside briefing the security team, and I rose from the table on shaky legs and went to the fridge for a bottle of water while I waited for him to return. Another cup of coffee might put me right over the edge. I'd chugged half the bottle when Rhett returned. One look at my face was all it took for him to read me.

"What did you find?" He came toward me as he asked the question.

"Didn't you say Heath had taken himself off the IA investigation about your dad because of a conflict of interest?"

Rhett nodded. "That's what he said."

My belly flopped like a fish dying on the banks of the

lake. "He's on the reports about your dad. All of them. For the last year."

Rhett's expression turned to stone. "What? That's impossible."

I set the water bottle on the counter and wiped my hands on my shorts, clutching the hem. "He's not just part of the investigation." I paused, meeting Rhett's gaze. "He's leading it."

Rhett's face drained of color, leaving it ashen. "Why the fuck would he lie to me about it then? It doesn't make any goddamned sense. He knew that I didn't care either way. I just wanted the truth. He could've told me he stayed on it, and I would've been happy that someone competent was working it."

I swallowed. "That's the other thing that doesn't make any sense. His reports are like a fifth grader put them together. Totally basic. Lacking any useful information. It was almost like . . ."

"What?" Rhett demanded.

"Like he was stalling."

"Why the hell would he—"

"I have no idea. Could he have been trying to help?"

From his narrowed eyes, it didn't look like Rhett was ready to give Heath the benefit of the doubt. And, honestly, from what I'd seen, I was having trouble too.

"Show me."

I grabbed the copies I'd printed out and handed them over. Rhett flipped through the pages, the line between his eyebrows deepening until they nearly touched. He kept his head down as he started to speak.

"Heath's a competent cop. This isn't even rookie work. I

don't know how his superiors didn't kick him off the case for this shit."

"It doesn't make sense."

Finally, Rhett looked up, his mouth set in a grim line. "There are only two possible explanations. Either he was trying to help and stall the investigation, or someone didn't want him closing the case and so he deliberately dragged it out as long as he could." He skipped to the last report and held it out. "This is what they were using to arrest him, and this information could've been in the first report, over a year ago. It doesn't make sense for Heath to sandbag this."

I glanced down at the sheet, and it sounded like an intelligent human being had strung together the sentences, which was at odds with the reports for the year prior.

"Could Heath . . . would he . . ." I didn't even want to voice the possibility that my brother could have been deliberately blocking the investigation for whoever it was going to implicate.

"I don't know. But we need to dig deeper into your brother and any possible motives." Rhett looked pointedly at me. "Can you do that?"

Disloyalty burned through my veins like acid, but if Heath had done something . . .

"If he's the connection from the department to me, and then me to Carlos, then this all starts to make a little more sense. I have to look."

FIFTY-FIVE
RHETT

Ari pulled Heath's phone records and I spent hours going through them. The number of burner phones contacting him on a regular basis did nothing but raise the level of my suspicion.

What the hell did you get yourself into, Heath?

While Ari dug for more information, my phone rang.

"We've got a package out at the front gate. Flower delivery van dropped it off, didn't wait for one of us to get there for signatures."

A feeling of foreboding slithered over me. "What the fuck is it? Do we need the bomb squad?"

Ari's fingers froze on the keyboard as soon as I said *bomb squad.*

"One of the guys on the team worked as EOD for a couple months. He's assessing it before we open it."

"I'm coming out. Don't open it until I get there."

Still unmoving, Ari stared at me. "A bomb?"

I shook my head. "Not likely, but we're not taking any

chances. If someone is trying to get to you, they're going to have to go through all of us first."

She bolted out of her chair. "You are not getting blown up for me, Rhett Hennessy. No way."

I crossed the room and yanked her into my arms. "This fucker has already proven he's resourceful and fucking dangerous. You're not taking any chances."

"What about you? I refuse to let him take you too."

I grasped her shoulders. "We're going to be careful. Wait inside. I'll go see what the hell is going on out there, and I'll tell you when it's safe." When she opened her mouth to argue, I put a finger over her lips. "*Safe*, Ari. Just let me keep you fucking safe."

"Okay. Fine."

I pressed a hard kiss to her lips. "Thank you."

As soon as I walked out the front door, I was glad I made her promise. The guys had created a perimeter around the box in the driveway outside the front fence, and one approached it carefully.

When I shut the door, Carver turned toward me to ask, "Who else knew she was staying here?"

"The article in the paper made it clear she was in town, but at this house? Just family—mine and hers—and a couple of her employees."

"Well, someone clearly knew her well enough to send a delivery."

The man approaching the box stared at a piece of equipment he held in front of him. "I'm not getting any readings off it that would suggest ordnance."

"So, let's cut the fucker open," Carver said.

The former EOD tech pulled on a mask, clearly worried about possible chemical threats. "Everyone get back."

The two other guys out front backed away, and Carver and I took two steps toward the house as well. Were we handling this with proper police protocol? No way in hell. We didn't have time for that shit.

The EOD tech cursed loudly at the same moment Ari's scream split the air, so loud I could hear it in the driveway.

As I broke into a dead run back toward the house, I heard them yell from behind me.

"It's a head."

FIFTY-SIX
ARIEL

N*o. No. No!*

The image on my computer screen that someone just sent me was so gruesome, I couldn't comprehend it at first. It had to be photoshopped. It wasn't real. But I couldn't stop screaming because something told me it wasn't a hoax..

The photo featured Erik's head sitting on a table next to a cardboard box. His eyes were open, but lifeless.

Arms wrapped around me from behind, and I turned. The tears spilling down my face blinded me, so I fought.

"It's me, Red. It's me," Rhett whispered.

"Erik. He's—" I couldn't say anything else. I leaned over and threw up on the floor.

Footsteps pounded in the entryway before someone else burst into the kitchen. "We need pictures to make a positive ID—"

The buzzing in my head nearly drowned out Carver's voice.

"I think your positive ID is on the screen." Rhett pulled

my hair back over my shoulder. "Come on, Ari. Let's get you to a bathroom."

I shook my head, wiping my mouth with the back of my hand, not even caring that it was disgusting. "No, I can't. I have to analyze the picture. It could be fake. There's no way it's real. It's not. It can't be."

Rhett held me tighter. "Ari, we need to get you cleaned up."

From his forced calm, I knew there was something else.

"What was in the box? The package? Oh my God. Please don't tell me—"

"I'm so sorry, Ari. So fucking sorry." Rhett's grip on me tightened.

"Nooo!" I screamed, tears burning paths down my face. My stomach rebelled again, and I gagged and choked on bile.

This isn't happening. This is a nightmare.

I wanted to close my eyes and pretend this day had never started. *Erik* . . . My body shook with sobs as a hundred emotions crashed into me at once.

Esme . . . My chest ached. My insides were shredded. My gaze dropped to the floor to see if there was blood puddled beneath my feet from the gaping hole in my heart.

"Why?" My question came out ragged. "Why would someone do this? Erik didn't do anything to anyone."

My phone rang from its position beside my computer. Too close to the horrific picture on the screen for me to take a single step toward it.

Rhett didn't hesitate. He reached out and snatched it up.

Esme. On the secured line.

"I don't know if I can do this," I choked out. "How do I tell her? I'm not strong enough."

"We'll do it together."

I answered the phone, and all we heard were sobs until she started wailing.

"He's dead! Someone . . . someone sent me a text message. With a picture. And one of Jan too."

My knees buckled, Rhett's hold the only force keeping me upright. "Esme, where are you?"

"In an Uber. Going home."

"Don't go home," I croaked, the words sounding broken. "Don't go home."

"Oh God, they sent it to you too?" Her voice rose to a screeching level. "How is this happening? This can't be happening!"

"I'm so sorry. It's all my fault."

"No, it's those motherfuckers, and we're going to take them all down." Esme's hysterical tone took a turn for the dangerous.

Rhett grabbed the phone from my hand. "What you're going to do is go directly to the airport and get on a flight to Vail. You're going to lay low until this is over."

I jerked my head around to look at Rhett. "Vail? Why not here? She should be here. With me."

He gave me a hard look and repeated himself. "You understand me, Esme? Don't take a damn thing with you. Tell the driver right now to change direction. We'll get you a ticket and message you the details through the secure app."

"Okay. Okay." Esme's voice shook as she repeated herself. "Colorado. Pot's legal there. I'll get so stoned, I won't remember what happened. I'll forget. I'll . . . *Erik* . . ." She broke into sobs again, and I pulled myself together enough to take the phone from Rhett and form words without crying.

"Listen to me. We will take them out. We'll get revenge. No one is getting away with doing this. *No one.* We won't just hurt them, we will *destroy* them." I didn't care if I sounded like a bad movie villain.

"Okay. Pot and destruction. I can do this." Esme's voice quavered, but she sounded steadier as we heard her tell the driver to go to the airport instead and she'd pay him cash. He agreed, probably not about to argue with the hysterical woman in his backseat. "Send me the ticket. I've got Erik's computer. I'm going to find out exactly what he was doing, and then I'm going to track down these mother-fuckers—"

"And give us the information so we can take care of it," Rhett finished for her.

"Only if you promise—"

"I swear to God, we will get them, E. I will not stop until we do." I'd never made a more serious vow. "Call me when you get to the airport and are checked in."

"I will."

We hung up, and I turned in Rhett's arms and soaked the front of his shirt with my tears.

"How can this be happening? What did I do?"

He smoothed my hair back from my face and held me close. "This isn't your fault. You didn't do this."

"But Erik wouldn't have been a target if not for me. Jan either." I looked toward my laptop and the other message mocking me for not clicking on it. I couldn't. Not right now. I didn't know if I could handle seeing more.

"And you wouldn't have been a target if not for someone else. There's a hell of a lot more going on here than we thought. Now we pull our shit together, find the answers, kill the people who need killing, and get Erik and Jan justice."

I looked up at him, blinking away my tears. "I need to call my brother."

Rhett nodded in agreement. "*We* need to call your brother."

After we arranged for the plane ticket to Vail for Esme, and Rhett's brother Rock agreed to pick her up and keep her safe, we had Carver call in two security guys to watch over my dad at the rehab center. We weren't taking any risks with the people we loved.

Rock knew there was a threat, and he promised he would take good care of Esme and Mrs. Hennessy.

Between Rhett and me, we called Heath six times. Each time, his voice mail picked up.

Rhett ended the last call and turned to me, his expression serious. "I didn't want to believe it. Fuck, I still don't want to."

In this moment, I had some idea of how Rhett felt when faced with first, the possibility of his brother being a dirty cop, and then his dad.

The choking disbelief. The visceral denial. The fear that it could be true. The last shred of hope I held on to that we could have gotten it all wrong.

I walked back to the printouts of the IA reports on the table and picked up the papers, hating that my brother's initials were on each one.

"He had to have a reason, right? He wouldn't do this without a reason." My logical, rational mind was fracturing under the weight of emotion.

Rhett turned, his lips pressed into a flat line. "We need to talk to him. That's the only way we're going to get answers."

I heard what he wasn't saying—*the kind of answers I never got from my dad.*

I took a deep breath and pushed the emotion out of the picture in favor of cold, impersonal logic. "Why would a cartel care about someone in IA? Does that even make sense? Wouldn't they want someone in another department?"

"IA has total oversight over the department. They police the police."

"If I were cartel, total oversight sounds attractive then."

Rhett nodded. "It makes a sick sort of sense. In his position, Heath can get into everything happening in the department. Very little information would be off-limits if he had even a shred of a reason to need to know it."

If I were brutal and cunning, it sounded exactly like where I'd strike.

"I hate this. I hate it so much. What if . . . What if he didn't have anything to do with it, and we're condemning him because he's not here to defend himself?"

"Ari, I know—"

I cut him off. "We have to find him!"

"Track his cell. Find out where he is, and we'll go pick him up if he won't answer the damn thing."

If I'd been thinking clearly, I would have already come to that conclusion myself. I rushed to my laptop. "On it."

FIFTY-SEVEN
RHETT

Ari couldn't get a lock on Heath's location, and my guess was his phone was off. I grabbed the stack of call records and scanned the list. Plenty of numbers I didn't recognize. Burner phones. Throwaways. The kind that CIs would most likely use . . . or possibly cartel connections.

"Can you get any info on these two numbers he called regularly?"

Ari's fingers flew over the keys. "I can try."

Within minutes, she'd identified the point of purchase of the burner phones as a small town on the Texas-Mexico border.

Her jaw clenched. "I really don't like this. Not at all."

I leaned over her and rested my chin on her head. "I don't either, Ari. But he wouldn't be the first cop to make a bad decision and have it go a lot further than he thought."

We both knew I was talking about my dad. Even now, I wondered what the hell he had to do with this.

Why would Heath drag out the investigation? There was one other possibility . . .

"Heath could have been keeping my dad from getting arrested so he didn't talk. He had to know that if Dad got arrested, the cartel would assume he'd roll over, and then they'd take him out. Maybe your brother was protecting him by not closing the case."

I wanted to believe it. It could make sense. Maybe this was Heath's way of trying to protect a man he considered a second father.

Ari turned around, hope lighting her gray eyes. "I hope that's true. I really, really hope it is."

My phone vibrated in my pocket.

"Keep digging," I told her. With a kiss to the top of her head, I stepped away. "I'm going to take this."

"Okay."

I fished my phone from my pocket to find it was my brother Rome calling. "Hey, what's up?"

"Why the fuck am I seeing the name Hennessy coming up in cartel chatter? I just got off the phone with my computer geeks, and they said they caught a couple mentions of the family name. It sure as hell isn't because of me this time."

"What chatter?" I'd stayed out of Rome's business before because I didn't want to know what he was doing down in Central and South America, but if he could help me in any way now, I needed to know.

"We listen. We monitor. We gather intel. After walking into enough situations blind, we decided we had to step it up. Now we watch for key phrases and all identifiable names."

"Got it. So, what the fuck was the chatter about?"

"You're on the radar, and I want to know why."

"We've got a situation here."

Ari's gaze searched my face as I turned around.

"Does it have something to do with Dad?" Rome asked.

"Maybe. We're still piecing it together. But we do know that Carlos Alberto Moreno Herrera is involved somehow."

Rome went quiet. "Do you have any clue who the fuck you're dealing with? That family is way above your pay grade, brother."

"I don't have a pay grade anymore, *brother*."

Rome made a sound of disgust. "You know what I mean. That family is bad news. Brutal. Ruthless. They'll send you a friggin' head in a box—"

"Yeah, got one of those this morning."

Ari turned away, and I reached out to grasp her hand.

"Are you fucking kidding me?" Rome shouted.

"I wish I were."

"And you didn't call me? You think you're equipped to handle this shit by yourself?"

"Heath was supposed to be handling it. He was working with the Feds to take Carlos out. Now he's in the wind, and two of Ari's employees are dead."

"*Shit*. They've upped their ante. Let me start working on my end to see if I can tell what's going on. You need to lay low. I'm not ready to come home for another fucking funeral. Tell me everything you know, and I'll get my people on it."

I laid it out. Every detail we knew and suspected, from the beginning. When I was done, my brother was quiet for a long moment.

"This shit is fucked. My world makes a lot more sense, if you ask me. None of us pretend to be good. We're all in it for the money, which is what I'm guessing both Sampson and Dad were in it for."

"You don't know that." The protest was automatic, even

though from what Mom said, he was right about Dad's motives.

"You might be older than me, but that doesn't make you smarter. You've always believed that everyone should have a code of honor like you. News flash—they don't. Everyone's in it for themselves. That's how the world works. I'll get back to you when I have something. Try not to get dead."

My brother hung up before I could tell him to fuck off.

"Who was that?" Ari asked.

"Rome. Apparently, my little brother knows a hell of a lot more about the cartel than we do. He's working on his end. Now we need Heath."

Ari shook her head. "I can't trace him. He's gone. I don't know what else to do."

"What about Carlos?"

"Nothing. He hasn't used the number I have for him since he called and texted me."

"He has to have another. Or he just uses burner phones and swaps them out constantly."

"I can locate those. The numbers that were on Heath's phone records . . . if you think that maybe—"

"At this point, it's worth a shot."

I needed to get out there and find him. I didn't want to leave Ari alone, but without anyone on the streets looking, we weren't going to find Heath. Shit, even that was a long shot. With the heat this was drawing, I wasn't about to ask anyone else to step into the line of fire.

My phone vibrated before I could figure it out.

Rome. Again.

"You forget something?"

"No, I'm just really fucking good. One of the G6s that's part of the Herrera family fleet filed a flight plan with New

Orleans as a destination. If I were you, I'd get my ass to Lakefront Airport and get this fucker as soon as he hits the tarmac."

"I'm on it."

I pulled the phone away from my ear to hang up, but Rome's voice came through. "Make sure to bring the big guns. Guaranteed they're coming in hot."

"Done."

I hung up, and Ari stood.

"What's going on?"

"Your ex-boyfriend is on his way here."

FIFTY-EIGHT
ARIEL

I'd made Rhett promise to be careful and he swore he would, but that didn't make me feel any better. Fear had settled into my bones and dogged my every step. There'd already been too much loss.

I wanted to curl into the fetal position and pretend none of this had happened. But that would accomplish nothing.

My eyes burned from tears waiting to fall as I thought about how terrified Erik and Jan must have been in their last moments. My chest felt like it had been crushed beneath an avalanche. The tendons in my hands ached from furiously typing, but I didn't know how else I could help.

Lockdown got real this time. I wasn't allowed to leave the panic room. No one would know if I tucked myself into a ball and sobbed. But what good would it do me? None.

The time for mourning was after everyone was safe. Until then, I'd hold it together and dig deeper, try to find answers.

As I put my fingers back on the keyboard, an instant

message popped up from a chat service I rarely used but had never bothered to uninstall.

HEATH: I really fucked up, Ari. I shouldn't have tried to fix this on my own.
ARI: Where are you?
HEATH: I fucked up and we're all paying the price. I'm sorry.

ARI: Just tell me where you are. We can help you.
HEATH: No one can help me now. It's time to face facts.
ARI: DON'T YOU DARE QUIT ON ME!

I yelled the words as I typed them.

HEATH: I'm sorry.
ARI: LET ME HELP YOU!

But he didn't reply. No little dots popped up in the dialogue box to show him typing. And then thirty seconds later, the program showed he was off-line.

His phone. He has to be on his phone. My fingers flew as I ran the trace. Heath might have closed the app, but his phone was on just long enough for me to get the location.

I sucked in a breath when the address popped up.

My dad's house.

Heath was home?

It didn't make sense. I tapped Rhett's contact, but there

was no answer. Before I could leave a voice mail, another call interrupted, and I looked down at the screen.

Unknown Number.

My hand shook at the knowledge who was probably on the other end, but I forced myself to answer the call. “Hello?”

“You want to see your brother and your father alive again? Or do you want their heads delivered next?”

My stomach twisted at the visual. My brother and father’s eyes as lifeless as Erik’s. I gagged.

“What do you want, Carlos?”

“If you’re as smart as I’ve always assumed, you already know exactly where I am, so I’ll tell you when you get here. Bring your trusty little laptop. If you call Rhett Hennessy, I swear he’ll die before he can get out of the airport parking lot.”

It seemed like every cell in my body trembled with fear. No, *terror*. There was a difference I’d never truly appreciated until now.

When I didn’t respond, Carlos kept talking.

“If you’re not at your father’s house, alone, in forty-five minutes, I’ll personally slit their throats. You want them to live out this day, you won’t be late.”

“Why are you doing this?” My voice shook, but I managed to get the question out.

It didn’t matter, though—no one heard it. Carlos had hung up on me.

He had my dad and my brother. My only family, both in the hands of a psychopath.

Logic told me that I shouldn’t go. I couldn’t go. It was suicide.

But logic’s role in this decision was overridden by terror.

Rhett tore himself apart for not answering his father's phone calls when he had no idea what his father was facing. How could I live with myself knowing Carlos had my family and I did nothing?

I couldn't.

It didn't matter that my father might not remember any of this, or that my brother might be a dirty cop. There was no way I was going to let them die while I sat locked in a safe room where nothing and no one could touch me.

I shoved the terror aside and considered the problem before me.

How do I get to my dad's house in less than forty-five minutes?

FIFTY-NINE
RHETT

The tires of the SUV squealed as we rounded the corner that led to the airport entrance. A private jet was lowering its landing gear on approach.

"You think he's here yet?" one of the security crew asked from the backseat.

"We're about to find out."

I slammed on the brakes, parked in the fire lane, and jumped out. As soon as my feet hit the ground, another SUV roared up beside me and stopped. I pulled my pistol as the window rolled down.

"What the fuck are you doing?" Rix shouted. "I've been following you for two miles debating whether I should pull your ass over after someone called in a possible drunk driver. You're lucky I was the closest unit."

"Not now. Busy."

"You care to fucking share why you're in an SUV owned by Lachlan Mount, hauling ass to a private airport with a bunch of his guys?"

My head jerked to the side as I looked at Carver. "What the fuck is he talking about?"

He shrugged. "You needed backup. The best. I got it for you."

Jesus fucking Christ. "Don't have time to explain," I told Rix.

The cop slammed his vehicle into reverse to park behind my SUV. He jumped out, gun in hand. "Something's going down. Don't know what it is, but you're not doing this alone."

"You can't be here."

Rix glared at me. "Too late. I'm here."

I shook my head. "Fuck it. Be stubborn. You want to help take down the cartel before they get to Ari? Then let's go get this motherfucker."

I tucked my gun away as I headed for the door. Private airport. No security. God bless rich people who don't like walking through metal detectors.

I walked up to the information desk and slid the slip of paper with the tail number Rome had texted me across the counter. "I need to know if this plane has landed."

The woman folded her hands. "I'm sorry, sir. For privacy reasons, we can't disclose that information."

Rix pulled out his badge. "We're overruling your privacy reasons."

Her eyes widened slightly. "I'm not supposed to provide any information without a warrant."

"You want to be invited to the funerals you contribute to by not sharing the information?" Rix countered.

"No." Her head shook vigorously. "If it's a matter of public safety, I can make an exception."

"We'd appreciate that," I replied.

She took the slip of paper, typed the info into the computer, and frowned. "This flight came in ahead of schedule. It landed about fifteen minutes after they filed the flight plan, but of course, we see that when people want to keep their destinations as private as the FAA will allow."

"Wait. You mean they're already on the ground?"

"Yes, sir. A couple of hours ago. They were here and left."

My mind racing, I spun away from the desk with Rix, Carver, and another one of the crew following me. "Fuck. *Fuck.*"

"This had to be planned," Carver said. "You think they wanted us away from the house? Away from Ms. Sampson?"

My stomach hit the floor.

"He's not going to touch her." I cut my gaze to Carver. "Get on the phone. Call the guys at the house. Make sure she's still in lockdown and there's been no movement."

He already had his phone out as I reached into my pocket to see a missed call on mine from Ari.

Fuck. I called her back, but got no answer.

"She's in the safe room? You're sure?" Carver asked. "Can you confirm via camera feed?" We waited for several moments before he froze. "What do you mean, the camera feeds are down?" He asked the question quietly, but it blared through my brain like he'd shouted it.

No. Not fucking happening.

I called Ari's phone again and let it ring until it went straight to voice mail.

Where the hell are you?

I snatched the phone from Carver's hand. "Have there been any disturbances? Anything?"

"No, sir. Well, something tripped a sensor on the back

perimeter, but there was nothing there when we checked and none of the house sensors were triggered. I went to check the feed to see what it was, and just saw it was black. We're trying to figure out what happened. The safe room door is still engaged."

I thought of the day the man came up on a boat and scared the shit out of Ari while she was outside, and how she'd locked herself in the safe room without setting off the alarm for Carver to know. None of that system was fool-proof. If she could get around it, so could someone else.

"Any boats? Coming or going?"

A moment of silence. "Now that you mention it . . . I heard a boat motor as we came around the house to check."

Fuck. "We need confirmation Ari is in the safe room. Go pound on the fucking door, if you have to. I need to hear her voice. Call us back."

"On it."

I hung up and handed the phone back to Carver.

"Where's Sampson? He know his sister is locked down in a safe room?" This came from Rix.

"No fucking clue where he is. MIA. But we got a head in a box from the cartel this morning. One of Ari's employees. Saw pictures of another one. Now the asshole who did it is here, and I'm not stopping until we put him down so he can never touch her again."

Rix's eyebrows went up. "You're gonna need more backup if you're going to war with the cartel." He'd done it before. He would know.

"You offering?"

"I can't do it officially, but I'm here. Let's do this."

I glanced to Carver. "We got another body on the team. Now we gotta figure out where the fuck this asshole went."

SIXTY
ARIEL

One stolen boat and one borrowed car later, I knew I made a huge mistake the moment I walked into my dad's empty house and someone grabbed me, wrenching my arms around my back. All my training deserted me, and I froze when I saw Carlos standing in the living room, his white shirt perfectly pressed but spattered with a faint spray of red. *Blood.*

I could hear Rhett's voice yelling in my head to *fight*. I yanked, trying to twist out of the grip of whoever held me, but all I did was waste my energy.

Carlos waited until I stilled to speak, shaking his head. "You should have done what I told you to do, Ariel. Instead, you had to be foolish."

Foolish? Foolish was coming here alone.

"What did you do with them? Where are they?"

There was no sign of either my dad or my brother in the room. Movement came from my right, and I whipped my head around.

Two men in black suits. I wasn't sure why I was

surprised. Apparently, Carlos had increased his security as well.

My gaze cut back to him to find his face twisted into a mask of displeasure.

"I am the only one who gets to ask questions here. Like why you let another man put his hands on you?"

He stepped toward me, and fear curled up my spine.

"Whore," he spat. "I thought you were smarter than the rest of them. You couldn't keep your legs closed for five minutes."

My first instinct was to fire back with his transgressions, but I snapped my mouth shut before the words flew free. This Carlos wasn't the guy I'd dated sometimes when our schedules connected. He was the son of a drug lord *who had my dad and brother captive*.

"Where are they?"

He stepped forward again, this time to backhand me on the cheek. "I said no fucking questions! Do I need to fuck the sense into you right here? In front of an audience? Maybe you'd like that too."

Tears stung my eyes as pain radiated from my cheekbone. *He just hit me.* No one had ever hit me. I jerked my arm, instinctively trying to cover the spot with my hand.

"I should have kept you in line with the back of my hand this whole time. Then we wouldn't have this situation. Now I'll drag you home to Mexico like the disobedient bitch you are, and I'll put you to use. My father has a pack of dogs that will break you if I can't."

The visual rising in my head threatened to empty the contents of my stomach.

"Why?" I dared another question. "Why are you doing this?"

A cruel smile twisted his lips. "Because I can. Because no one offers me something and then tries to take it away. You were part of the deal, you and that brain of yours, and I don't renegotiate."

Part of the deal?

"I didn't make a deal. I don't know what the hell you're talking about, but I'll pay you to let me go. As much as you want, just let me walk out of here with my dad and Heath."

Cruel, mocking laughter burst from Carlos's lips. "I never understood how you could be so naive and so brilliant at the same time. I have more money than my children's children could ever spend."

"Then what do you want?" I yelled.

His expression turned forbidding, and he gripped me by the chin and squeezed before flinging my head to the side. "You will learn respect!"

The tears burning my eyes tipped over. "Where are they? Just tell me. Please. They're all I have left."

"The fact that you risk my wrath for that piece-of-shit brother of yours tells me just how stupid you are. He doesn't deserve your loyalty." He nodded at the large flat-screen TV mounted on the wall. The one Heath and I had gotten Dad for Christmas two years ago.

One of his goons turned on the power. As soon as Heath's battered face filled the screen, I froze. He was tied to a chair. A chair I recognized.

My gaze cut to the breakfast nook and my dad's table. One chair was missing.

Heath spat blood at whoever held the camera, and it spilled over his lip and down his chin. "Fuck you."

"No, fuck you." It was Carlos's voice. "You thought you could show her that picture without paying the price? Didn't

I prove you wrong when they put your father in the hospital? Did you not get the message?"

"I'm done. I'm fucking done!"

Bloody spittle coated Heath's lips as he yelled, and a man stepped into the frame and swung a fist at Heath's face. My brother's head jerked sideways when it connected, and the crack of bone on bone had me crying out as he cursed.

This time, when the man stepped back, Heath coughed up teeth with his mouthful of blood. That's when I realized it wasn't bone on bone, but metal. Brass knuckles were secured on the man's fingers.

"How do we get into the safe room?"

The question Carlos asked Heath caught me off guard.

"She'll come. She's gonna come."

The man backhanded him and Heath coughed, blood bubbling up on his lips.

"The safe room."

"I don't know how to get in."

"Bullshit. You inspected the whole fucking house before she got here. Don't lie to me."

Another punch, this time to the gut, left Heath doubled over. I shut my eyes and turned away. I had asked him to check out the house before I rented it, just to make sure it wasn't too good to be true. But the safe room wasn't something I'd mentioned, nor did he.

"Stop. Just stop," I whispered.

Carlos wrapped his arm around me and closed his fingers over my throat. "Oh no, we haven't even gotten to the good part yet. And you and I are not even close to done. We're just getting started."

My breathing shallowed as Carlos put pressure on my

windpipe. "Is he alive?" I whispered. "Just tell me . . . did you . . . *please tell me.*"

I tried to control the shivers racking my body, but I vibrated against Carlos.

"Control yourself, or I'll do it myself."

His voice once again came from the video. "You're going to be selfless for once in your life and save your sister from me rather than cover your own ass? I'm shocked. I never expected in the choice of her life or yours, that you would choose her."

"What do you mean?" Heath asked.

"It's simple. You give me the safe room override and I let you walk out of this room alive. I get her and that brain I'm going to put to work. Then you get to live."

"That wasn't the deal."

"No, it wasn't, but since you didn't hold up your end of the bargain and take out all the Hennessys when you had the chance, things have changed."

"They were never together. After wiring the house, there was no way to take out the rest to make it look like an accident."

Realization slammed into me like a runaway freight train. Heath killed Mr. Hennessy? And had agreed to kill the others? That couldn't be possible. My knees buckled, and I clawed at Carlos's grip as I fell. He yanked me back up, my lungs burning and my entire body shaking as tears coursed down my cheeks.

No! Why would he do it? How *could he do it?* The man on the screen covered in blood looked like my brother, but the man I knew would never . . .

"It was no accident that you threw your sister at him either. Did you think by pushing them together he could protect her from me? A Hennessy, of all people? The fucking family that has cost me millions? And now you'll all die."

"Fuck you, asshole. You used her to keep me in line, and I did what I had to do. There were no guarantees."

"And you can't trust a dirty cop who steals money from the cartel either."

I fought for another breath. *Stealing money from the cartel? For what?* The remaining shreds of hope that my brother was innocent withered and died one by one.

In the video, Heath took another fist to the face, and my stomach lurched.

"Fuck off. I needed the money. Fucking greedy pigs. You got more than you'll be able to spend. It was getting seized anyway. You were never going to see it again."

"Greedy pig? No, that's you, you piece of shit. You should've known better than to gamble with money you can't repay. Should've known better than to fuck with us."

The backhand that struck Heath across the face was more of an insult than anything, but I still flinched.

"Where is he?" I asked, the words sticking in my throat.

Carlos twisted my head so he could look me in the eye. "What? You don't want to see the good part?" He turned me back to face the TV as a knife flashed in the goon's grip and slammed into Heath's hand, pinning it to the arm of the chair.

I projectile vomited on the floor for the second time today.

Carlos flung me away from him, and I landed on my knees. "Disgusting." He snapped his fingers, and one of the men in black suits disappeared into my dad's kitchen and returned with a roll of paper towels. Carlos snatched it from him and shoved it at me. "Clean up the mess."

It was from my knees, next to my own vomit, that I watched the rest. Heath refused to give up the safe room override code—until a second knife pinned his other hand to the chair and my stomach rebelled again.

"Fine! I'll give it to you!"

My brother's words slammed into my chest, knocking me back on my ass as he rattled off a series of numbers. *He . . . he gave me up. Sacrificed me to save himself.*

"No family loyalty. Disgraceful. Especially when you rushed here to save him," Carlos said as he stood above me, looking down.

On the screen, they ripped the knives out, unpinning Heath from the chair, and he rose to his feet on unsteady legs.

He sold me out. Gave me up to these brutal men to save himself.

The same person who taught me to ride a bike, and cleaned up my skinned knees when I crashed. The brother I always thought would come to my rescue. The brother I was willing to undertake a suicide mission to save. The brother I didn't want to believe would willingly offer me up to a psycho.

But he did.

He'd lied to everyone.

Me. Dad. Rhett.

But he was still my brother.

"Where is he?" On my knees, there was no doubt I was begging. "And my dad. Please."

Carlos laughed and nodded at the screen.

I stared at the TV as Heath turned his back on the camera and walked toward the door, pain evident in every uneven step.

"Tell your little sister good-bye, Heath."

My brother's head whipped around just in time for someone to draw a pistol with a long barrel and pull the trigger three times.

"NO!"

My screams echoed through the house as my brother dropped to his knees, clutching his chest where the bullets had penetrated, and collapsed on the floor.

SIXTY-ONE
RHETT

When we got to the house, Ari still wasn't answering. I pounded on the door to the safe room, but no noise came from inside.

"You have the override?" Rix asked.

"No."

Carver burst into the closet. "I've got the override code." He flipped open a hidden panel to reveal a keypad and punched in the numbers.

The door slid open silently, and I rushed in. "Ari!"

The room was empty. She was gone.

I spun around to face the men behind me. "How did this happen? How the hell did she get out of here and not a single one of you noticed?"

One of the men spoke up. "There was a car that drove by a couple times, real slow. I went out front to check. Then the back sensor went off, and we cleared the front threat to go check that one out."

Rix walked into the safe room. "There's no sign of struggle. My guess is she left on her own."

"Why the fuck would she do that?" I strode out of the safe room, but I already knew the answer as soon as I voiced the question. "Heath or her dad. Herrera has one of them."

Carver shook his head. "Mr. Sampson is at the rehab center. I called to check."

That left only one possibility.

"If they had Heath, she would've gone." I knew it down to my bones, because that's how loyal Ari was.

Carver's phone rang, and he glanced down at it before picking up. "What? Wait, at the Sampson house?" His gaze cut to mine. "We're on our way."

"What the hell is going on?"

"Got a guy monitoring police radio. Call just came in from a neighbor about the Sampson house. Said she was worried about a possible domestic disturbance because of the yelling."

"That has to be them." My heart jumped into my throat. "Let's move."

I'm coming for you, Ari.

SIXTY-TWO
ARIEL

Neighborhood dogs barked outside, maybe because my screaming had set them off. Or maybe it had been the sound of Carlos's fist connecting with my jaw to silence me, or the sound of my head smashing into the edge of a table or the lamp shattering as it hit the tile.

"Shut up. Your brother doesn't deserve your sympathy. Worthless piece of shit. He showed you that picture of me, used it to push you away. That's why your father is lying where he is. To teach him a lesson. Look where his actions got you all."

I curled into a ball, shielding myself from another blow. "Where's my dad?" My voice was raw, destroyed from crying.

Carlos dragged me back up to my feet, this time by a fistful of hair, and my scalp burned as a chunk ripped free. "Same place he's been all day. You think security would make a difference if I wanted him dead? I didn't need him. I knew you'd come." He shook his head. "Oblivious, trusting Ariel."

He was right. I was. I'd missed it all, and my brain struggled to piece together what I'd learned. My brother stole money from the cartel to pay back gambling debts. He'd worked for them, had been responsible for the explosion that killed Ronan Hennessy.

"Now, we wait to get your boyfriend here, and I can eliminate another Hennessy before he causes me any more trouble."

The disgusted tone of Carlos's voice made it sound personal, which I didn't understand. Had Ronan somehow double-crossed the cartel? Was that what he'd done to earn his end?

"Why?"

"You want to know just how tarnished a bloodline Rhett Hennessy comes from? His father was dirty for over a decade. He facilitated all cartel business in the city for years. Then the oldest son decided to make taking down the cartel his top priority. Like that would keep drugs off the streets." Carlos laughed. "It's a losing battle. The cops will never win. We have money, power, and resources they'll never fully comprehend. We will always win, always get what we want. And we'll always take out anyone who gets in our way."

My jaw and head throbbed, but my heart ached for Rhett. This would wreck him.

"You killed Robin?"

Carlos snorted in disgust. "Like I would lower myself. I have more important things to do." He paused. "But I ordered it. Too bad the father finally found his conscience and had to join him."

Coming closer, he nudged me with the toe of his expensive shoe. "How do you think your boyfriend is going to feel about you when he learns your brother killed his father? It's a good thing you won't be here to find out. You're going to make me the most powerful man in the world instead. You're going to give that facial-recognition software to all the police departments in the country, and then we're going to use it against them because you're giving us a back door. We will know their every movement as it happens."

He was crazy. Insane.

"I'll never—"

My declaration was cut off by a knock at the front door.

"Is someone in there? Ariel? Heath?" Mrs. Thurman's shaky voice called. "I called the police, just in case something was wrong."

Carlos waved a hand toward the door and one of the goons moved toward it, pulling out the same gun that had killed Heath. *Heath.* My heart ached for him.

I couldn't save him. He'd been beyond saving.

But I can save her.

"Everything is fine!" I yelled toward the door, and the goon paused and glanced back at Carlos and me. "Just doing some redecorating before Dad moves back in. We got into a little argument about paint, and I knocked over a lamp with the roller. I'll stop by when I'm done, Mrs. Thurman."

Carlos grabbed me by the hair again. "You'll learn only to speak when spoken to." Then he nodded at the goon. "Kill the old bitch. No witnesses. And make it quick. We're leaving."

Another protest left my lips as Carlos dragged me toward the back door, right beside a tarp wrapped around what had to be my brother's body.

When I struggled to untangle his fingers from my hair without success, he growled in my ear. "If you don't cooperate, I'll send someone to the rehab facility to kill your father."

He dragged me out the back door and down the steps into the backyard.

Dazed, I fixed my gaze on the rosebushes. My dad had planted one every year on my mom's birthday. They lined two fences now, and I wished I'd been here to help him do it instead of spending so much time away. Maybe then I would have had a clue what was going on, and Heath wouldn't have done what he did.

Carlos jerked to a stop, and I stumbled in front of him. He wrapped an arm around my body and pinned me to his front as a familiar voice rumbled in a menacing growl.

"Let her go."

Rhett.

SIXTY-THREE
RHETT

I couldn't get a clear shot. First the trees, and then Ari being too close to the target. Now that I saw her face, bruised and bloody, I cursed myself for not taking the risk.

"He killed Heath," she croaked. "They're going to kill Mrs. Thurman from across the street. You have to stop them." Her wrecked voice matched her appearance. "Don't let them hurt her!"

One of the crew peeled off and ran for the front of the house as Carlos gloated.

"You won't take the shot, Hennessy. Too worried about harming the woman whose brother killed your father. Pathetic."

Heath killed my father?

The information sliced into me but I didn't let it show. Right now, all that mattered was getting Ari away from him and taking this motherfucker out.

The back door to the house burst open and shots rang out. A round punched into my shoulder but I ignored it and did the only thing that made sense. I dived at Carlos and Ari, knocking them to the ground before he could pull his weapon.

Bullets flew over our heads as Ari snapped into action, maneuvering her body and wrenching Carlos's wrist back to get him in an arm-bar like she had the morning I saw her with Carver. I leaned up and landed a punch to his face.

"You don't fucking hit a woman. Didn't anyone teach you that, you piece of shit?" Blood spilled from my shoulder, and I hoped like fuck it blinded him.

"You're going to die," he said, his accent thickening.

"Wrong, asshole. That's you."

When I reached for the gun in my ankle holster, Carlos yelled, "Kill them!"

As I rolled back up, Ari's entire body jerked and she lost her grip on Carlos. He shoved up to his knees and I didn't hesitate. I pulled the trigger, putting a bullet right between his fucking eyes. His body fell sideways as I crawled toward Ari. Bullets still flew, but all I saw was the blood gushing from her neck.

"We need a fucking ambulance!" I roared the words as I yanked her shirt up to put pressure on the wound to slow the bleeding, but her eyes were closed.

Someone behind me unloaded on the last man standing, and the gunfire died away.

"Ari, wake up," I pleaded. "Stay with me. I won't fucking lose you now, goddammit!"

Rix skidded to a halt beside me. "Ambulance won't be quick enough. We gotta get her there now."

I ripped my shirt off and wrapped it around her neck before we lifted her and carried her to the SUV.

"Five minutes. She'll be there in five minutes." Rix met my eyes. "She's gonna make it."

It was the longest five minutes of my life, and then the longest two hours.

Rix, Valentina, and I sat there with Carver and the security guys, waiting for an update on Ari's surgery.

"Any word?"

I jerked my head to the side, shaking off my stupor as Con Leahy sat down beside me.

"Where'd you come from?" I asked, shocked to see him here.

"Valentina called Vanessa. You got people who care. We're here for you. Whatever you need."

Ten minutes later, Lord walked into the waiting room and took a seat with a chin jerk. They waited with me for hours. Ari had never even met them, and I prayed she'd have the chance.

Our lives were a shattered mess of lies, death, and betrayal, but I didn't care. Together, we could figure out how to pick up the pieces. Without her . . .

I didn't even want to think about it.

Finally, a surgeon entered the waiting room and I stood. Rix got to his feet beside me and placed a hand on my shoul-der. My heart stuck in my throat as I waited for the verdict.

"Ms. Sampson's family?"

"Right here," I said.

The surgeon nodded, and my entire body tensed until he said, "She's going to be fine. She's in recovery now."

He continued with a long-winded explanation of what they'd done to repair the damage, but only one word stuck with me, echoing in my head. *Fine. Fine. Fine.*

"Can I see her?"

His gaze cut to me. "Give us a half hour to get her settled in and for her to hopefully wake up, and a nurse will bring you back."

"Thank you." My voice hoarse, I reached out to shake his hand. "Thank you for making sure she had a shot."

"You stopped the bleeding and got her here. If you hadn't acted so quickly, we might have lost her. Today is Ms. Sampson's lucky day." He released my hand and turned to walk out.

Her lucky day? The day her brother was murdered and her ex-boyfriend nearly killed her?

As soon as I decided the surgeon and I must have different definitions of the word *luck*, it hit me that Ari and I had survived it all and were getting our shot at picking up the pieces.

Together.

SIXTY-FOUR
ARIEL

Everything was fuzzy when I opened my eyes. My mind kicked over into fight-or-flight mode, but a hand clenched mine and Rhett's voice calmed my panic.

"Right here, Red. I got you."

My throat was sore and my head swam, but fractured memories sliced through my head.

"What happened?" The memories felt like bad dreams. Nightmares. Like they couldn't be real.

"Doesn't matter right now," Rhett said, but his tone told me so much more. The nightmares were real.

My brother sold me out to save his own life, and had wound up losing his anyway. He'd betrayed my family and his best friend. All for money.

My eyes burned as tears broke free, splashing hot on my cheeks. "Heath killed your dad. You must hate me."

Rhett's grip on my hand tightened. "*Never*. You had nothing to do with any of it. This isn't your fault. You don't get to take this on yourself."

The words were so much like the ones I'd said to him

once upon a time when we both thought my family had the moral high ground. All that had been shattered now.

"But—"

"He made his choice. It wasn't your fault, Ari. None of it."

I tightened my hold on his hand. Absolving myself wasn't so easy. "I should've—"

Rhett pressed a finger to my lips as his gaze turned serious. "If my father's sins aren't mine to bear, then your brother's aren't yours."

His words echoed in my head. How could I disagree with him when he put it like that? His father's actions didn't reflect on the man Rhett was . . . therefore the corollary should also be true.

But sound logic couldn't wipe away my guilt.

"I'm so sorry, Rhett. Your dad . . ."

"He wouldn't hold it against you either."

I wanted to disagree. Argue. Rage that he was wrong and I was to blame, but I couldn't without Rhett taking on the blame for his father's actions. I couldn't let him do that. He had borne too much responsibility for things he didn't do. Now it was time for him to let go . . .

But I had no idea how I could. My brother's betrayal was too fresh and too raw.

"I have to tell you the rest."

Rhett climbed into bed beside me and held me as I told him everything, never letting me go, even as I cried through the end of it. His strength held me together, and eventually, my tears ran dry and a head poked through the doorway.

Carver. "I don't want to interrupt, but I had to see for myself that you were okay."

Rhett's expression darkened as he turned to look at the

man. "You can report back to your boss that she's going to be fine and no longer requires your services."

His boss? Did he just fire Carver? I'd missed something here. Carver didn't protest, only nodded.

"It was a pleasure serving you, Ms. Sampson. I wish you a speedy recovery."

With that, he left the room, and I looked at Rhett.

"I'll tell you later. You need to rest."

My eyes were already heavy, and I drifted off.

SIXTY-FIVE
RHETT

"*If my father's sins aren't mine to bear, then your brother's aren't yours.*"

I replayed the words I'd said to Ari while she slept, but I wasn't sure I believed them as they applied to me.

Eventually, the nurses had kicked me out of Ari's bed, but I refused to leave the room. I wasn't letting her out of my sight for a long damned time.

Her chest rose and fell with even breaths while I wondered, *Where do we go from here?*

I wasn't sure I'd ever be able to let go of what my father had done. Likewise, Ari would carry her brother's actions with her for life.

It still shredded me to realize that two of the most important people in my life had betrayed me and everything I believed in. Heath had been closer to me than my brothers, and somehow I'd been completely oblivious to what was happening beneath the surface. I should have been a better friend, a better son, and maybe . . .

There I went again.

It was going to be a hard habit to break, for Ari and me both.

Separately, we were two broken people struggling to make sense of things, but together, maybe we could heal each other. I wasn't going to consider any other alternative, so I hoped like hell I was right.

My phone vibrated and I stepped outside the room, still watching her from the cracked door as I answered.

"Please tell me she's really going to be okay." My mom's voice carried a heavy dose of fear, even though I'd kept her updated by text.

"She's going to be fine, Mom. I promise."

"Thank the Lord." She paused. "And I swear, Rhett Hennessy, you've damn near given me a heart attack for the very last time. No more of those *I'm in the hospital* messages. I'm done."

"I know."

"You going to talk her into staying? Plant some roots back where she belongs?"

I had to smile. My mom could jump from subject to subject without any hesitation. "We've talked about it."

"Well, stop talking and just do it. Life is too short to waste time. I learned that the hard way."

The sorrow in her voice gutted me.

"I wish I would've found out something different, Mom. I wish we would've found out he had nothing to do with it."

She got quiet for a moment. "Me too, but it doesn't change the fact that he was the love of my life. Good people do bad things, Rhett. Sometimes for good reasons, sometimes for bad ones, but that doesn't mean all those memories we have are somehow worth less. And it surely doesn't mean that what he did has any bearing on you. *You* didn't do this."

"Ari said something along those lines."

"And she's right. Focus on the future, Rhett. Ari will need all the support you can give. You both deserve to be happy. I love you."

"Love you too, Mom."

I ended the call and watched Ari sleep.

She was alive. I was alive. And that was all that mattered right now. Everything else could wait.

SIXTY-SIX
ARIEL

Mist blanketed the cemetery as the priest said the final prayer to lay Heath to rest. My heart broke as my father wiped his eyes with a handkerchief. He'd finally been seen by a specialist who determined that he wasn't suffering from dementia due to early-onset Alzheimer's, but due to a toxic cocktail of the drugs he'd been taking. It had been another blow to realize that only Heath had the ability to switch out the pills in one of his arthritis prescriptions to cause it.

As my brother's ashes were now being interred, we couldn't ask him why, but had to assume that it was because my father must have asked too many questions and Heath had needed them to stop.

As much as I wanted to assign a noble motive to what Heath had done, this was the final nail in that coffin. He couldn't be exonerated, and I would have to live with that knowledge. But Rhett and I made a deal—we wouldn't assume responsibility for actions that weren't our own, and even though it was difficult to adhere to, I was trying.

Rhett's arm tightened around my shoulders as the priest said the final amen for the service.

I'd held Esme as we both cried what seemed like a million tears for Erik. Nothing would ever be the same without him, and Esme had been apologetic when she handed me her resignation. She couldn't be in the office without him. It hurt too much, and I didn't blame her. I'd offered her the capital she needed to start her own company, no strings attached, and she was still considering my offer. We'd said good-bye to Jan the next day in a small service as well.

Too many funerals in too short a time. Too much loss, heartache, and regret.

It was time to start fresh. But how?

Rhett pushed my father's wheelchair beside me, and assisted him into the van that would take him back to the rehab center. He was scheduled to move home in a couple of weeks, but he'd surprised me by saying he'd rather check out a senior-living community because his house was too empty and quiet after the hustle and bustle of his current place.

If my brother weren't already laid to rest, I would kill him for what he did to Dad.

Stop. Right there. We're letting things go.

It was easier said than done, obviously.

Forgiveness was a process, or so I was told, and I was still working on it.

Two hours later, we were finally home again. It wasn't technically "home" yet, though.

"Who did you say owns the house?" Rhett asked when I got off the phone with the leasing agency.

"Some guy named Lachlan Mount." The name rang a bell, but I couldn't remember why.

Rhett spun around in the kitchen and stared at me. "You're fucking kidding me right now."

I shook my head. "No. That's what they said. They said he'd consider selling for the right price. They told me to make an offer."

"No. Not a chance. We're packing our shit and leaving." His tone was implacable.

"Excuse me?"

"This guy is fucking everywhere. Has his hands in everything. He's Carver's fucking boss. Owns the security agency you used, and at least half the city. We are not living in a house he's probably still got wired with his own surveillance."

I raised an eyebrow. "Then we rip it all out and start over. This is where I fell in love with the real Rhett Hennessy, and I want to stay."

Rhett froze. "What did you say?"

"I want to stay." I felt strongly about it, and I wasn't going to let whoever owned this house run us off.

"Before that. You said this is where you fell in love with me . . ."

"Yeah, I did. So there. If you've got a problem with living here, then *we* have a problem."

His face softened. "You love me."

"You're just figuring this out?"

"You've never said it before."

I opened my mouth to protest, but then I realized he was right. I hadn't. To me, it was a given, something that went without saying. An irrefutable fact that was simply accepted as being true. It never occurred to me that I had to put it into words for him.

"Neither have you."

"I thought it was obvious."

"Then I guess we're even."

He closed the distance between us and pulled me against him. "I fucking love you, Ariel Sampson."

"I love you too."

A voice came from the entryway. "Then I suspect you should probably marry the girl before she changes her mind."

We both spun around. No alarms had sounded. The hinges hadn't even squeaked, and yet somehow a man in a dark suit exuding power laced with menace stood there.

"What the fuck are you doing here, Mount?"

He barely gave me a lazy shrug before crossing the floor. "Came to give the place another look before I decide whether I want to let it go."

So, this was the guy.

"You weren't invited," I said, pleased my voice was steady.

The smile that twisted his lips fell into the category of ruthless. "I don't require an invitation."

"It might be your house, but I'm the one with a valid lease, and therefore I say you do."

His eyes narrowed on me before shifting his attention to Hennessy. "Good luck with this one. You're going to need it." And then he turned and strode away.

As soon as the door shut behind him, I spun to face Rhett.

"You sure you want this house?" he asked.

I gave him my most mulish expression. “I’m not going to let him scare us away.”

“Then I guess we better make him an offer. He did have one good idea, though.” Rhett winked at me, and my heart stuttered in my chest.

Is he talking about . . .

Before I could finish that thought, Rhett’s fingers tangled into my hair and his lips met mine.

Everything else fell away as I lost myself in his kiss.

Whatever else happened, as long as I could end every day like this, I would be just fine.

EPILOGUE
RHETT

"A couples baby shower. Really?"

Ariel sounded like she couldn't quite get the concept through her brain. Probably because in the few months since she'd permanently moved her company to New Orleans, she'd met the rest of the guys and their women. Like I'd hoped, Valentina, Elle, Vanessa, Charlie, Yve, Delilah, and Eden had taken her into their fold and become the girl crew Ariel had never had before.

After everything that had gone down with Heath, she needed the support system. Ariel had hoped that Esme would move to New Orleans if for no other reason than to stay close, but she'd decided to stay in Vail and make her own mark.

The one silver lining was that Skip Sampson had regained all his normal cognitive function, and Ari spent as much time with him as possible. It had surprised us both when he'd invited us to dinner to meet his girlfriend. After being a devout bachelor for Ari's entire life, he'd met someone at the retirement community.

Ari was thrilled.

Every day, we all felt the hole Heath had left in our lives. The shock of betrayal hadn't faded completely, and I doubted it ever would. Instead of drawing into her shell because of it, or taking refuge in that big brain of hers and shutting me out, Ari had leaned on me more, and being there to support her had helped us both.

We'd never forget. I wasn't sure I'd ever forgive Heath—or myself for not seeing the signs. No one walked away from that mess without dragging some of the blame with them, including Ari. We were working on it.

But today wasn't for regrets and recriminations. Today was for something completely different.

I turned to look at Ari from where I sat in the driver's seat of her fancy Fisker electric car. "You've been to a baby shower, right?"

Her expression turned contemplative, and a couple of moments of silence followed. *Considering. Processing.* That's how Ari worked.

"I actually don't think so." Her chin jerked toward me. "Oh God, how terrible is that? Does that make me a freak? The company held baby showers for employees, but Erik and Esme always handled it . . ."

When she trailed off, I reached over to grip her shoulder. Our losses stayed with us, no matter where we went.

"You're not a freak." I squeezed harder so she'd look at me.

"I'm not normal," she countered.

"And thank God for that, because I wouldn't want you any other way than exactly how you are."

A quiet *awww* left her lips, and I rubbed my thumb across the engagement ring on her left hand.

Ari was going to be my wife. In less than two months, we were heading to a beach on a tropical island to start fresh. Rome was picking the most secure place, and I didn't want to know what criteria he was using. Sometimes, I had to just trust my younger brother.

Mom was over the moon and kept asking when we were going to start a family. Neither Ari nor I were quite ready for another upheaval, so we'd agreed to wait a few years, unless life had other plans. I was hoping Rock would take one for the team and knock up some girl in Vail, but so far, that wasn't the case.

I turned down the driveway of the massive lake house that belonged to Con and Vanessa Leahy, which was lined with blue balloons. A Shelby Mustang turned down the driveway behind us, and I took pride in knowing we weren't the last to arrive. I pulled the Fisker onto the edge of the cement, and we climbed out as Elle parked.

"If you say one word about me running that light—" Elle's voice came through the window as she pushed open the door.

"I ain't saying shit about shit, sweet thing. I'm smarter than that."

"It's only because I wanted to make sure we weren't late. That wouldn't be fair to Valentina."

"We're here, and I'm damn sure she wouldn't hold it against you even if you were."

"Crap! The gift!"

Lord reached into the backseat of the car and retrieved a blue bag with tissue. "Like I'd forget that." With his other hand, he grabbed what looked like a fifth of whiskey, much like the one in my hand.

"Great minds," I said, raising the bottle in Lord's direction.

"Smart man," he replied.

"Come on. We gotta get inside. I promised I'd help set up, and I totally lost track of time. She's going to kill me."

"I'm pretty sure she could stage a foreign invasion, so . . ."

Elle shot Lord a look. "Don't tell me my best friend doesn't need me."

Wisely, he held back his answer, grabbed Elle's hand, and followed Ari and me up to the house. We passed an Aston Martin, which meant the Titans were already there, and the BMW that Simon and Charlie Duchesne drove. Delilah and JP's Vespas were parked next to Bishop's woman's ride, near the steps that led up to the raised lake house, which meant the entire crew was here.

For a couples baby shower.

Elle must have been thinking along the same lines because she giggled as we climbed the stairs. "I *really* hope Vanessa planned some ridiculous games. I would pay good money to have you guess what kind of baby food was in a diaper."

Ariel's eyes widened. "Oh God, is that what happens at baby showers? I googled, but everything sounded too ridiculous to be true. How could anyone think it would be a good idea to cut a piece of string to guess how big around Valentina is? I mean, what if your string is a foot too big? How embarrassing."

I wrapped an arm around Ari, wondering what exactly she'd gotten as a gift that fit in the envelope she carried. She'd been in charge of it, and I hadn't asked questions. Knowing her, there was probably information to access a bitcoin account with the equivalent of college tuition or startup capital inside.

"It's a couples shower, so that means no dumb games. I made Con swear it on his life," Lord said, and I hoped his answer eased Ari's anxiety.

"It's going to be all right, Red, I promise."

We reached the top step, and the door flew open before she could answer.

"Good deal. Now we can get started," Con said as he ushered us into the house. He looked like he'd stepped off the set of *Vikings* with the shaggy hair and beard he was growing.

Across the wide-open space, Vanessa was pouring Valentina a glass of what I assumed was non-alcoholic champagne.

"That better be the fake shit," Rix said as he stepped up beside her.

She shot him a look. "You have no room to talk. This kid isn't playing soccer with your bladder."

Rix's expression softened as he lowered himself to his knees and put a hand on either side of her belly. "Come on little rock star, take it easy on your mama. She looks so damn beautiful, waiting for you to make your appearance. But when you kick her organs, she gets this little frown, and we know you don't want to make your mama frown." He pressed a kiss to his wife's belly, and Valentina's eyes turned shiny.

I clutched Ari tighter against my side. She knew the whole story about Rix and Valentina. "Things worked out exactly the way they were meant to," I said, my voice low as I looked over at her.

"I might be biased, but I have to agree."

There was no doubt in my mind.

Vanessa spun toward the door, looking like she might cry over the scene happening in front of her. Her expression turned into a vibrant smile, warding off the tears.

"You made it! All of you!" She pointed at Elle. "You're lucky I hired a cleanup crew. Otherwise, I'd be sticking you with that job since you bailed on setup."

"It wasn't my fault. I swear. Blame Lord and his—" Her words cut off as soon as she saw Charlie readjust the baby on her hip. "You brought her!"

Elle rushed toward the baby girl Charlie held with Simon beaming down at her. I could swear the guy had been wearing that same expression for months. Ari had missed that baby shower, but I had a feeling, from the slight bump Eden was sporting, that Ari would get more chances soon. There was clearly something in the water.

I scanned the room, taking in the people who'd all come into my life because of the badge I'd given up. They'd all become as close to me as family. Sometimes life worked out the way it was meant to.

"Just to give you fair warning, I need to steal your genius fiancée for a few minutes before this is over. I have a problem that I think she'd enjoy helping to solve."

The voice pulled me out of my thoughts and I looked over at Lucas Titan.

"Steal?"

"Borrow," he said, correcting himself with a smile.

The billionaire wasn't as big of a prick as I'd originally thought. Even though I wasn't as close to him as I was to Lord, Con, and Rix, I wouldn't hesitate to call him if shit went down again—which it wouldn't, I hoped. Rome had promised to take care of any blowback from Carlos's death, and he'd given us the all clear a few weeks ago.

Regardless, I kept an eye out, and I felt better that Ariel and I spent most days locked down in her lake fortress, working. I was already at max capacity for missing-persons investigations, and had a waiting list. Word spread quickly that I was the guy to call, and I had a certain Vietnam POW to thank for it.

"Borrow is better." I looked at Ari. "If she's game."

She was practically salivating at the chance. "You're joking, right? Lucas Titan needs an extra brain to solve something? I'm in. But I don't work cheap. There better be crawfish involved."

"I'm sure we can make that happen."

Yve returned to his side, coming from Vanessa's direction with two champagne flutes. "I got the good stuff. None of that fake sparkling-cider crap."

Titan turned an indulgent look on her. "You just say the word when you're ready to change that, love, and we'll get to work."

Yve rolled her eyes. "Get to work? I'm sure you'd just have to snap your fingers to impregnate me. He wills it, it shall be done." She clinked the champagne glasses together for emphasis.

"Mmm, I think I'd rather enjoy the work part more."

Yve handed off the extra champagne flute to Ari instead of Titan. "Don't listen to him. We're too busy conquering the world to have babies yet. I figured you two would understand that better than anyone else here."

When I laid a hand on Ari's hip, she nodded. "Someday. But not too long. I want three, so it's going to take a little while."

My head jerked to the side. "Three?"

Her smile widened. "I was going to say four because there were four of you growing up, but I think that's a touch excessive."

"Two. That's plenty."

She raised an eyebrow. "Then we'll agree to disagree."

"Hmm, sounds like y'all are gonna have fun with that," Yve said. "God knows Titan will probably knock me up with triplets because of his super-sperm."

Titan chuckled, and I decided to stay silent on that subject.

"Sorry to barge in," Delilah said, "but I've got the good champagne and JP has the fake shit. Whoever has a bun in the oven that hasn't spilled about it is about to be outed because Vanessa insists on a toast."

When Titan and I both reached for the real champagne, Delilah rolled her eyes. "As if I thought there was a question there."

"You've all met my home girl, Honor, haven't you?" Elle asked as she joined the group, carrying Charlie and Simon's baby.

We all nodded as Elle ran down the list of reasons Honor was the coolest baby ever, and why Rix and Valentina and Eden and Bishop had their work cut out for them if they wanted to have a cooler kid.

I couldn't get over her name and the innocent aqua eyes staring back at me.

Honor. I'd thought that was the only thing that mattered for so long, but I'd been wrong. It was people who mattered. Principles were cold company if you had no one in your life to share the good times and the bad times with.

Sitting in that hospital waiting room, not knowing

whether Ari would make it through surgery, everything had become crystal clear. I would have done anything, given everything, to guarantee she'd come back to me. And maybe there was a certain kind of honor in that—the willingness to do whatever it took to protect the people you loved.

I would lie, cheat, and kill if it meant protecting Ari or any one of the people in this room, and I wouldn't lose a minute of sleep at night because of it.

"So, who wants to play a game?"

The entire room filled with groans at Vanessa's question.

"I thought you said no games?" Ari asked.

"Hey, y'all pipe down. This is a good one. The ladies are going to come up with an idea for a tattoo to grace your significant other's body . . . and then Con, Bishop, and Delilah are going to draw them up for you and ink them all this week." She paused. "But there's a catch—you're getting a matching tattoo, except for the girls who are knocked up. You get a rain check. No backing out. No pussy shit. Who's in?"

Everyone looked at Vanessa and then at their partner before voicing their agreement. Ari's *okay* had been quiet.

"You don't have to, Red. You might be the only person in this room without ink, and no one's going to push you into it."

Her gaze swept up to meet mine. "Oh, hell no. I'm doing it. But the pressure's on. I have to make this perfect."

I could practically hear the gears turning in her brain as her focus turned inward.

Never before would I have thought watching a woman *think* could be so damn sexy, but that was another way Ari changed everything. She was the exception to every rule, and she was *mine*.

A glance around the room revealed gleeful smiles and contemplative looks. This was going to be an interesting week at Voodoo Ink, to say the least.

Vanessa came around with sketch pads and pencils, and Ari accepted one with another glance at me. She grinned and began to draw.

Simon

Voodoo Ink, later that week

It had been a while since I'd sat in this chair, and all I could think about was how much my life had changed since the first night I'd walked in. Charlie's aqua eyes had slayed me then, and now I see them every time I look at our daughter. We've had plenty of challenges over the years, but together we've grown stronger as we've overcome each one.

"You going to show me before they do the transfer?" I asked, wondering what my former notorious runaway had thought up to be inked on us both, although hers would be put off a few months because she was breastfeeding.

With a smile, Charlie turned around the sketch pad to show me the design she and Delilah had created. The corners of my mouth tugged up.

It was a red-and-black Mardi Gras mask, and the significance hit me immediately. It was a replica of the one she'd worn the night her true identity had been revealed, the night that had changed everything for us. Charlie faced her past, and together we'd fought for this incredible future. I looked closer at the drawing to find there were two dates along the bottom edge—our wedding day and the day

Honor was born. Two of the most important dates of my life.

I threaded my fingers through Charlie's, tugging her close to steal a kiss. "I love it."

She pressed her forehead to mine and trailed her fingertips down my cheek. "I'm so glad. Thank you for never giving up on me."

I made her a solemn promise. "Never. I will *never* give up on us. I love you, Charlie."

"I love you too."

Con

A few hours later

"All right, princess, whatcha got for me?"

I waited for Vanessa to finally show me the design she and Bishop had worked on. I was already covered, so I was curious to see where this piece would even fit. But since this was Vanessa's idea, one she didn't run by me, I might add, I was going through with it. She was too, before we left the shop today.

"You sure you're ready?"

"Lay it on me."

She flipped the sketch pad around and showed me a pair of boxing gloves drawn in the traditional style with the words FIGHT FOR LOVE written around them. Instead of an emblem on the back, they had a fleur-de-lis matching the one I'd tattooed on Vanessa in this very same chair.

I met her gaze as she held her breath, waiting for me to

say something. Anything. She was crazy if she thought there was a chance in hell I wouldn't like it.

Her impatience took over. "So? What do you think?"

I reached out and grabbed the sketchbook before sliding a hand around the back of her neck and dragging her down for a kiss. "I fucking love it. You killed it. Now, where is it gonna fit?"

Vanessa pulled back and studied me. "I was thinking hip. You've got just enough room left down there, don't you think?"

"If you want me to take my pants off, princess, all you have to do is ask." I winked at her.

Vanessa's laugh filled the room. "What are you talking about? I barely even have to do that."

Once her laughter died down, I threaded my fingers through hers and tugged her close again. "You know I'll fight for you every day. I'll never stop fighting to be the man you need me to be."

Her eyes turned shiny. "You're already exactly the man I need. You challenge me, push me, and dare me to take more from life than I ever thought possible. You were the wild card. The one thing I never planned on. And you're the best thing to ever happen to me. I love you, Constantine."

I hauled her into my lap and covered her mouth with mine. In between showing her exactly how I felt, I told her.

"Fucking love you, princess. Always."

Lord

A few hours later

Elle had a surprise for me, but I had one for her too. Con left us alone for the unveiling, and I couldn't wait to see what she'd come up with.

"You going to keep me in suspense?"

She shook her head. "You know I suck at surprises."

It was true. She did. Too impulsive to keep a secret to save her life. She flipped the sketch pad around and there it was, like she'd snatched the image right out of my brain.

A chain, links shattered at the ends, but more and more solid as they came together in the middle. The part I hadn't imagined? A small pocket watch in the middle.

"What time is that set to?"

Elle smiled. "The time I started my job interview."

I huffed out a chuckle. "You mean the time you came into Chains and demanded I hire you?"

"Call it whatever you want. Perfect timing. Me saving your ass. Fate. The time you changed my life." She shrugged with a grin.

"Let's go with the best thing that ever happened to me."

"That works for me." She studied my face. "So, do you like it?"

I nodded and reached into my pocket. "I love it. But not nearly as much as I love you."

I dropped to one knee on the floor of my brother's tattoo shop, and Elle's mouth fell open.

"Oh my God." Her eyes went wide and filled with tears. "Are you—"

"If you'll let me talk, you'll find out."

Her lips snapped shut.

"You blew into my life like a hurricane, and I've never been so caught off guard. You're not just my better half, you're my partner in everything I do. You make this life an adventure, and I can't wait to wake up every morning to see where it's going to take us next."

Tears slid down her cheeks as she smiled down at me, so I figured I was doing this right.

"Eleanor Marietta Snyder, will you marry me?"

Elle dropped to her knees in front of me. "Only if you promise that you'll never say my full name ever again," she said with a laugh. She flung her arms around my neck, and I wrapped mine around her, squeezing tight.

"I can promise that." After all, once we said our vows, she'd be Eleanor Marietta Robichaux, and I'd say it whenever I wanted.

She lifted her teary face to mine. "Yes. My answer is *hell yes.*"

A champagne cork popped outside the room, but I didn't need alcohol because Elle's answer already had me buzzing.

I wondered what she'd say when I told her we were getting married next week. I wasn't waiting any longer to make her officially mine.

Lucas

The next day

"You sure you want to do this?" I asked as Yve and I walked into Voodoo Ink. She had a sketch pad from the baby shower under her arm, and she'd refused to show me what she'd worked on with Con.

The man who'd once been my rival was now one of my best friends. Two years ago, if someone had told me I would be walking into his tattoo shop with my wife to get matching tattoos, I would have laughed them out of the room for being insane.

Apparently, life had different plans, and there was nothing I would change because it all led me here, to this moment with this woman.

Yve raised an eyebrow at me. "Of course I'm sure. Although I'm not sure how I'm going to be able to keep myself from attacking you once you've been inked."

This time my eyebrows rose. "Is that right? What exactly am I getting tattooed on me anyway?"

She flipped open the cover of the sketch pad and turned it so I could see.

The meaning hit me like an avalanche, which was appropriate considering I was staring at a mountain range. She knew what this meant to me. How it had haunted me until I'd finally granted myself absolution. When I met her eyes, she rushed to explain.

"We've both conquered our demons, even when they seemed insurmountable. I think we need to celebrate that instead of pretending they didn't exist. Mine brought me to you. Yours made you into the man I love. There's nothing to hide."

She was right. But then again, my wife was always right. I had the superior taste it took to choose such an amazing woman—and she'd knock that arrogance back down my throat every time she felt it was necessary.

I nodded. "So, where is this going?"

"I was thinking your forearm, so when you roll up your sleeves in your meetings . . . delicious." She punctuated her statement with an *mmm.*

"It sounds like we'll be having more meetings at home then."

"I think that's an excellent idea."

"Where are you putting it?" I asked, and I read the hesitation in her expression as her lips pressed together. "What?"

She bit her lip before finally speaking. "I'm going to have to take a rain check for a little while."

My gaze sharpened on her. "Why? What's wrong?"

"I'm pregnant."

The words hit me harder than the meaning of the tattoo, nearly taking me out at the knees. I stumbled backward into a chair in the empty waiting room, glad that asshole Leahy wasn't out here to see.

I looked at Yve, her face the picture of anxiety. "You're pregnant."

She nodded, even though it wasn't a question.

"When?" I meant when had she found out, but coherent questions were beyond me.

"My doctor confirmed yesterday. I'm eight weeks along."

I shoved out of the chair and swept her into my arms. "Just when I think you've given me enough to keep me happy forever, you shock the hell out of me with something I never even dreamed about."

Yve whispered in my ear. "You're going to be a daddy, and I can't wait."

I squeezed my eyes shut, the wave of emotion threatening to overwhelm me. "I promise I'll never be anything like my father. Our son or daughter will never—"

Yve pressed a finger over my lips and her whiskey-colored eyes were serious when they met mine. "I know.

You're going to be an amazing father. You'll never let yourself be anything else."

I wrapped my arms around her and gripped her tight. My whole life was in my arms, and it was a glorious one.

"We putting some ink on this asshole today, or what?" Con asked as he walked into the lobby.

"Fuck off, Leahy. We're busy."

Yve giggled.

Somehow, Con knew something monumental was happening in that moment, and he backed off. "Let me know when you're ready."

When he disappeared, I stared into Yve's eyes. "I love you. With everything I have, and everything I am, I love you."

"I know. I love you, Lucas."

We held each other for long minutes in the lobby of Voodoo Ink as I thanked God for letting a bastard like me find his happily-ever-after.

Rix

"Let's see it, duchess. What do you want inked on me?"

Valentina, soon to be mother of my son, handed me a sketch pad, and I stared down at the drawing on the page. Simple. Strong. Perfect.

"It's a coronet. Fit for a duke and duchess."

"I'm not the one who should be royalty here, though," I told her.

She shook her head. "That's where you're wrong. You're

the best man I've ever known, even when I thought you were . . . someone else."

I knew what she was talking about, and hearing those words meant a lot. My woman was the daughter of a judge and had been half dating a cop, but she'd fallen for a man she thought was a criminal. If taking that risk wasn't a sign of true love, I didn't know what was. It had killed me not to tell her the truth, but I would protect her at my own expense every time.

And now she was giving me the greatest gift ever—our baby. A family of my own. Something I'd never had.

"You probably deserve better, but damned if I'm ever letting you go to look for it."

Valentina met my gaze. "How could I deserve better when I already have the best? I love you, Beauregard Hendrix, and don't you dare ever question me on that."

I looped an arm around her waist and pulled her toward where I sat on the chair so I could whisper to her belly. "Mama's fierce, and that makes us the luckiest men in the world." I glanced up at her. "And we'll never forget it either."

Her lips curled up into a beautiful smile. "It goes both ways."

"Then bring on the ink. I'm ready. Ready for every damn thing."

Bishop

All week, we'd had friends in here cementing their bonds with ink, and something about it struck me as poetic, not that I was a romantic kind of guy.

I'd been waiting my turn. Delilah had volunteered to help Eden with the drawing, and I couldn't wait to see what she'd come up with. Like Con, I was starting to run out of real estate, but I was determined to make whatever mark Eden wanted to put on me fit in perfectly. I trusted my sister's hand, and I knew it would.

Eden wasn't getting hers done for quite some time because she was carrying our little boy or girl. We'd decided not to find out because we were both rebels like that. We also hadn't told her father yet, and I expected the mob boss would have something to say when he found out. Not that it mattered much because Eden was mine and that wasn't changing.

When our turn rolled around, I sat in the chair where I usually worked on clients, and Eden handed me a sketch pad.

"What do you think?"

It took me a minute to realize what I was looking at. The New York City skyline. I jerked my gaze up to meet hers.

"I know what you're going to say—that we both have bad memories tied up with New York, but it made you who you are. It made me who I am. I'm incredibly grateful for that, and I want to celebrate it, not hide it. But if you hate it, we don't have to go through with it."

I dropped my attention back to the sketch pad for a few moments and wrestled with the image.

New York was the scene of my biggest failure, but also my greatest triumph. Indisputably, it was a city that would always hold intense meaning for us both. She was right. It wasn't something I needed to hide anymore. Eden knew everything, and because of it, I'd gotten her. It was a fair trade.

I cleared my throat. "I think it'll fit in the open spot on my rib."

"You're sure?"

I met her eyes again. "As sure as I am that I'm going to spend the rest of my life loving you. You changed everything, Eden. I love you."

A tear slid down her cheek. "Stupid hormones," she said, snuffling. "I love you too. And as soon as I can, I'm getting it tattooed on me."

I pulled her close and placed a hand on her small belly. "We've got more important things to worry about before that."

She laughed. "Like how I'm going to tell my dad . . ."

"Maybe it's time for a trip home."

Her eyes lit up. "Are you serious?"

I nodded. "Yeah, no more demons in New York."

"Thank you," she whispered. "Thank you."

Rhett

Ari had been quiet for days, and I knew it had to do with the tattoo situation. She was a perfectionist, and with something this permanent, she'd need a lot more time to process and consider.

I was in the chair while Con was working on the transfers, and the suspense finally got to me. "Are you going to tell me or make me wait until after it's done?"

Ari bit her lip nervously. "If you think it's stupid, we can do something different."

"Come on, Red. You know if you thought of it, I'm not going to think it's stupid."

She nodded and handed me a folded piece of paper. I peeled it open and stared at the single line of ones and zeros. For some reason, with Ari's brain, I'd expected something complicated and intricate, but this I couldn't interpret.

"What is it?"

"Love."

That's when it hit me—the ones and zeroes were binary code.

This woman . . . she constantly amazed me.

A true measure of genius was the ability to take the most complex concept and break it down to the simplest expression. And that's exactly what Ari had done in her own unique way.

"Do you think it's dumb?"

I shook my head. "No. Not at all." A lump rose in my throat when I pictured her racking her brain for something so perfect.

"It was either that or the first ten thousand decimal places of pi, because the infinity symbol seemed too bland. I thought this was a more elegant expression."

I yanked her into my arms and pressed my face into her hair. "It's perfect. I love you, Ari."

"I love you too."

Nothing else needed to be said, in any language.

The End

AUTHOR'S NOTE

If you were intrigued by Lachlan Mount, you don't want to miss the Mount Trilogy. All three books are available now!

Have you read the entire Beneath series? If not, there are more deliciously addictive alpha males and strong, sassy women in the Beneath world to devour:

Beneath This Mask (Book #1 - Simon and Charlie)
Beneath This Ink (Book #2 - Con and Vanessa)
Beneath These Chains (Book #3 - Lord and Elle)
Beneath These Scars (Book #4 - Lucas and Yve)
Beneath These Lies (Book #5 - Rix and Valentina)
Beneath These Shadows (Book #6 - Bishop and Eden)

Visit www.meghanmarch.com/subscribe to sign up for my newsletter and receive exclusive content that I save for my subscribers.

ACKNOWLEDGMENTS

To the readers who have followed this series from the beginning—thank you. Thank you for making my dreams come true by falling in love with this world and these characters. Please don't be sad that it's over. I promise they'll make cameo appearances in future books. I'm not ready to say good-bye to them either.

To my Runaways—You are an amazing group of souls. Thank you for being my constant cheerleaders.

Jamie Lynn—You found me with *Beneath This Mask*, and look how far we've come! What an amazing ride, and I can't wait to see where we go next. Thank you.

My JJL crew—I love you, bitches. So fucking hard.

To every blogger who has read one, all, or some of my books—Thank you for investing your precious time in my words. You make this indie book world function with your dedication, and it is truly appreciated.

To my kick-ass beta readers—Thank you for your time and intuition. I appreciate the gift of your feedback more than you'll ever know.

To my family—Thank you for understanding when I disappear into my book worlds and am incommunicado for days or weeks at a time. I love you all.

To my author friends who share insight and encouragement—I can't thank you enough for being the best damn colleagues in the most amazing industry out there. Hugs to all of you.

To JDW—You're in every hero I write, but none of them can even come close to the real thing. Thank you for showing me what it is to be truly loved. You make my dreams come true, and without you, these books wouldn't be nearly what they are. I love you.

ALSO BY MEGHAN MARCH

MAGNOLIA DUET:

Creole Kingpin

Madam Temptress

LEGEND TRILOGY:

The Fall of Legend

House of Scarlett

The Fight for Forever

DIRTY MAFIA DUET:

Black Sheep

White Knight

FORGE TRILOGY:

Deal with the Devil

Luck of the Devil

Heart of the Devil

SIN TRILOGY:

Richer Than Sin

Guilty as Sin

Reveling in Sin

MOUNT TRILOGY:

Ruthless King

Defiant Queen

Sinful Empire

Savage Trilogy:

Savage Prince

Iron Princess

Rogue Royalty

Beneath Series:

Beneath This Mask

Beneath This Ink

Beneath These Chains

Beneath These Scars

Beneath These Lies

Beneath These Shadows

Beneath The Truth

Dirty Billionaire Trilogy:

Dirty Billionaire

Dirty Pleasures

Dirty Together

Dirty Girl Duet:

Dirty Girl

Dirty Love

Real Good Duet:

Real Good Man

Real Good Love

REAL DIRTY DUET:

Real Dirty

Real Sexy

FLASH BANG SERIES:

Flash Bang

Hard Charger

STANDALONES:

Take Me Back

Bad Judgment

ABOUT THE AUTHOR

Making the jump from corporate lawyer to romance author was a leap of faith that *New York Times*, #1 *Wall Street Journal*, and *USA Today* bestselling author Meghan March will never regret. With over thirty titles published, she has sold millions of books in nearly a dozen languages to fellow romance-lovers around the world. A nomad at heart, she can currently be found in the woods of the Pacific Northwest, living her happily ever after with her real-life alpha hero.

She'd love to hear from you.
Connect with her at:
www.meghanmarch.com

www.ingramcontent.com/pod-product-compliance
Lightning Source LLC
La Vergne TN
LVHW091035201224
799595LV00021B/66

* 9 7 8 1 9 4 3 7 9 6 0 2 1 *